DUSTED
AN ANTHOLOGY OF
SHORT STORIES

EDITED BY
CHRIS BARTHOLOMEW

DUSTED
AN ANTHOLOGY OF
SHORT STORIES

EDITED BY
CHRIS BARTHOLOMEW

STATIC MOVEMENT

TABLE OF CONTENTS

CLOWNS ALL AROUND YOU
Emma Kathryn

The black limousine cruiser (grade B) slid out of the GaragePort version 3.2; its cargo safely locked in the back. Tinted windows hid the neurally-programmed driver from the world, which shot by like a blur of spilt and wasted paint. He was dead to everything but the vehicle he was in charge of. No emotions flittered through his brain. Only speeds, directions, airways, and addresses. Gliding through the night air, the driver punched in an access code and the destination co-ordinates unlocked and confirmed with an electronic voice. Location Granted. With dead eyes, the driver returned attention to the airways.

***

Cacophony stood on the roof of a ludicrously tall building with her hands resting in the breast pockets of her jacket, elbows jutting out at dangerous angles. Half of her jacket was red and the other was black. The lapels matched each opposite colour. A black lace skirt stuck out wildly, poking out over a pair of red leggings. She stood like some caricature of a comic book villain. Brightly painted eyes watched headlights whiz around the world, forever in a hurry. Sighing past lips of harlot red, she produced a tarnished silver pocket watch from her right pocket. It flipped open to reveal a face with backwards numbers and no hands. It was missing the number 3 altogether.

"'Tick tock, tick tock; White Rabbit's gone and broke his clock," she grumbled, closing the lid and flicking the defective timepiece from the roof. It tumbled into the abyss, missing the sidewalk and falling down and down and down, vanishing into the putrid fog below, which had killed the last inhabitants of this damned planet. "Lend me a minute, sweetheart?" she asked her sister, Silence, who was lying on her belly, using her hands as her pillow and one leg hanging dangerously over the edge of the building. Silence gave a non-committal shrug of her shoulders and continued her survey of the tiny streets below the current, which the air-borne traffic was passing busily along.

"Liar," Cacophony grunted, rolling onto her toes and stretching her arms above her head, knocking off her hat as she did so. Silence sat upright and swung around to face her sister, folding her legs under her as she did.

Black sleeves, ending in white gloves, pointed upwards. One arm stayed where it was, while the other dropped down before arching back up and settling about 45 degrees from the other. A living clock sat, staring up at her foolish sister.

"The hour of ten, why thank you my dear," Cacophony said, bowing to Silence and fetching her hat in one theatrical movement. At times, she resembled a silent movie star, with far too much to say for herself. Silence drew a wide smile across her own painted white face with her forefinger. There was something disturbing about the woman's silent grin. "Yes, I'm very happy now, princess," Cacophony replied, tilting her hat at an extremely jaunty angle, like a twisted 50s pin-up girl. "Where would I be without your time-telling expertise, lovey?" The other woman rolled her eyes, which were adorned with painted black tears, and made a scuttling motion with her gloved hand. "With the rats in the gutter? My prediction exactly, poppet."

Silence slid back to her position on the building's edge, chin on her hands, slippered toes pointed skywards. She sighed overdramatically, stretching her body in her skin-tight catsuit. But as soon as her head was down, it perked back up again and she raised her hands to her eyes like binoculars. The black limousine cruiser was nearing. She twisted back into a sitting position, clapping her hands enthusiastically, the noise muffled by her white gloves. Cacophony turned to where her sister now pointed and her wide smile stretched even further.

"Good job, my sweet dove," she said, reaching for Silence's hand and pulling her to her feet. The pair stood together, eye to eye, exactly the same height. "Time to fly."

They waited until they saw the cruiser enter the current their building was situated on. Cacophony removed her hat and looked at Silence, winking with a flash of bright eye shadow, before they plummeted, hand-in-hand, from the rooftop in a suicidal plunge.

***

The driver of the limo-cruiser jumped as two thuds sounded on the vehicle and he flicked up the visor, which covered his eyes, and glanced above him, his A.I. reacting to the odd incident. His eyes were the palest grey, devoid of life and personality.

"Driver 693," said a voice, warbling through the speaker, which linked the driver to the world behind the sealed partition. "693, what's going on?"

"Unknown occurrence, sir," the driver said, holding down the communication switch as he did. "Emergency procedure in operation. Unscheduled stop required." He punched in a few more codes and access keys and the cruiser changed course smoothly. Visor flicked back down, scrolling various speeds and updates to the air current he was travelling on across the red plastic which now covered his eyes.

"No!" the speaker-voice snapped. "You will continue on route as planned!" Driver 693 flicked the communication switch again, not bothering to remove his visor this time.

"Cargo has been compromised. Checks must be carried out."

"For the love of God! Turn this machine around!" the radio screamed with a hiss and a crackle. Something banged in the background. The driver's A.I. estimated that it was the passenger's fist against the partition. The partition was shatterproof, though and the driver decided that precautionary action against the passenger's futile attack would be unnecessary.

"Nearest safe stop located: 7.5 seconds."

The cruiser slid into a street on the middle grounds. It pulled up by the paved curb and the engine shut down. The vehicle rolled out a short metal landing deck, for all passengers to exit the cruiser. The driver opened his door and took a step onto the lamp-lit sidewalk, via the landing deck. Before he had the chance to turn, Silence – who had been perched on the roof of the vehicle since the sound of the thump – threw him from the cruiser, shoving him forward with a strong push with both slippered feet. Quickly, she slid from the roof and into the driver's seat, pulling the door shut and locking it behind her.

She settled herself into the seat and smiled smugly. From beneath her thin and skin-tight attire, she could appreciate the luxury, leather seat she now perched her behind on. She would love a cruiser like this. Gloved hands slid lightly over the steering wheel and then the control panels. What a beautiful machine. The radio barked angrily at her, ruining her enjoyment of such a charming piece of engineering.

"693, what the hell is going on?!" Silence watched the speaker and gave a shrug before starting to hack into and override the cruiser's internal systems.

Outside, the driver scrambled to his feet and rushed at the cruiser, slamming his fists against the heavily reinforced windows. His A.I. was in overdrive this time, calculating the risk of this woman as Code Red.

"Hey!" Cacophony shouted from where she sat on top of the limo. "Tin cars can't race with dents in them!" Issuing a hard kick to the face, she sent him spinning backward where he landed face down on the pavement. With a bounce, she landed on the ground, striding toward him, flicking a spade-shaped dagger from beneath her red sleeve – which was her left side. She bent over him and pulled back the collar of his shirt to reveal a square of discoloured flesh on the back of his neck. Luckily, she had kicked him so hard that it made it difficult for him to struggle. With the blade, she made a small incision around the scar and, with a single cry from the man; she flicked the small, square microchip from his flesh. It landed on the dry pavement; hissing, crackling and curling in on itself as it met the night air, leaving only a tiny puddle of blood and gore. The street cleaners would pick it up later, assuming that a cat had been in a fight and lost.

Fetching a MedPatch version 6.0 from her back pocket, Cacophony unpeeled the seal and slapped it over the wound. There was a brief moment, as the patch fizzed. Then the man sat upright, his back deadly straight. All the colour came pouring back into his eyes. It turned out he had green eyes with a little brown in them.

"Where am I?" he asked, rubbing at his head as the painkillers swiftly met his bloodstream. Cacophony smiled at him.

"Not far from home, sweetness. Your name is Tristan and your Iseult is waiting for you. Six long months have been wasted. Somewhere down the street, you'll remember which way to go." Staring at her blankly, he nodded slowly, getting to his feet and shambling away in the direction she'd sent him. Soon enough, he would remember his life before his time as a driver. In a gasping breath, which brought a flood of tears and memories, he knew exactly where home was.

Standing up, she straightened out her jacket and dusted off her leggings, then strolled back toward the vehicle. She adjusted her hat again, removing a pin from somewhere in her thick blonde hair and using it to fix the accessory into place. Totally the wrong place, but it was a place nonetheless. Bending her top half over to stare into the tinted window of the driver's seat, Cacophony tapped out a beat on the glass with her gloved knuckles. Still she tapped, even as the window slid down and her sister's face appeared. Silence shook her head and grabbed Cacophony's fist, signalling for her to stop.

"Shall we let Jack out of the box?" Cacophony grinned, lacing fingers with her sister. The mime nodded and flicked a switch on the dashboard. "Good job, petal," the painted fool said, kissing Silence on her blanched cheek, before slipping her head out of the window and strutting down the length of the limo toward the passenger door. Grasping at the handle, she threw the door open in a dramatic fashion.

"Hello, my childr..."

Gasping for breath, she didn't see the gun until the bullet had hit her in the chest. Lowering her head, she looked at the smoking hole in her jacket, hand sliding toward it. It had pierced the red lapel on the black half of her jacket. Heavily adorned eyes lifted to meet those of her shooter. A young man; neatly combed hair, new suit, new gun. He still had it pointed at her, hands shaking and eyes wide.

"First time's always awkward," Cacophony whispered to him with her crimson lips. Breathing heavily, she stared hard at him. "Bet you're glad one of us remembered the protection," she added, climbing inside the car and slipping onto the seat beside him. She unbuttoned her jacket to reveal a heavy bullet-proof vest beneath.

"Try pointing your weapon elsewhere next time."

Taking the gun, she pushed him to the floor where a large steel casket rested. With a quiet whirr, the partition between driver and passenger slid down and Silence turned around with raised eyebrows. Cacophony picked the bullet from her vest and tossed it to her sister.

"For the collection, sweetie," she said, doing up her jacket again. "That'll bruise like the moon," she grumbled, tapping the young man on the shoulder with the gun. Silence eyed the obscure bullet carefully, before turning her white face to their hostage and waving a gloved finger at him in a reprimanding fashion. "You tell him, gorgeous," Cacophony nodded, gun still pointed at him as she crawled to the side of the steel crate.

The sisters' eyes met. Silence gave Cacophony a nod. *Ready when you are.*

"Right, Pandora," Cacophony sang, eying the keypad on the container, "open her up." Silence gave a whistle, attracting the other woman's attention.

Fingers folded and counted out numbers. 3. 1. 4. 1. 5.

"I always preferred the Mississippi Mud variety, to be honest," Cacophony laughed, shaking her head at the stupidity of whoever thought that code was clever.

"Has she scored the jackpot?" she asked the man sitting on the floor with her, tilting his chin up with the barrel of the gun. His already-laboured breathing quickened still.

"Yes," he said, sweat running from his forehead. "Yes." Cacophony continued to stare at the prisoner, her head cocked slightly to the left. Silence whistled again. She pointed at him.

"Looks like you'll be doing the touching, Midas," the fool grinned, pushing him toward the casket.

"I'm not supposed to compromise..." he began, receiving the butt of the gun to the back of his head. A little blood pooled under his well-oiled hair. "Alright, alright!" he cried and lifted a trembling finger to the keypad.

"Shake the pig, out comes the pennies..." Cacophony babbled while Silence watched, leaning through the partition.

3 1 4 1 5. The silver box omitted a strange clunk and the lid was pushed up, air rushing out with a hiss. Finally, all went quiet; the box awaiting hands to open it.

"What present hides under this wrapping?" Cacophony asked the boy, her fingers toying with the metal's edge.

"I don't know."

Hammer cocked back, bullet in the chamber.

"Reason!" he screamed, eyes clenched shut, starting to pour

out this classified information. "They call it Codename: Reason. I think it's a computer system or something. It's the most intelligent thing known to man. I'm just here to transport it for the guy who owns it."

Silence and Cacophony held one another's gaze, listening to what he had said. Silence gave a small nod; her face seemed even whiter than her make-up made it.

"You can run all the way home now, little piggy," Cacophony told him quietly.   He hesitated a moment. The gun was lowered. Slowly, he crawled to the car door, shaking hands clutching at the handle and letting the night air in. Stepping out of the car, he took a deep breath, hand still on the door, about to close it over.

"Hey, kiddo," Cacophony called out, forcing him to turn around to face her, before she put a bullet through his skull. As his body slumped to the pavement, she leaned over and closed the door behind him.

Silence started the engine and pulled the cruiser out of the street, slipping into the busy current above. Cacophony was still staring at the box as Silence punched in their destination co-ordinates. A mechanical voice agreed with her decision. *Location Granted.*

Slipping her supple body through the wide partition, Silence joined her sister in the back. The women took hands and faced one another. Calmness filled the spacious limo. *Ready when you are.*

Together they slid off the lid and looked upon the cargo.

Reason. A sleeping, young woman; naked, slim, long blonde hair, angelic face. Wires plugged her into the padded box, keeping her unconscious.

"Princesses were made for glass coffins," Cacophony said mournfully, looking down upon the sight. The mime slipped an arm around the fool's shoulder, letting her head rest on her shoulder. "Welcome home, little sister," Cacophony said as the triplets were finally reunited.

About the author: Emma Kathryn is from Glasgow, Scotland and has an honours degree in English studies. Her writing has appeared in the likes of *Pandora's Nightmare: Horror Unleashed*, *Haunted*, Static Movement, Ethereal Tales and Dark Eye Glances.

You can find her blog at bewarethevampirebunnies.blogspot.com. She is rather tiny and rather mad.

ANOTHER SMASHING CONCERT
Jason Barney

The luxury liner *Glittering Stars* entered the system several minutes before zero hour. The assembled guests observed the random floating objects far from the sun and were mildly impressed. They'd seen plenty of meteoroids and dwarf planets. There was enough to comment on, but little else. Most were a frozen mixture of rock and ice. Some had moons but weren't much different than in a million other star systems.

The conductor ordered his orchestra to begin playing common tunes, ones that would quietly comfort and relax the crowd. He wanted to build anticipation for the climax of the musical performance.

The schedule was tight, but not unmanageable. They needed to be within the orbits of the inner planets in an hour. The crowds were excited and their mood was jolly. The navigator maneuvered the vessel through the dust clouds and large space bodies. Then he set a course for the gas giants. He banked the cruise ship against the gravity of one of the most remote dwarf planets, and dazzled the hundreds of thousands of passengers with the closeness of their approach.

When they descended upon the first gas giant its sky blue atmosphere and light clouds invited them for an orbit or two. The hull of the *Glittering Stars* screamed through one stupendous arch, and the crowds excitedly exploded in applause. People observed the eye shaped splotches of clouds, which the captain, through the intercom system, announced were some of the largest storms in the solar system. The crew was satisfied that the passengers were impressed and the vessel moved on.

The ship bolted for the next planet and the mob sighed as the bluish sphere fell behind. Some folks tried to glimpse it for as long as it was possible; other's turned their attention forward in anticipation as the next gas giant approached.

It was less remarkable than the first. People seemed to yawn as its brightness became clear. The details of its atmosphere were normal and disappointing. The captain pointed out a minor system of rings circling around it, and that its poles were where most planet's equators where supposed to be. The science of the announcement impressed a few, but didn't interest most, and the captain checked their speed and schedule. They'd known they could not please everyone, so he ordered the ship into a series of quick start and stop maneuvers, like a flee jumping around on a pets back. With each mini-jump *Glittering Stars* accomplished a quick swirling orbit around twenty-seven different moons. The five closest to the gas giant were spherical and caught some of the planet's reflective light. The others were darker and more shadowy. The passengers seemed to appreciate the vessel's ability to execute precision turns and awkward rolls.

With each course change the conductor commanded the orchestra to mix the tunes. Stringed instruments commanded the journey between the lunar objects, while drums pounded like thunder during the close approaches.

The captain commanded the engines to full for a couple of seconds. The passengers were dazzled as the star field swirled and disappeared. The engines were disengaged and the ship decelerated. A massive planet with enormous rings blossomed before them. Its girth was mostly different shades of light brown; along the equator it was tan, like sand on a beach. Rings of auburn curved around the globe.

It was the rings that grabbed everyone's attention. The navigator brought the ship over the disks, and the passengers looked on in awe and wonder. The gray, gold, and chocolate tinted rings passed under the ship like a vehicle traveling over a pavement.

The band's music intensified, led by the soft sopranos and brass. The spectator's breath was taken away as the ship descended into the layers of dust and rocks. Small clumps of powder sprinkled against the thick observation glass, while some stones and rocks ricocheted into space. It was like water splashing.

Some pieces of space debris shattered, and as the distant sun's light captured the expanding discharge, it looked like it was snowing outside the passenger liner. The crowds erupted into thunderous applause as the music calmed and slowed, and visions of winter fields came to people's consciousness.

The *Glittering Stars* dropped from the rings as quickly as it entered them, and the observers witnessed a ceiling of space debris resting above. Random large chunks rolled and tilted away as they brushed against the outside of the craft.

They moaned in impressive disappointment, the band quickened the pace of the music, and the engines blasted the ship away from the gas giant. Moments passed, the sound and intensity of the melody increased, and hungry eyes searched the heavens for the next destination. Time passed. Some members of the crowd expressed displeasure; that they may have over paid for tickets, then yet another gas giant appeared in the distance.

The music softened and slowed, like the sound of a breeze flapping the cloth of a banner at dawn. Most of the witnesses were transfixed as the size of the world slowly increased, and the rhythm of the instruments quickened.

At first the atmosphere was indistinguishable and bland. The distance lessened and details were revealed. Peach, orange, and eggshell cloud swirls made up the atmosphere, and they all spun in different directions. Some bands swam against and away from the others. Everyone's attention quickly focused in on an enormous red splotch chaotically swirling in the southern hemisphere. It was oval and churning, and seemed to grab at the clouds around it.

The viewers were abuzz as the massive world grew and grew... and everyone became silent as they realized the ship was heading directly for the Great Red Spot. It loomed above the protective transparent hull, and darkened as the ship got closer.

People tensed as they suspected something was wrong with the engines. They quietly asked others if there might be something wrong with the guidance systems. Heart rates increased, and folk's nerves became frayed. Anxious hands covered shocked mouths as a gush of exasperation passed through the audience.

"This isn't in the program," they cried.

"Are we all going to die?" they asked.

Aware they'd frightened their wealthy patrons, the captain and director of the liner got on the intercom and made a calming announcement. They hid their satisfaction and obscured their glee at striking fear into so many hearts. They were in the business of providing a memorable show, and were confident they were accomplishing their goal.

"We are on schedule and we are safe," the captain's voice boomed through the halls, theaters, and public areas. "Please remain calm. The hull of the *Glittering Stars* can easily tolerate the gravitational stresses of this world."

A collective sigh spread through the people.

The captain and conductor giggled. The music became dreamy. Stringed instruments delivered long, slow notes that were as comforting as a warm summer sun.

"Please be prepared for a very violent display," cautioned the captain. The people tensed again, and wondered if they had decided to go on the wrong cruise.

The Great Red Spot consumed the entire view now, the breath of the intimidating planet lost to the edges of everyone's ability to see. The stormy panorama of angry orange dominated the view.

There was a slight shift in the gravity as the ship's systems measured and compensated for the natural tugging from below. The assembled watched, cringed, tensed, and looked away. They couldn't help reacting as though they were on a runaway vehicle about to smack into a solid wall.

An orange hue encircled the ship and thunderous applause exploded from everyone. Citizens and wealthy patrons from a thousand worlds laughed and tried to project they never thought there was any danger. The crew observed the reactions, and knew they were providing a most memorable experience.

Blue flashes burst from the billowing clouds and countless "Ohs" and "Ahs" escaped everyone's mouths. Streaks of lightening hundreds of kilometers long flashed outside of the hull. Some were jagged and pointy and lasted only a brief second. Some bolts looked solid and left the impression of crooked stairs in the eyes of the beholders.

"Please take your seats, ladies, gentleman, and assembled gender neutral life forms," said the captain. "We will be approaching this system's asteroid field. The vessel is going to briefly accelerate. In a few moments the asteroids will be around us. We hope you enjoy it."

The people grumbled and complained about being asked to sit.

"We pay good money," they said. "We should stand whenever

we want."

Some agreed, some chastised the control being placed on them.

On cue, the band turned to rapid tunes, which were joined by deep male vocals. The music had the desired affect and the passengers envisioned gods and the birth of empires.

Suddenly the flashing lightening and cauliflower clouds were left behind, and the lonely blackness of space surrounded everything. People wondered how long the wait for the asteroid field would be, and the anticipation for another spectacular event grew.

The wait did not last long, and people quickly understood why they'd been asked to take their seats. *Glittering Stars* instantly decelerated, and people struggled to deal with the sudden inertia. The director of the cruise smiled as he remembered the secret agreement he had with the crew to tamper with the gravity and inertia controls. A broad grin wouldn't let go of his mouth as he watched everyone struggle to keep their balance.

One instant the blackness of space dominated everything, the next there were more hunks of debris taking the place of the stars. En mass people leaned into a hard turn as chunks of space rock and ice exploded into view around the craft. Some were tube shaped. Others were circular, lumpy, and large. A few approached the size of dwarf planets. Most were battered with depressions and impact craters. Uncounted numbers were tiny and bounced off from the glass hull like sand thrown up by a running foot.

Everyone ducked as the ship edged closer to a massive potato shaped rock. It had an irregular spin and everyone brought their hands above their heads as though they were attempting to prevent pieces of a falling ceiling from crushing them. No impact came, and everyone got an upfront view of the rock face. Questions rumbled and chatter increased as they saw glittering and sparkling from the surface that was too close for comfort. People's eyes and necks remained locked in place, and they wondered what naturally occurring substance could provide such random beauty.

The ship dipped as part of the imposing asteroid came dangerously close to the hull, and once again cries and complaints expanded among the patrons.

"How dare they scare us like this," some cried.

"I didn't pay for such a display of negligent driving," said another.

And the orchestra and chorus zipped through jingles that suddenly made everyone think of flapping wings and rambling waters.

Everyone noticed the direction of the flight. It took them awkwardly close to another chunk of space rock. The ship raced through several patches of randomly floating pebbles and descended toward a jagged and irregular shaped floating ledge.

Just before impact, the ship turned, swerved, and descended into an obsidian cavern.

"Ladies and gentlemen," said the captain. "The Tunnel of Love. This is the time for romance. If that special person is sitting next to you, squeeze their palms with affection or give them a quick kiss. Let them know how special they are..."

Shadows grew as rock formations passed only meters away. Some found the intimacy that had been suggested over the intercom, others quaked with fear from claustrophobia.

Glittering Stars left the asteroid as people clutched at one another. It twisted course to avoid more random debris.

"We will be approaching the inner planets," the intercom said.

"Complimentary bottles of wine are being distributed. The ship will move at high speeds once again, and we will toast a wonderfully red orb".

The mini-jump occurred, the blackness of space settled, and several different conversations erupted among the passengers. Some were drawn to witnessing the unique characteristics of this system's habitable zones. Others yawned at the prospect of viewing another random planetoid.

One person pointed, others glanced up, and a bright red sphere expanded as the ship approached. The vessel's speed declined, the destination continued to get bigger, and viewers began to notice the redness of the world. Less distance provided more detail, and it was soon revealed the planetoid wasn't really red at all. As the free and vintage wine made it to the goblets and glasses, then moved to the lips and tongues, arguments broke out about the exact hue of the world before them.

"It's brown-orange," one viewer said.

"It think it's more reddish pink," another countered.

"More wine," a third demanded.

The crew, the captain, and the director of Space Lanes Vacations smiled at the interest and enjoyment they'd created.

"Assembled guests," said the director into the intercom. "I would like to draw your attention off the port bow of the ship. For you non-navy types, I am asking you to look out to your left, about half way up the curvature of the glass shielding. The engines are going to be engaged for a really brief speed burst. So small will our jump be that you will still be able to see the red world behind you.

"I would ask you to not let your attention remain there for too long, as you'll miss the main event... our grand finale.

The crowd became silent.

"I would also like to introduce you to our orchestra conductor, Hobnix Flort Bidva, who has been leading our one thousand band members and our three hundred choir members."

The applause began and sounded like water flowing over a waterfall. Its intensity increased to booming ovations and loud calls for the music to continue.

"Ladies, gentlemen, and assembled non gendered types," said the director. "I would like you to consume as much wine as you would like, sit back and enjoy the last portion of our show. The composer named it... *Above and below*... please enjoy it."

The orchestra director raised his wand.

The engines surged.

Wine was hastily consumed.

And the music played. It started out as a near classical piece. Visions of bale' dancers and opera performances settled into everyone's imagination. The male vocals were light and soothing, like a mild wind blowing through a deep forest. The female vocals sung quick spikes and elevating slides, and it was tough not to imagine birds swooping through air

The thrust of the engines diminished, and the ship appeared behind and below massive pieces of tumbling rock and ice. Its surface was smooth in some areas, like the flat beaches of so many worlds with liquid water. Some places looked mountainous and treacherous and had long towering blades of ice projecting out into space. People realized it was a comet as they saw the long trail of dust, gas, and debris dragging behind.

People gawked at the display as yellow, gold, and green pebbles fell away from the main section, like a braid of long hair thrown behind a woman as she turns.

Glittering Star's speed was slightly faster than the enormous comet's, and people were awe struck as they traveled directly under the comet's tail. The ship approached the main bulk and people got their first close glimpse of its physical form.

They also got their first view of what lay beyond.

In the distance, large and imposing, was the sun. It was bright and yellow, and its heat caused the entire front face of the comet to bubble, froth, and burn. Spectators were mesmerized by the close view of nature's rawness. The back of the tail fell behind and curled in a long arc.

The full view of what was before them emerged, and everyone's attention was drawn to the front of the ship. The music intensified and echoed as though a great rite of passage was underway.

Almost everyone saw the blue-white world emerge around the rim of the comet. It was in front of the star, a jewel reflecting the light from the sun. It had a single moon, pale with a ghostly gray shine to it.

People gasped at the world and commented on its beauty. Wispy white cloud formations circled much of the blue, green, and brown sphere. It hung in front of the brilliant sun, like a child playing in front of its mother.

"Ladies and gentleman," said the director. "All announcements will be ceased at this time to allow you to enjoy our final display. We've come to this remote star system to witness the coming together of this comet and the world in front of you. Such events are not uncommon, but we believe our orchestra has composed a wonderful piece of music for this event. It should be quiet remarkable... enjoy."

Some people gulped down more wine. A few started frantic conversations and speculated on what they would see. Many eyes bounced to the enormous mass edging closer and closer to the world in the distance.

Slow, calming tunes floated through the assembly.

Glittering Stars maneuvered closer to the tumbling rock. The sun side churned and bristled with activity. The movement of the body continued on, leaving behind a lengthening blanket of debris.

The world sat in space, its rotation spinning the jagged landmasses out of view, like characters walking off the stage during a play.

The music got louder, and floated through the ship. The tension built as everyone began to wonder where the impact point would be.

The ship maintained its proximity to the comet, and onlookers got a surgeons view of the rolling momentum. The surfaced boiled and sputtered.

Everyone noticed the relative size of the two space bodies. The comet's approach brought it in line with the blue sphere, and the world dwarfed the oncoming object.

People speculated how much damage would be caused. They wondered about the length of time before the impact. Some postulated the event was a sham, that the cruise had arranged for them to observe a near miss, and that the real event was still to come.

The level and intensity of the band and chorus increased again. Songs boomed through the assembly.

Folks looked around in confusion as *Glittering Stars* pulled ahead of the comet and circled its jagged form. Everyone understood the potential devastation they were about to witness. If the star in the distance was the parent to the world before them, the comet was a runaway vehicle.

The music again spiked, and even the doubters realized there would be no near miss. Everyone counted down the seconds and wondered where the impact point would be. Some thought they would witness a straight on collision. Others believed it would graze the surface and then the real contact would occur.

*Glittering Star*s pulled in front of the comet, as the depth of the planet's atmosphere became observable. People were able to see the world in three dimensions. The curvature of the landmasses and oceans was obvious, and the atmosphere surrounding the globe shined and reflected sunlight.

The drums thundered. The symbols crashed. The strings produced short breathtaking strands, and all the other instruments played short beats and pulses that rapidly came together.

The ship arched against the atmosphere of the planet and everyone got one heart throbbing view of its surface. Bright lights stringed the ground and came together in splotches shining yellow. The onlookers wondered what they were as the girth of the comet passed directly below them.

The impact happened quickly. For an instant everyone was able to see the sizes of the two objects. The clouds in the upper atmosphere rippled apart like the surface of a pond after a stone has been thrown in. A ring of brown and black was ejected upwards and outwards. The landmasses and oceans wrinkled as the surface was crushed like a plaster unable to stop an angry fist. A fraction of a second later a halo of fire and lava squirted into space. The planet's crust was broken; its mantle bruised.

The observers gasped and applauded as tunes light and dreamy melted into the background. The ship circled the crash zone and everyone saw the two space bodies became one.

The comet fell into the globe. Pieces shattered and crumbled as momentum and gravity pulled it down. Lava splashed up and outward.

People held their hands over their mouths as they wondered how much devastation would envelope the world. A circular, blazing wave covered the continents, islands, and oceans. A deadly blow the comet had dealt to the planet. Magma rose over the entrance point, forming a crown of displaced rock and lava that the cold of space quickly seized.

Death and chaos did not take long to spread over the shattered world. More and more of it was consumed by the spreading fires, and soon only a charred spherical corpse remained.

The comet no longer existed. The world continued on, mangled, deformed, and dead. The after affects of the collision continued to dazzle the alien observers. Even in the moments after such a violent meeting, the planet's orbit around the sun continued. Its form was unbalanced. The tail of the comet stretched out from behind the mashed world.

The music ended.

Silence fell over the crowds of people on the *Glittering Stars*. One pair of hands came together in thoughtful applause; then others joined in. Soon the entire ship burst with appreciation and admiration.

The navigator steered the ship over the wounded world and people were able to get a final view of what had transpired. The impact area protruded from the rest of the globe like a broken bone hanging through torn flesh.

The ship changed course and did a quick flyby of the sun.

***

"Thank you for your time and we hope you enjoyed your experience with our cruise," said the voice of the program director hours later. "We will be returning to star port shortly and hope you consider another trip with us."

Glittering Stars entered the port area and prepared to let the passengers disembark. They chatted and remarked how impressive the show had been. They remembered the journey they'd been on and the awesome display about the randomness of nature.

***

The composer sat in his cabin. He was at his desk trying to find inspiration for the next cruise. Such originality was a difficult thing, and it was rough trying to create the right mood and musical writing experience.

"Computer," he said to the simulation screen. "Could you please show me the most recent recordings of gaseous activity within the Orion Nebula?"

Fuzzy greens, swirling yellows, and exploding reds appeared on his screen.

And he began to write his next piece of music.

About the author: Jason Barney lives in Vermont. He tries to write one new short story per week and send it out to different SF markets. He has had work accepted by *Lame Goat Press*, *Static Movement*, *Pill Hill Press*, *Twisted Tongue Magazine*, *Absolute Press*, *Resident Aliens*, *Enscorcelled*, *Wicked East Press*, *This Mutant Life*, and the *Pennsylvannia Literary Journal*.

Tiny Bubbles
Jessy Marie Roberts

William fiddled with the hot water knob, twisting it back and forth, until he slid his fingers into the pulsing stream and found it the right temperature.

He opened a pink bottle of strawberry-scented bubble bath and dumped a couple of capfuls into the cascading water, inhaling deeply as the scent of sweet fruit filled the bathroom. He looked over his shoulder to where she sat perched on the toilet lid, her eyes empty and fixed on the wall behind him.

"Now, now, love, don't be angry. I'll get all cleaned off in just a bit," he said, smirking at her look of distaste. He pulled his white t-shirt over his head and threw it into a duffle, and then let his black jeans slide over his thin, muscled hips. His thumbs hooked the elastic waistband of his boxer shorts, and they followed the rest of his outfit into the bag, waiting to be laundered.

He wandered over to the sink and lit a pink four-wicked candle. "Adds a touch of ambiance, don't you think?" he asked, blowing out the match. The stark stink of sulphur challenged the strawberry smell, both masking something more unpleasant.

She was starting to rot.

He sighed, realizing he was going to have to get rid of her soon before the neighbors started to complain of the cloying perfume of death reeking up the place. He enjoyed the pungent odor of decay on occasion, but preferred to bathe with strawberries lingering in the air. He could lose himself in the filth of putrefaction later, for one last thrilling night, until he had to dispose of her remains in the morning.

There would be another. There always was.

Looking again at the young woman slumped over on the white porcelain stool, he smiled. Thirteen.

Twelve had come and died before her.

He remembered each of their names, their looks, their smells. They were waiting, patiently and eternally, for him to bring their thirteenth sister home—hacked to pieces and thrown into a pit shaded by trees and cloaked with isolation.

His private paradise.

He slithered his arms above his head, his leer accentuating the gaunt chisel of his upper cheeks. He wiggled his hips back and forth, swaying to the rhythm of the knife stabs he had used to kill her. His hips beat frantically as he envisioned pounding the blade into her chest and stomach, side and thighs. One hundred slashes and gashes and it was over, done.

He stumbled to sit on the side of the tub and leaned over to the knobs to off. Bubbles brushed against his nipples, the light, airy touch arousing him as thoroughly as the death dance before his girl had.

She would take care of *that* later. First, he would relax in the bath.

A glass of burgundy rested on a small table next to the tub, condensation sliding down the stem to puddle on a coaster. He slid into the bath and reached for the wine when, out of the corner of his eye, in the center of the largest bubble, he saw eyes.

Blue eyes, with long, black eyelashes sweeping up in a wicked expression of hate.

Startled, he dropped the glass, the delicate stemware shattering as it collided with ivory tile. Crimson liquid splashed onto the thick bathmat, splattering up the sides of the Jacuzzi tub, dripping into the grout of the expensive, imported floor covering.

He sighed; grateful he was not in his own house. The wine was sure to stain, especially if left alone—it was worse than blood.

"See that, pet?" he asked the corpse watching him from across the room. "Something's got me spooked. The house owners shouldn't be back from England for another week, but I'm going to cut my little vacation here short. I think I'll go home after I dump you. One last night on those silky sheets."

Ignoring his spilled wine and thirst, he dunked his head under the steaming hot water, using his long, slender hands to sluice soapy water out of his eyes. He shrieked when he opened them again, seeing two eyes peer at him through the translucent glimmer of a bubble.

Taking a deep breath, he caught the offending bubble in the palm of his hand and brought it to eye level. Squinting, he recognized the eyes.

Number one. Jenny Resaveck, age nineteen, sophomore, home from college visiting her family when he found her staggering out of a bar, fake ID snuggled into the plastic identification holder of her faux-leather wallet.

He found her real ID stuffed into the zipper pouch of her designer purse knock-off along with a half-empty pack of spearmint gum and a yellow cigarette lighter.

Her blue eyes stared at him, accusation evident in the narrow slits of her pretty orbs. His hand itched for a soup spoon, envisioned scooping out those eyes again, wrapping them up in a ribbon-tied jewelry box and having them delivered to her parents.

It was all of their daughter they had to bury.

He shook his head, clearing his thoughts. He must be more tired than he realized, seeing dead eyes in his bubbles. He laughed, the fake and hollow sound echoing off the bathroom's walls. Finally, he poked the bubble with his index finger and the opulent globe burst into perfumed droplets.

His eyes burned as tiny flecks of the soapy sphere connected with his corneas. "Bloody Hell!" he shouted, grabbing a hand towel from the rack by the tub and wiping his eyes. He opened and shut them in rapid succession, tearing in an attempt to drown out the strawberry burn.

Eyes shut; he switched on the water to rinse the soap from his face, scalding himself as it shot out piping hot. With blind inefficiency, William twisted the cold temperature handle until tepid water poured from the tap.

He cupped his hands and splashed fresh, clean water against his face, then scrubbed it dry with the Egyptian cotton towel.

His vision was a little blurry when he reopened his eyes, but it was manageable. "What is in that bubble bath?" he asked dead girl thirteen. "Acid?"

She did not respond, but he did not expect her to. Dead friends made the best listeners.

He saturated the towel with clean water before turning the knobs to the off position. He folded up the towel and leaned back in the tub, the wet fabric over his eyes.

Something tickled his big toe. Irritated, he flicked his foot out of the water, wiggling the digit, and then re-submerging it under the hot, fragrant wetness.

The itching intensified, as if a hundred miniscule bugs raced up and down the length of the toe, underneath the nail and around to the calloused pad.

With an exasperated sigh, he removed the cloth from over his eyes and sat up to inspect the toe.

A large bubble encapsulated the offending appendage, and inside the effervesced cylinder was another pair of reproving eyes.

He recognized them at once by the gaudy green eye shadow clashing with the stormy hue of her blue-grey irises. Reina Gilbert, twenty, waitress at an all-night truck stop a couple of hours north of his home. Number two.

Her toenails had been painted red, white and blue to celebrate the Fourth of July, and he had been so taken with them he had cut them off, starting with the big toe, working his way to the smallest. Her widowed mother had received nine toes, but he kept one for himself, wrapped in shiny paper and hidden in a pound of hamburger in his deep freeze.

"Oh, I've really lost it, have I?" he asked Miss Thirteen, glaring at her before turning his attention back to his aching, throbbing toe. He moved his hands to either side of the bubble and clapped his hands together sharply.

The radiant bulb did not explode, but stayed latched around his swelling metatarsal, the base squeezing the joint where toe met foot. The tickling turned to burning, and he screamed as he watched his toe blister.

Frantic, he tried to burst the bubble again with his hands, to no avail. He spied a razor sitting next to a can of women's shaving cream and grabbed it. Hands shaking, he disassembled the razor until the plastic lay in a broken heap on the wine-stained bathmat and the sharp silver blade was clutched in his right hand, his carving hand.

With practiced ease, William lowered the blade to the outer perimeter of the bubble and sliced along its membrane. He could see the tip of the razor inside of the bubble, but its shiny, viscous skin remained intact.

Frustrated, he withdrew the blade and swiped at the bubble a second time, nicking the top of his toe with the edge of the razor.

Blood squirted out of the wound, trapped within the globe, pooling.

"Damn it," he muttered, distracted for a moment by the malicious glint of eyes floating around his toe. "Oh, so you think that is funny?" he asked the eyes, and then swiped the blade down, through the bubble, through the mocking eyes, and through his toe, slicing it to the bone.

His eyes widened in shock and pain, the bath water turning a light shade of red as blood seeped into the aromatic liquid. He dropped the razor blade into the water and clutched his toe, trying to staunch the bleeding.

It was obvious to William he needed stitches. "I'm going to get dressed and go to the hospital, love," he told the rotting girl watching from the toilet, standing in the sudsy bathwater. "You stay here and keep an eye on things. I'll be back as fast as I can and we'll play."

The dead girl said nothing, staring past him. For a second, he thought he saw the corners of her mouth turn up in a light smirk, but disregarded it as a pain-filled figment of his imagination.

He tried to lift his right leg out of the water, to step out of the tub, but found he was rooted in place, unable to move. "What now?" he shouted, nude and vulnerable, scented beads of bloody water dripping onto a cloud of bubbles. Glancing down, William counted ten more sets of eyes watching him, paralyzing him, keeping him in the tub.

"Let me go," he cried, struggling to detach the soles of his feet from the ceramic basin. "You're dead! What do you want from me?"

In the flicker of candlelight, he was sure lucky number thirteen smiled, her cracked and desiccated lips exposing perfect, straight teeth.

"You," he screeched in blame, "you're the reason this is happening to me! I should have hacked you apart and gotten rid of you yesterday! What was one more night, you selfish bitch?"

There was a rumble and the knobs of the water turned, opening the valve and letting water jet into the tub. The cap on the plastic jug of bubble bath twisted off and floated across the room as the bottle fell to the side and emptied its fragranced contents into the cascading stream of hot water.

The stink of strawberries was overwhelming, reeking of

compost and spoiled food rather than sweet and succulent. As the torrent of liquid splashed into the puddle of pink soap, more bubbles sprung to life, glistening and hateful circles of vengeance.

Sudsy water spilled impossibly fast over the side of the tub and streamed toward thirteen. She waited patiently as the water pooled and collected around her, forming a lake inside the bathroom.

He glanced at the open doorway leading from the bathroom to the master bedroom, appalled to discover an invisible buttress forcing the water to stay gathered in the small room, unable to escape in rivulets into the bedroom and the rest of the house.

"This can't be happening! Not to me, not now! This is impossible!"

The water rose past the porcelain toilet, thirteen slipping into the pungent abyss, floating face down toward him, guided by the twelve bubbles housing the eyes of his previous victims.

Her blonde hair spilled out, caressing the top of the bubbly wetness, the tips of the silken tendrils wrapping around the back of his knees. Panicked, he tried to push the corpse away from him, but the water's current outmaneuvered him.

Suddenly, dead number thirteen jerked her face out of the water, her hair still wrapped around his legs. With a shout he lost his footing, no longer entrenched in the tub, and fell backward, his skull colliding with a *crack* as it impacted with unforgiving hardness.

Dazed and dizzy, he tried to lift his head out of the water, but found something was on top of him, keeping him submerged. He opened his eyes, ignoring the sting, shocked to find thirteen straddled atop him, her dead weight ensuring his airways could not breach the surface.

Floundering for breath, he kicked and hit, thrust his hips and strained his neck, but it was too late. Scorching water wrought with tiny bubbles swam into his mouth and nose to his lungs until he thrashed no longer.

Thirteen shut her dead eyes for eternity, resting upon her killer, the water soothing and cleansing. She drifted away to forever sleep intact, her body left in a stranger's bathroom to be delivered to her family.

And then twelve bubbles popped, at peace with their thirteenth sister.

About the author: Jessy Marie Roberts lives in a "haunted" house with her husband and two dogs. She is originally from Morgan Hill, California.

Against Death
Michael C. Pennington

The message runner burst through the door, stumbling on the threshold into the inn, barely clothed, skin and blond hair streaked with road grime, dripping sweat. He leaned over, hands propped on his knees.

The common room went from uproarious to silent in an instant. Every head turned his way, the teenager's urgency evident. Community runners were never used for trivial matters.

The messenger's head jerked up, his desperate eyes searched the room and sought them out.

Ulrich sighed with false exasperation at the interruption. There was no avoiding the kid. The two were obvious, dressed in issue forest camouflage. In contrast to the homespun or frayed clothing of an age gone by that everyone else wore.

He had foolishly hoped for a little time off, the two of them were always after some rogue beast or homicidal mutant. They had just returned that morning from an outlying homestead investigating the murder of an entire family.

The pseudo vampires were the number one suspects, only God or the devil knew what motivated them to drain and drink the blood from their victims. They were a scourge on the rest of mankind.

Ulrich sat with the master hunter, each with their back to one wall in the back corner. He had loudly enjoyed the midday meal, shoveling in food to fuel his large frame. Until, the messenger disturbed his peace.

The kid dodged around the tables to reach them, his chest heaving. Between heavy gasps, in a wheezing whisper he spilled out his dire news into Rolf Thorson's ear.

The journeyman hunter watched his friend's face turn grim. "Six?" Rolf asked to confirm.

The messenger nodded his head.

Ulrich anticipated that they would be leaving at any moment and stuffed the last part of his meal into his mouth. Food was scarce, a quality meal even rarer. He privately raised his flagon of red wine to fighting Death and gulped the bitter sweet concoction down.

Only then did he wipe his sweeping brown mustache with his cloth napkin, rise and pull the dark hand-woven balaclava down over his ears. He lifted his and Rolf's gear from the pegs on the wall near the table. Discreetly, observing the crowd of local business scions and their lackeys. There were few prosperous professions that would allow a man to take his midday meal in an inn. Those present were the town's cream of scoundrels.

Unlike the rest of the inn's patrons, he didn't strain to eavesdrop on Rolf's inquiry. Soon enough he would face whatever awaited them. More than likely, he really didn't want to know what manner of beast caused the haunted fear on the teenager's face.

He sized up the possibility of a new recruit, if he could be persuaded to leave the Sheriff's employment.

The hunters' talents were in constant demand these days. Amongst the destruction, the disease, the famine and the monsters that crept out of the dark. Few wanted to venture outside the confines of the human enclave, let alone fifty miles or more in any direction. It took nerves of iron to stand against a raging man-eating tiger, a maniac with a meat cleaver or something that shouldn't exist, but did.

Together all three of them left the dining area. Rolf ignored the questions thrown at him as they passed several tables. The patrons' voices burst into a roar of worry and curiosity as the door closed behind them.

With grim purpose they strode up the street for the town's northern border. Running vehicles were in short supply and fuel rationed, the gas kept mostly in reserve for farm equipment. The hunter's were used to travelling on foot.

Ulrich heard the door to the inn slam open. He rolled his eyes and turned with his longbow in one hand. His right hand upon an arrow half drawn from his quiver. Ready to assert that they were not to be followed, he coldly stared down the men sent after them. He shook his head, dropped the arrow back in the quiver and stabbed his index finger back at the inn.

Not a single set of eyes met his. Most knew him well. There wasn't a one he wouldn't thrash. No doubt their own employers would deride them, but better for them than an arrow in a foot or a sound beating.

The last thing they needed was the town's folk mucking up the crime scene. Ulrich turned and lengthened his stride to catch up with the master hunter. The gossips would just have to wait.

When the terrorist's activated their satchel nukes, the dirty kind, they devastated multiple American and European cities. The radiation spread and vital areas became uninhabitable. The terrorists had planned well. For all the good it did their nuked out countries.

The world shifted into a change twenty years ago. The War on Terrorism forced the enactment of the United States' Continuation of Government. America deployed her troops, retaliated for years and eventually brought what few soldiers that were left back home. Men like Rolf.

The borders closed and aid stopped going out to solve the rest of the world's problems. America faced a hard enough time just caring for her own citizens. While the rest of the world fared even worse. The world plunged into anarchy after the United States, the United Kingdom and the rest of her allies waited out the aftermath in a defensive posture while the Four Horsemen reigned.

The grassroots of democracy were just now springing back up around the scattered pockets of civilization. The United States only a shadow of her past glory. The appointed COG officials claimed the terrorists hadn't won the war. However, they would have a hard time convincing the rest of America's survivors of that.

The everyday citizen not only fought corruption, but still had to face the more serious risks of starvation, multiple diseases and the weather. Plus, the wide spread radiation caused gene mutation in beasts and man. A person could harvest a deer, catch a fish, plant a crop or open an old can and die within a few days of radiation poisoning. Death took more forms than Ulrich could imagine.

***

An hour later, Rolf conferred with the Sheriff. His hand hovered about the revolver strapped to his waist. While Ulrich waited with the two deputies a dozen yards away. They wore expressions of men that would prefer to be anywhere else than at the scene of slaughter. Each kept glancing at the sun in the west, no doubt calculating the time before sunset.

It was more than just superstition. Statistics proved more people died after dark. The numbers also showed that folks were more likely to be murdered than pass peacefully in their beds.

"What do you think did this?" Ulrich asked them.

"F'en Vampires!" Stu blurted.

These weren't the old movie vampires that Stu was worried about, or the kind that a person read about in books. They were changed humans, afflicted with radiated virus that caused an insane craving for blood. The majority weren't restricted by daylight or bound by arcane rules. More often than not, they couldn't be distinguished from normal humans, until it was too late.

"Vampires don't dissolve and strip the flesh from the body and leave nothing but a pile of bloody bones." Deak shook his head at his partner's ignorance. "You watch yourself Ulrich. I've never seen the likes of this. Ghouls or something new."

Ulrich shrugged, keeping his eyes on Rolf.

"I wish they'd hurry up," Stu complained.

Rolf motioned for Ulrich to join him as he turned away from the Sheriff.

Ulrich said in parting, "I'll see you two back in town. I'd keep this quite if I were you. There's no reason to scare everyone half to death."

"You mean like the two of us?" Deak called after him. The deputies were good enough men, just out of their environment.

Ulrich joined Rolf and the two surveyed the campsite. "They're about ready to crap themselves." He whispered to the middle aged hunter.

"I don't blame them." The skin beneath Rolf's left eye twitched.

Ulrich leaned forward and traced the prints on the ground.

"See that." Rolf pointed at multiple spike holes in the soil, each set surrounded a blood stained pile of bones. Torn remnants of clothing and metal implements lay amongst the mayhem.

Most of the victims' packs, boots and personal possessions were undisturbed where they had stacked them before bedding down. Ulrich flipped the top of one pack open, noting the quantity of gadgets and precious metal versus clothing and food. Rolf grunted at the sight. Ulrich wondered if they had been scavengers or thieves.

He switched his attention elsewhere. "What leaves that kind of tracks?"

Rolf glanced up at Ulrich, the twitch more evident. "I've no idea."

If Rolf Thorson had told him he was a winged fairy, Ulrich would have been less surprised. The man was the best tracker and woodsman in the northwest. "Oh, great."

"How many do you think we're facing?" Rolf asked as he usually did to test Ulrich's skills. "What do you see?" He pointed at each pile of bones.

"I..." Ulrich stared hard at the scene. Only the spiked holes overlay the earlier scuff marks of the encampment. Not a single spiked hole had been scuffed out. "There's no sign of a struggle. It took them in their sleep."

"Right. What else?"

Ulrich stepped away from the site. He prowled the entire perimeter then concentrated on one area. Coming back, he eyed his friend and then ventured his assessment. "There's only one trail in or maybe out. The spike holes only seem to lean in one direction, all angled away from the site. The other thing is; depending on how many legs the beast has that did this..." He pointed at the spike marks around one pile of bones counting the number. "Eight legs. It looks like only one beast did this."

"Exactly."

"Lord Almighty! It had to kill each one of them without the others even knowing."

"My thought too." Rolf stared off at the sun and then to the north at the upper slope that the old forest darkened.

"A giant spider?" Ulrich ventured.

"You ever see a giant spider?" his friend asked sarcastically.

"No. Not yet. But this thing's appetite, six men..." Something caught Ulrich's eye and he looked closer.

"We're done here." Rolf motioned him to take the load.

"Wait." Ulrich pulled an arrow from his quiver and picked at a pile of bones. He teased out a set of false vampire teeth and picked them up with a scrap of cloth.

"Pseudos!" Rolf grabbed the fangs. "Well this is a turn of events."

"They won't be missed and it explains the booty."

Rolf signaled the Sheriff and went to meet him.

Ulrich knocked the arrow across his bow and followed the trail up the slope a little ways despite his inner fear. He had long since learned to confront his terror. He had a job to do, but that didn't stop his imagination or the nightmares.

He observed Rolf wave farewell to the Sheriff from the corner of his left eye and heard Stu bawl out his relief.

"Thank God! I thought they would never finish." The two still had to gather the men's processions, before they could join the Sheriff and runner in the open jeep.

Ulrich was ready to bet that Deak would keep the throttle floored on the way back to town.

***

The rainforest towered over the pair. Several deadfall lay scattered about, each heavily encrusted with lichen. Fern and low bush crowded the ground between the trees near the forest's edge. However, the deeper they trekked, only the lichen and a rare fern grew from the thick mulch.

Tracking the beast became difficult, finding an occasional scuff amongst the lichen. The failing light threatened to make the task impossible. His eyes never stopped scanning the ground, the trees about him and the branches above him. His cautious heart pounded at the thought of being ambushed.

They found a game trail, just a hint of brown in an indentation in the lichen. It followed the easiest way through the trees. The slope steepened and the dark shadows pressed in.

"Psst."

Ulrich froze in place. His neck craned back to pick out Rolf leaving the path. The master hunter placed each foot down with deliberate caution, careful to leave as little sign as possible. Ulrich followed; paranoia and terror amplifying his senses. Tracking a rogue monster in the dark was one of his least favorite tasks.

Rolf stopped and prepared his climbing equipment. He pointed at a tree close by for Ulrich to mount. "I'll take the first watch." He growled out in a low monotone, the higher pitch of a whisper tended to travel further.

"Do you think it can climb?" Ulrich reciprocated.

"I'm not sure. Now be quiet and get up the tree."

Ulrich strapped the spikes to the inner side of his boots, flung a fat rope about the bole of the tree and adjusted the length at his belt. They both humped up the tree about twenty feet, high enough to get a vantage point, low enough to get down fast if the need arose. The two positioned themselves where they could see the trail and each other, and then lashed a padded platform to the tree that they could sit on.

The hours of the night passed, and just the slightest hint of false dawn crept beneath the forest's canopy. Ulrich scanned the trail and the forest around him. The wind had picked up and every rustle of the branches caused his eyes to jerk about. He peered up into the tree above him, afraid to make a sudden move with anything but his eyes.

He shuddered, the thought that all anyone would ever find of him was a pile of bloody bones occurred to him. Well aware that Rolf had purposely set them in place to ambush the beast. His eyes dropped back to the trail.

A large deer with several tines stepped into view. Hesitant, it paused with one hoof in the air. The buck took a pace forward, head bent down to nibble and then moved on.

Another buck followed, just as cautious. Ulrich's eyes flowed about the forest, half expecting the deer to be attacked. The first passed by, before he noticed the strangeness to the shadowed outline of the second. When he perceived the deception, his heart raced and the hair rose on the back of his neck.

The head and antlers were there, but what he thought to be the animal's legs were too spindly. The body looked like the deer's hide, but was too lumpy. A hot rush of revulsion swept his mind.

Something wrapped about the deer, not even its companion seemed to notice. In one fluid motion, he lifted, drew back the bow and let the arrow fly. The long shaft buried deep into the torso of the deer, just behind where the front shoulder should have been.

What looked like an umbrella shaped batwing spread out from the far side. The deer collapsed to the ground, a mess of bowels and blood spilled. Pinned by the arrow to the deer, the monster thrashed about to free itself.

He had observed Rolf jerk awake at the thrum of the bowstring. Ulrich freed the rope that held him to the tree stand. He dropped a coil of line to slide down. Intent on putting an end to the creature, he leaned out from the tree to belay down.

Blackness fell about his body, as if a leather hide was thrown over him and tightened. He felt himself fall, struggling to free his arms and face from the smothering interior that engulfed him. A scream of terror escaped his lungs, when he realized that one of creatures had him. He slammed against the ground, the wind knocked from his lungs.

The sharp scent of expelled putrid musk assailed his nostrils and fouled his taste buds with his first inhaled breath. Spiked dew claws punctured his skin and something sucked at the stocking cap trying to get at his scalp. In a second wave of terror and hysterical strength he thrashed about. His hand closed on his knife just as he and the beast that enshrouded him rolled down the slope.

He stabbed the knife deep and slashed down. Then again and again; until the creature's flesh parted and he struggled out from its fetid insides. They both rose up in confrontation. The monster stretched out before him, maybe eight feet in diameter with triangular teeth lining a mouth like ring in the center of the inner surface. Far larger than the one his arrow pinned to the deer.

He backed away wishing he had a boar spear. He thought to look for Rolf, expecting help to come to his aid. A mistake, the beast must have observed his distraction.

The monster sprang toward him, like a circular net cast by a fisherman. Ulrich fell on his backside and kicked out in panic. Legs entangled in the shroud, he frantically slashed at the monster with his climbing spikes. His left hand automatically closed about one long claw where the thick skin flapped loosely from one of his earlier cuts.

Ulrich rolled and dragged the thick hide of the shroud with him. He heard a snap of hollow bone. The monster was surprisingly light. He sheathed his knife, hoping his impulsive idea didn't fail him.

A second spiked claw stabbed out at him and he grabbed it. He pulled the other one in his left toward his right hand to clutch them together. Scrabbling to the top of the outer surface, he folded the shroud back upon itself. Articulated joints popped when separated, and the snap of bone seem to weaken the beast with each fold. With his last effort he tied the claws together with a game strap from his belt.

Scrambling away, he climbed to his feet to look for Rolf. Another shroud enfolded the master hunter's upper torso and arms. Knife back in Ulrich's hand, he ran to his friend's aid.

Rolf flopped on the ground, his legs flailed at the air. Ulrich grasped a leg spike, applied the knife's edge and sliced upward toward Rolf's head and the monsters center. His nerves on edge, because the shroud had a lot more time to work on the hunter. He peeled back the shroud, folding the monster back upon itself like he had the other. Dew claws ripped from Rolf's skin and clothing.

Free from the shroud, Rolf rolled away, desperate his hands wiped at his reddened face. Ulrich finished securing the shroud, leapt for his fallen pack and tore the goatskin water flask free from its strap. In another second he was beside Rolf to drench his face and hair hoping the water would dilute the acidic burn of the saliva.

Perhaps instinct warned him, maybe it was just a noise, but he looked up in time to see the shroud he pinned to the deer, tear itself free. Like an undulating jellyfish, it sprung into the air. To spread its umbrella like shape to drift down some distance away, furled its self and then sprang into the air again.

Ulrich went for his pack. This time he freed the double headed woodsman's ax. He crouched to wait for the attack. Only the shroud flapped away in the opposite direction, headed deeper into the forest.

Rolf staggered to his feet, wiping at his face. "How many?"

"Two bound up, the first is getting away."

"Go get it. I'll be right behind you."

Ulrich took off with only the ax and his knife. He ran as hard as he could. The shroud disappeared ahead amongst the trees

With the ax gripped to his chest, he burst into a clearing. The shroud stood ballooned up in front of him. There were several black spots near the top, spaced about the center. He wondered if the spots were eyes. He couldn't even guess which way the monster faced.

Behind the shroud a white nest of strand like material

squatted on eight stubby legs. He charged the shroud. His ax lifted up above his head at the last minute.

He drove it down into the motionless creature. Unsure and confused why the shroud didn't try to fight back. Or at least flee into the nest to take refuge.

When, he pulled back on the ax to free the blade. The shroud pulled away from another beneath. He didn't hesitate and stomped down near the center to gain enough leverage to free the ax.

The ax sucked free to take a swipe at the other one, just as the shroud sprang toward the nest. Its legs scrabbled to pull down a trap door in the side. Ulrich had no intention of letting it get inside, terrified to go in after it.

Desperate, Ulrich arched his back with the ax once again held high. He hurled his body forward letting it fly. The heavy blade tumbled once and clove into the escaping shroud. Without hesitation he surged forward to finish the kill. Ax back in his hand, he lifted his head to check the nest.

The open trapdoor, and dark interior frightened him. He backed away, not taking his eyes from the gaping hole. His imagination at work, he was ready for more monsters to swarm out.

Rolf stumbled into the clearing, with Ulrich's bow over his shoulder, exhaustion evident from his heaving lungs. He bent over hands supported on his knees to keep watch the open trap door. "Anymore?"

"I don't know."

The hunter pointed at the smaller forth one. "Did that come from inside?"

"No. I think it cloned off the larger one."

"Like cell division? Mitosis?"

"Yes."

"Lord, help us sinners." Rolf looked back the way he came. Perhaps thinking of the two they left behind multiplying. "I wonder how fast they breed."

"I thought monsters like this were just science fiction stories," Ulrich complained.

"Me too."

"What do we do?" Ulrich asked, unsure of his next move.

"Use that ax and drop a tree on the nest. A big one."

A half hour later, the tree gave a sharp pop and a low pitch squeal as it leaned toward the machine. Ulrich in quick succession slashed the ax twice more into the cut to direct the trunk's fall. The remaining wood snapped and fibers pulled as it fell exactly across the hatch, flattening the nest down the center. The tree completely sealed the trap door beneath its weight.

But the nest burst open from the side and emitted a high pitched scream that the men felt more than heard. The pressure on their eardrums was relentless. The two hunters backed away from the nest that Ulrich now suspected was alive.

Ulrich traded Rolf his ax for the bow. He quickly knocked an arrow just in time. A stack of shrouds burst out of the torn side. They were smaller than the originals ambushers, each about the size of a large pumpkin. A second stack followed.

Ulrich put an arrow into the first stack. The second stack popped one shroud off the top, then another and another until they faced three in the air. The first stack, unable to disperse, scuttled straight for Ulrich.

Rolf intercepted and buried the ax in the stack's top shroud, while the rest puffed up their skirts trying to break free from the arrow.

Ulrich launched an arrow to pluck a looming shroud from the air.

"Don't let any get away," Rolf yelled out. He hacked at the stack taking the lower legs out from under the bunch.

Ulrich's third arrow took a second one from the air, when the bottom one from the separated stack launched itself from the ground. He ducked, but the claws caught on his cloak and the shroud spread itself on his back.

He threw himself down with the intent to hurt the monster. He pawed at the shroud to get it off his back. Before, it crawled up on his neck.

Parachuting down, the remaining shroud in the air hovered above Rolf, who still flailed at the pinned beasts. "Look out," Ulrich screamed.

Rolf drew and fired the heavy caliber pistol with no effect, going down with the shroud over his head, spiked claws digging in. The hide rippled and ballooned. He cursed a continuous string of muffled profanity. While he beat and pried at the shroud, unable to get the blood sucker off his head.

He stumbled over the entangled mass that thrashed about at his feet. Rolf took a hard fall and rolled about fighting suffocation.

Ulrich latched on to a spiked claw that appeared in his vision. The gratifying snap of bone, momentarily panicked him afraid the leg would pull free from the shroud. He clutched at the hide instead and slammed it to the ground to stomp the lump into a quivering puddle.

Yanking his blade from his sheath, for the second time that morning, he rushed to cut a shroud away from Rolf. The hide sucked in close to the neck. He pulled it away, afraid for his friend, before pealing back the skin.

"Burn the nest! Burn it," Rolf scream in fury as the shroud pulled away from his face.

In agreement, Ulrich dug for his flint and steel as he strode toward the nest. He had no idea if the fibrous material would burn. He wasn't surprised when the sparks only smoldered amongst the damp fiber.

He ducked under an old tree and stripped dead branches from the trunk. Stepping back, he jumped and snatched at some dried moss. Then pealed at the red bark, until he could hold no more clutched to his chest.

Returning to the nest, he went to his knees to sort the kindling into a workable pile. He rolled the moss into a wad, dug in his pockets and pulled at the lent and what threads he could loosen to push into the center. Then once again, he raked the flint striker along the rod.

With each stroke a stream of sparks fell into the tender. At the hint of smoldering, he cupped his hands around the sparks and gently blew into the smoke. Flame flashed and he wedged the burning tender amongst his kindling.

Soon, he directed the burning pile against the nest, before jogging back for more wood. With worry, he watched the fire over his shoulder. The flame didn't seem to want to catch.

He kept adding wood to build the flame. The heat increasing as the size of the fire grew. Abruptly, the air boomed in displacement and the nest burst into flame.

Ulrich backed away toward Rolf, who still sprawled on the ground. He bent over to help him up. "Hey Rolf. What's the matter? You hurt? Or just getting old?"

Rolf shook his head and kicked at the nearby stack of skewered shrouds. "I guess we know how they took out the pseudo vampires. Dropped on them from the air and then walked out in a bloated stack."

"Damn scary."

Rolf nodded. "We'll have to get a bulletin out, in case more nests turn up."

"The bastards are smart. They set a trap for us."

"You know Ulrich, I've been thinking."

"What?"

"It's about time you took on an apprentice or two for these little sojourns."

"Why?" Ulrich bent over, manhandled the stack of squirming shrouds and hurled them into the fire.

"Times are changing. I prefer the simple vampire or rogue tiger."

"You're joking. You'd miss all the action." He hustled after the two with protruding arrows that flapped on the ground.

"No. I think it's time that I took on a desk. Someone needs to coordinate the overall mission, there's too much activity. You can handle the field work from now on."

"You'll get fat." Ulrich tossed the shrouds on the fire.

"I'll suffer."

"You're still going to pay for the meals, right?"

"I'll be feeding more than you if I have my way."

"What do you mean?"

"Death's rearing his mighty head."

Ulrich turned and gave all of his attention to his friend. He realized his friend spoke of something else besides retiring.

"The change is upon us again," Rolf pointed at the pyre.

"What can we do?"

"We'll gather as many worthy apprentices as we can muster. I want to create a new group of Death hunters."

"Where we going with this?"

Rolf glared at him intently. "We're going to fight back. I

refuse to just keep taking these monstrosities on as they come. We're going to hunt them out and kill them."

"You're speaking of a small army."

"Exactly. An army of rangers for the continuation of life."

"It sounds like a religion."

"If needs be. You Ulrich shall be our first captain."

"Rolf. Are you alright?"

"Never better. We're not going to stop at killing Death's minions either. We're going to teach the people how to survive death, how to grow their own food, fight disease and when the time comes stomp out the corruption around us."

"A tall order. What makes you think COG will let us?"

"Their local cronies won't be able to stop us. Which would you choose, a way of life that doesn't protect you from death, or one that promises life? Before they know it we'll be too strong."

"Always."

Rolf leaned on Ulrich. "Then the Four Horsemen don't stand a chance. A fifth rider will take the field for Life."

Ulrich couldn't resist asking. "Rider? And what color of horse do I get?"

Rolf laughed. "An old swayback appaloosa.

"Huh?" Ulrich turned to his friend in surprise.

Rich laughter echoed up into the trees. "It will represent what we have left to patch the world back together with."

About the author: Michael C. Pennington is the owner of Aurora Wolf Literary Journal of Science Fiction and Fantasy at www.aurorawolf.com

A Stopped Clock
Lee Hughes

Stan stood in the dark of his wardrobe, a digital clock wailed in the room outside.

He sat on the bed and rubbed his forehead. The alarm was set for 7:40. The clock had a twin, and its alarm was set to 7:25. Stan reached and thumbed the switch swapping the alarm to post meridian ready for the evening. He did the same to its companion. There was a third timepiece. This one a little more archaic than the cheap radio-alarm clocks. A pocket-watch with a gold casing. His fingers worked the catch. The delicately wrought and blackened hands stretched out to point at 7:32, the second hand stood static.

It had all gone strange since he'd found the pocket watch. He laughed the same bitter laugh as the same bitter thought trampled through his mind, *"You can't turn back time."* Stan's laugh soured, *"You can't get it to go forward either."*

Stan stared at all of the things he'd scrawled upon the walls throughout the sleepless night. Fear had brought obsession, and like every obsession it became dominant, visible, inked upon the walls.

***

The find.

Scotty shouted: "Hey, Stan, come have a look at this."
Stan went over to see what Scotty had found. Scotty was holding up a mucky magazine, turning it this way and that. Scotty flipped it over so Stan could see.

"Hot, huh?" Scotty said, grinning.

"Nice." It was half-hearted.

"Nice?" Scotty was shocked. "Nice? This is a hot piece of ass, Stan, Christ how long you been divorced now? Two, three years? That's more than enough time to stop thinking of it as just something to piss out of."

Carl slapped Stan's shoulder. "You know what he's like, mental age of a brick."

"The worst part is he has a point."

"You'll get back in the game when you're ready." He hiked

a thumb over his shoulder, "That dingbat, he talks a good game, put him in a room with that lass from the jazz-mag and he'd shit himself."

He stopped on the path. The headache was back, the migraines had been coming more frequently. He dry swallowed a couple of Paracetemol. There was a half dozen bulging bin-bags. Stan took a step back. Number 32, an old chap, always generous with his Christmas box. Stan looked up to the skies, he wasn't religious but he hoped the old feller had gone on to a better place. Stan grabbed up a couple of the bin bags he wasn't supposed to, because the rule was they only took what could fit in the bin. Stan thought those rules didn't matter, not in such circumstances.

Something shiny caught his magpie eye. It was gold, but stood out from the fake gold of the cheap pub trophies. He dipped a hand in and took the watch out. He found the tiny catch and thumbed it. The second hand performed its stuttered lap. He knew the old man lived alone, but there might be offspring that would like such a keepsake. He looked at the face of the watch. The second hand had become static. He put it to his ear and heard only silence. That was probably why it had ended up in the bin.

Scotty was setting up a bin. Stan saw the dirty magazine was rolled up in Scotty's back pocket. "Saw you bringing out those extra bags, why'd you bother?"

"The old man's dead. The stuff would just lie rotting."

"Anything decent?" Scotty asked.

"Just junk by the looks of it."

Scotty grabbed the lid. He took out a trophy. He held it aloft liked he'd won it. "Oi, Carl! I won the 2003 West District darts championship, what the hell did you do that year?"

"Bollocks you did."

"Yes I did, look, got a trophy to show for it." Scotty stomped off to the front of the wagon with the trophy. Stan moved on to the next bin, the weight of the watch in his pocket constantly playing with his morals. Just because it was broken shouldn't mean that any surviving family member wouldn't want it. Back at the depot he'd be able to ask a few questions, hopefully find someone to give the pocket watch to.

***

"Hello?"

"Stan?" It was Alice from the depot. She'd been divorced a little while longer than Stan and he reckoned she'd a soft spot for him. She'd managed to get hold of the phone number of Mr. McGee's only daughter.

"Hi Alice."

"Just phoning about the watch, I spoke with the daughter."

"That's great; she should have something like to remember her father by."

"That's why I'm ringing, Stan, she doesn't want the watch. Says that's why it's in the bin."

"Oh," Stan managed, feeling a little deflated.

"Stan, it was good of you to think about getting the watch to her. Good news though, it's yours if you want it."

"Mine?"

"Yeah, when I told her you'd found it and wanted to get it back to someone she said you can have it."

"I'll come get it. And thanks, you know, for doing this."

"You can always take me out for a drink."

His heart leapt a little, it was a good feeling. "Sure."

"When?"

"Friday night?"

"The Swan and Brick, about seven?" Alice suggested.

"Sounds good. I'll be popping in for the watch in a little while."

***

Stan was surprised to find six watch menders in the local vicinity. His pointing finger dawdled over Butler and Sons Watch Repairs; they fixed all manner of time pieces, but specialized in pocket watches and grandfather clocks, established in 1893.

***

The hanging bell alerted whoever was out the back. With the

old-school decor of the place Stan had expected to see a withered, hunched, bespectacled man come doddering out from the back. Instead the man was a little younger than he, no stoop and didn't limp.

The man smiled. "Good..." He paused and looked at the various clocks to garner the time. "... afternoon. Sorry, I stare so long at clocks; the time itself just becomes a background noise. How can I help?"

Stan pulled out the watch. "I was wondering if you'd be able to fix this." He set it down on the counter. The man picked it up, evaluating it by turning it this way and that. "Nice," was his whisper, "very nice."

"You wanting me to pop it open and let you know what's up with it and give you an idea of a repair price?"

"I was hoping you'd do that," Stan said.

The man sat down and pointed to a stool in the corner. "I'm Tom by the way."

"I'm Stan."

"A pleasure." Tom said. He carefully discarded the back of the casing and turned his professional eye upon the gala of springs and cogs that made up the music that the pocket watch should have been dancing to.

"Oohh," Tom said.

"What?" Stan asked.

"This is probably worth a few quid."

"How come?"

"Well, if the makers not above ground the price usually hikes, and it's a pretty rare piece. Arthur Covington was the maker. His chicken scratch mark is here. Only seen a couple of his, mind if I ask where you got it?"

Stan squirmed a little on his stool. "It was left to me in a roundabout kinda way." He fiddled with the inner workings for a few minutes and then looked up, his face a little embarrassed. "Everything looks like it should be working. I mean there's nothing that jumps out at me as to why it's not, ticking. But this to me should be running reliantly. Do you want to leave it with me?"

"No."

Stan put the watch into his inside pocket and patted it. He strode down the street, the afternoon sun bold above him. Stan didn't notice that everything that he passed re-worked its shadow, pointing to the hour that the watch had stopped. Once he was a few feet away the shadows snaked, worming after his ankles.

A voice called him from the doorstep of a closed down shop.

"I can smell it on you," The tramp said from his cardboard seat.

"What?"

The piece of diseased alcoholic in rags grinned. His mouth was a patchwork of teeth, the majority of which were absent or blackened. "The cancer, I have it too. It's in my lungs, all black, watch me cough." The man thumped his chest as if to loosen something and then hacked and coughed like a sixty-a-day-smoker. He spat onto the ground. Pointed to the mess and said, "That's my cancer. Cancer's eats away at you, just like time. You've gotten cancer of time, how long who knows. I could be dead tomorrow or next year, it's all just a waiting game, more so for you."

Stan wasn't even aware of his words as he asked. "What kind?" He was finding it hard to decipher the lunacy.

The tramp poked at his little puddle of illness and looked up. "Spare some change for a sick man?"

Stan shook his head, still bamboozled by the nutter's ramblings. The tramp snarled, "Then screw off."

Stan shut his front door and leaned against it. Every whacko that had something to say said it to him on the way home. The phone rang and he jumped. His hands were reluctant as they grabbed at the receiver. "Hello?"

"It's Alice." He wasn't expecting a call from her.

"What's up?" Stan wondered if she'd had a change of heart about their date.

"I've just had Mr. McGee's daughter on the phone again."

"What does she want?"

"She didn't want to tell me on the phone; she asked for your number, I told her I wasn't at liberty to divulge it. So she gave me hers, if you feel like calling it."

"What's the number?"

He put the phone down and picked it straight back up again, his fingers hovered an inch above the buttons, reluctant to start hitting them in case he heard something he didn't want to.

"Yes?" It was a woman's voice.

"I'm Stan Perkins; you were trying to get my number?"

"The man with my father's watch?"

"Yeah, that's me." He waited for her to say she'd changed her mind about the whole thing.

"I might have been a little abrupt with the woman from the bin centre, or whatever it's called."

"I'm sure Alice wasn't offended."

"Good. I was basically just calling to suggest you throw the watch away, to be honest it brought nothing but ruin to my father."

"Ruin?" Stan had always been a glutton for superstition.

"As in ruined his life."

"I'm sorry, you've lost me. It's just a watch."

"It sounds silly to me too, and I really am loathed to be talking about it to you. But before my father found that watch in a box of junk at the auctions he was happy go lucky. Soon afterwards he started to fixate about the watch. That it had stopped, but it wasn't broken, didn't need winding, and that it was a harbinger. Look, it doesn't matter to me either way, I've warned you, now it's entirely up to you what you do with it." Without another word she hung up. He took out the watch, turned it this way and that, it was a watch, nothing more.

He sat down at the computer.

He had Wikipedia up on the screen. Arthur Covington, watchmaker, born 1811, died 1876, not a bad innings. He started reading through his biography. Where he was born, where he was educated, He was married to Aphelia, his only child, a daughter Cecilia. Finding out how respected figures of the time craved to own a piece of his work and how he had suddenly retired and moved away, to where was only speculation. Where the mundane finished the hearsay started, the kind of things that if it was said in today's times it would end up with a court case and a serious lump of compensation. Clicking on a few of the links most of them to external sites it gave him more of the story involving the Watchmaker, the Earl, and the Watchmaker's daughter.

February 14ᵗʰ 1850

The light from the oil lamp burned as bright as he could get it. The recognition he was receiving was alarming. It gave him a sense of great pride for folks to think of quality when they heard the two words, *watch* and *Covington* in the same sentence. He used tweezers to settle a small spring into place. He ignored the sound of the shop door opening, his concentration purely on the work at hand. With the job done he left the workshop and walked through. On the inside he cringed and felt disgust, on the outside he managed a smile. "Good morning, my Lord."

The Earl was tall, broad at the shoulders and moved in a manner that let everyone know of his importance. "Arthur, fine day outside, don't you agree?"

"Yes, my Lord."

The Earl was moving around the shop. "That delectable daughter of yours not here today?"

The internal cringe turned into a knot. The Earl was renowned for his predatory like chasing of the ladies and of late Arthur's daughter Cecilia had been the subject of his hunt.

"I'm afraid she's helping her mother today."

Earl slapped his glove down on the counter. "Damn shame, I know how much she looks forward to my visits. But, alas, if she's not here it mightn't be such a bad thing as I have business to discuss with you, a commission."

The knot tightened. It was bad enough doing the repairs and the maintenance on the Earl's clocks without having to commit to crafting him one from scratch. The Earl also wasn't a man that was easy to say no to.

"You'd best come through to the back."

"Splendid."

***

"Cecilia," Arthur said, lowering the flames in the lamps.

"Yes father?" She was sweeping the shop.

"Be a dear and give the place a little bit of a tidy, I promised to go and have a look at the butchers clock, should be good for a leg of lamb."

"Of course father. Will you be heading straight home then?"

"My stomach feels as though its throat has been cut, so take that as a yes, you'll be fine to make your own way home?" He reached for his coat from the hook. Cecilia smiled, nodded and began to wipe down the surface of the work table.

Cecilia heard the front door open. She smiled, for a man with such precision for making watches her father was clumsy in the mind at times. She looked around the workshop wondering what he had forgotten.

A voice came from the front of the shop. "Arthur?"

Cecilia's heart froze. It was the Earl. She instantly wished she had followed her father through and locked the door after him. It was too late now for the fox was in the chicken coop. She took a few calming breaths, straightened the front of her dress and headed through.

The Earl smiled and raised an eyebrow. "I had expected to find your father but instead I find a gem of the purest beauty, my luck has turned, for the better. Is your father in the back?"

"He's popped out." She kept the counter between herself and the Earl.

The Earl's smile widened. "Lucky us."

"I can tell him that you called." Her mouth was running out of spit.

"Never, it's dark outside; there could be all manner of brigands afoot. I just could not live with myself if anything befell you, oh how angels would weep. No, I shan't hear of it, we can get to know each other a little better; you'd like that, wouldn't you?"

Arthur headed on home with a decent sized leg of lamb. It was good to get paid in money but there was something about trading that seemed to have a nobler feel to it. He hung up his coat and embraced the warmth from the fire before heading on through to the kitchen. Margaret was busy at the stove. She smiled as she looked back over her shoulder. The smile faded a little. "Is Cecilia not with you?"

"I left her to finish up at the shop. That was over an hour ago, there weren't that many chores. I'll pop back and see if there's anything the matter, mayhap she's just having problems with the locks again, won't be a tick." He headed back through to the parlour.

Arthur tried the door and found it unlocked, once or twice Cecilia had struggled with the lock, this time he decided that he would do something about it and get it fixed, but not tonight, his stomach wasn't the most forgiving of creatures.

He called "Cecilia?" But gained no answer. He ventured deeper into the shop. He could see that the lamps were still burning in the workshop. He didn't even get over the threshold before his legs threatened buckled. His stomach forgot about food and sickened. "Cecilia!" he ran to her. She was a crumpled mess in the corner. Her dress was torn, her hair dishevelled. She looked up. Her face was bruised, one eye blackening. She began to sob, the sobs grew louder.

***

It had been a week and Cecilia had barely said a word. She sat and simply stared off into some other place. Once Arthur had carried Cecilia home and had called for the doctor he had made straight for the constable. Arthur hadn't expected to get anywhere there, not when the buffoon was under the thumb of the Earl. He ended up buying a pistol in a rage.

Arthur looked at the clock above his workbench. The clock had been made by his father soon after he'd finished his own apprenticeship. The Earl had sent a message that he would be by a little before noon to see how the watch was coming along. Arthur couldn't believe the audacity of the bastard. The man was above the law, shielded by his position, even from rape and battery. Arthur opened the drawer and looked hard at the pistol, the shine of the barrel enticing, whispering to him about the justice it could deliver. There were some laws that even the likes of the Earl couldn't dodge. He heard the door open. He slid the drawer shut, steadied his fury and stood.

"Good day, Arthur." The bastard was all smiles as though he hadn't done anything to his daughter. The Earl marched up to the counter. "Right then, how are we getting on with my watch, and how's that daughter of yours?"

Arthur's jaw clenched. There was a look in the Earl's eyes

that was practically daring Arthur to say something. "She's fine my Lord, she's work to do at home. Come through to the back."

Arthur motioned to the half constructed watch upon the bench, nowhere near finished. Since the attack on his daughter he had wanted nothing to do with the Earl's watch. The Earl was leant over, staring into the casing as if he had half a clue as to what was what inside. Arthur's hand went to the drawer. Yes it would be murder, but justifiable, if not condonable under the circumstances. Yes he would hang, but justice would be served. He opened the draw a little way, the Earl spoke. "Oh, I nearly forgot. I hear you have been to see the constable over a mistake." He didn't look up from his musings.

"A mistake?" Arthur could hardly get the words out, he choked on every syllable.

"A mistake, an error on your daughter's part I should wager. It is not farfetched to believe the fanciful imaginings of a young girl besotted by someone of my stature."

"The bruises? The torn dress? The rape?" Arthur was shaking with his rage. The Earl looked up, his eyes narrowed. "I hear that rumour again besmirching my reputation and there will be consequences, very, very harsh consequences. Do you understand me? But for your piece of mind I will let you in on the facts of that night. I came to see you, but found only your daughter who how shall we say made certain advances that I rebuked but such was her desire I had to take a firm hand with her. And also I heard a whisper that this week you purchased a pistol. You wouldn't be having any foolish notions would you? As if I even suspected such a thing you would be straight to the gibbet."

Arthur slid the drawer shut.

The Earl smiled. "Now show me where we're up to with my watch."

That night Arthur didn't go home. He worked feverishly. He took parts from other watches to finish it as quickly as he could. The workshop broke out in with the chorus of midnight. Arthur stared at the watch as the lamps died down to darkness and he sat in the dark and began on something that there would be no coming back from. Before the chiming had ended the lamps relit themselves and Arthur began to weep.

"Magnificent," the Earl said, holding his new watch up to the light.

"I'm glad you like it," Arthur replied, his look switching from the watch to the face of the bastard that was working the fob through a button hole.

The Earl pulled free his purse and began to count out a small fortune. "I'm glad you managed to get over that earlier silliness and see sense."

"Thank you my Lord, I'm glad that I saw sense too. I hope you enjoy the watch."

"I'm sure I will, good day."

Arthur watched the Earl's back, no smile on his lips as he knew that revenge wouldn't taste sweet. He looked at the walls of the shop that had become his second home. Those feelings were gone, torn away along with his daughter's innocence. Arthur strode to the door and turned the closed sign over. His shop was shut and wouldn't be opening again. He checked the time. His family would be waiting for the coachman. It was time for a new life up North, far away from this place but regardless of where they went he would be getting that little bit closer to damnation.

***

The Earl tore free the envelope on the watchmaker's shop door. The watch had cost a fortune and within the space of a couple of hours it had stopped dead. He tore out the letter.

My Lord,

You are a consummate bastard and I wish you nothing but ill-fortune. I have refunded the money for the watch and left it with your crony the constable. Please do with the watch what you will. But know this, the time that it stopped is the time of your death, only you will not know whether it be of the morning, or of the evening. May the Devil welcome you to his halls when the time is right, I will already be watching from the galleries no doubt.

Yours faithfully,

Arthur Covington

The Earl crumpled up the missive and cast it to the ground. There was nought he could do. He'd been refunded, and permitted to keep the watch. He opened the watch and looked at the time. The previous evening when it had halted the hands had pointed to 5:15. The Earl sneered at the closed shop and stormed off. He noticed as he went that the shadows were acting out of character and seeming to bend as he passed them by, tuning their darkness to the direction of his supposed our of death. The Earl walked that little bit faster with a feeling of unease sprouting in his gut.

The unease grew. The wine no longer tasted fine. The beggars and the halfwits would harass and hound him. All issuing whispers about something they should not know. Slowly his madness and paranoia wrapped its slick grip about him until his death sixteenth months later.

***

Stan sat back in his chair. Most of the stuff he'd read had come from pages about ghost stories and urban legends. He opened the watch, even though he didn't believe in such absurdities it did make him feel a little unsure. The way it had been working, the way it had abruptly stopped and there being no way to get it going. It didn't help when he read that the Earl had gone a bit doo-lally and had been obsessed with the time of his death, right up to it.

When he mentally matched that with what Mr. McGee's daughter had said on the phone the feeling began to swell. It was like an uncontrollable wave that rolled through his core. The lunatic spitting bits of charcoaled lung onto the floor and what he had said. It made Stan dash for the front door. He rushed down the path to stand at the lamppost on the other side of the gate. Its shadow was pointing in the same direction as the rest of its brethren until Stan grew close. It snaked around and mimicked the hour hand of the watch. Stan walked backwards, the shadow returned to normal. His heart thumped in his chest and his hands began to feel sticky.

Back inside he clicked on link after link about watches and time until seven o'clock rolled around. He grabbed the radio alarm clock from the spare room and sat it next to the one in his own room and began setting the alarms. One to warn him it was nearly the allotted time, the other to inform him that the time had passed. He felt foolish letting his imagination get the better of him. He jumped as the first alarm aired. He switched the alarm off and didn't know what to do with himself. With one minute to go he climbed into the wardrobe.

The dark of the wardrobe seemed to hold the ability to stretch time into infinity. When the second alarm aired the sensation of relief was astounding. Stan practically burst out of the wardrobe cursing himself for having such notions. Then that feeling returned, reminding him that even a stopped clock is right twice a day, or he hoped, wrong twice a day.

Sleep was impossible and the next morning he found himself phoning in sick. He couldn't risk being outside and working when 7:32 rolled around so when the first alarm sounded he returned to the wardrobe and waited for the second, praying to hear it.

***

Alice pursed her lips. There was still no answer. Stan had phoned in sick two days ago and hadn't been in touch since. Their supposed date was tonight. She was starting to wonder whether or not he was using it as a way of chickening out of it. Her head started running through scenarios of what might have happened to him, all of which were not good. In his sickened state he might have taken a shower, slipped and banged his head. He might have fallen down the stairs. The sickness could have been worse than what he'd said and he might be in dire need of help. She got up, ran into the filing department and asked if one of the girls could cover for her so she could take an early lunch, medical reasons.

She peeped in through the living room; there was no sign of him. Something was up. She dug out her mobile from her handbag and dialled his house number. She let it ring as she lifted the letter box and listened to the unanswered ring through the slot. She hung up and dialled treble nine.

She put the backdoor window through with a cheap gnome.

"Stan?" she called as she moved from the kitchen to the

hallway. She checked what she guessed was the spare room and the bathroom, both of which were empty. The third room she figured to be Stan's bedroom. There was scrawling on the wall in marker pen that unsettled her.

She stared at one scribbling that read, '*Nothing is immortal, especially time.*' Alice turned around, her eyes found something familiar. The watch. It was dangling from the door of the wardrobe by a length of string. Her hands pulled at it. The wardrobe door came with it. Alice screamed.

She watched his body lifted into the back of the ambulance. All she could think about was what the paramedic said when she'd asked if he knew what had killed Stan. The paramedic had suggested that by the bloodshot eyes and the way the body was laying he may have died of a brain aneurism. He might not have even been aware of it. Maybe just some headaches for symptoms maybe a bit of blurry vision. He said they were like time bombs; anything could be a trigger, undue stress to it just being ready to blow. She asked how long he had been dead. The paramedic had said at another guess maybe as little as five hours. She looked to her wrist, it was a little after twelve. That would have him dying around seven o'clock.

Alice walked away from the house. The road seemed to stretch on forever as she walked. The image of Stan haunting her. Her car was still parked outside his house. She felt she needed to walk, she didn't know where. Just to walk. She couldn't help herself. She dipped a hand into her bag and felt relieved by the touch of the watch. She had just wanted to take something away, something of his. It wouldn't be worth anything, the watch had stopped a few seconds after she had opened it. She walked on, ignorant of the shadows that migrated positions as she went.

About the author: Lee Hughes' writing can be found in print in Cern Zoo: Nemonymous 9,Deep Space Terror, Flash! 365 Days of Flash, Don't Tread on Me, Howlupcoming in, Daily Bites of Flesh and Caught by Darkness. His onlinewriting can be found amongst many of the online haunts and hecurrently edits horror for the eZine Thrillers, Killers 'n' Chillers.To find out more visit www. LeeHugh

IN THE BEGINNING
Dorothy Davies

In the beginning was the mushroom cloud, many trees tall into the sky and from the cloud came fine dust. It burned the ground and tore the skim from the bones of those who ran.

IT stood in the centre of the square in its own hut, the wooden casing marked with rain, the flimsy back which housed the electronics slowly dissolving, colourful wires falling out.

There were some people who ran to burrow in the ground like the rabbit in his hole, there to live until the dust should cease to fall.

Gil hated IT. He didn't know why and he didn't feel he could tell anyone how he felt, either. It was just a blind hatred for a blind thing. The blank stare disconcerted him and he would make elaborate detours to reach his hut rather than pass IT by.

There were some people who fell to their knees and cried to the Unseen Spirit. It heeded not their cries and they were burned. Their bones littered the ground.

Mother would complain if yet again he was late with the precious copper bowl full of water, but somehow it seemed, well, childish, to tell her that he didn't want to walk past IT. She would laugh at him and at thirteen it hurt to be laughed at, even by his mother. Or was it because she was his mother? But detour he would. And he did.

There were some people who ran to the woods, where they lived as the animals do, sleeping on the ground and eating of the berries and leaves of the trees and bushes. Of these, many died, but some lived. They that lived joined with others who came from their holes in the ground. There was a Gathering together of those that did not die.

"Where have you been? Why are you always so late with the water?" Annoyed, his mother turned away into the shadowy interior of the hut, still grumbling about her need to tend to Zita and how late he was. Gil sat on the ground outside, picking at the grass.

"Look after Zita for me while I milk the cow." Before he could reply, she walked away, stoop-shouldered and tired, down the narrow beaten track toward the pasture. Were all the women stoop-shouldered and tired? He knew the answer even as he framed the question. Gil was growing up fast and questioning every aspect of his life. He was worried by the things he thought about.

When the people ran to hide, they took nothing with them but their skills. And when the dust was gone and there was silence in the world, they went back to look in the broken buildings for that which was of value. They found many things.

Where in this Gathering is there a suitable mate for me? Gil asked himself. The girls were young and thin, not one of them seemed ready to help build a hut and start a new corner of this Gathering. If there should be no suitable mate... He examined the thought of leaving: it filled him with dread.

There were books, many books, which told of the ways to build the things which made the mushroom cloud. And in their anger and hate they burned all the books. They made fires which could be seen for many trees' distance. And more people came, to bring books to the Burning. It went on for many days.

Zita gurgled and chuckled to herself and Gil went to pick her up. For a baby sister she wasn't so bad, at least she wasn't missing any vital parts and she might one day be as pretty as her name. He waved a flower in front of her eyes to amuse her and she reached out to grab it from him.

And they found the Television, which we were once proud to care for in our Gathering. It was one of the earliest founder members who discovered it, complete among many broken ones. May his name live forever.

His mother came back, walking slowly so as not to spill a single drop of the precious milk. That would be for Zita, it always was. Gil's young stomach rumbled with the need for the food he had not had for the past two days. The harvest had been bad this season and the pasture was getting scarce.

"Everything's all right," he said as his mother passed him. "I was just playing with her. She didn't cry."

"There's a funeral this afternoon," his mother commented as she disappeared into the hut with Zita.

Gil followed her in. "Anyone I know?"

"An old man. I don't think you ever spoke to him."

Gil sighed wearily. A funeral meant a compounding of the nightmare which tormented his sleep. The black stare of IT came closer and closer, threatening to engulf him. The dead person's face would be captured in the square box and Gil would rise up from his bed, screaming. For, after every funeral, IT was brought out into the open, available for any bereaved grieving person to commune with it.

They say that in the time before the cloud came down, all the persons in the world had a Television. They say that people walked and talked behind the screen. They say the picture came from far away, people would talk to the screen and it would answer them. It must have been a wonderful thing.

In the afternoon the male members of the Gathering – Gil among them – took their sharp pointed sticks and tramped into the forest to the burying ground. There they scraped the hard earth away to make a shallow grave. The Leader of the Gathering came with the men who carried the body and they slowly lowered it into the cold unyielding earth.

Every member of the Gathering came forward, took a handful of earth from the side of the grave and threw it on the body. Then they turned and walked away.

The burying was silent, sombre. Gil knew that the nightmare would be back that night, whether he had known the old man or not...

The Television stood in the centre of the Place we had then and all who passed IT revered it. The hut was sheltered. IT was never left to fall apart. The children were taught to stay away from IT. IT stood proudly among us and we were proud that it was there.

Gil ran with his friend Dani, tossing a ball from one to the other, then, thrusting it inside a rough home-made tunic to climb trees, Gil joined Dani and they swung dangerously from creaking branches before dropping to the hard earth where they could watch the blazing sun die in the vermillion sky.

"At the end of the day comes the dying," sang Gil softly.

Dani laughed. "Been listening to the Song Man too much!"

"I like the Song Man," Gil defended himself vigorously. "I like the Story Man, too."

"He only talks of the past," said Dani with all the confidence of fourteen years. "I look forward, not back."

"Don't we all?" responded Gil, showing – outwardly at least – equal confidence.

"Gil..." Dani rolled on his back and stared at the black lace pattern of branches on burning sky. "I want to talk to you ..."

"You're talking; I'm listening, what's new?"

"No, *serious* talk now. You won't tell anyone, will you?"

"I won't tell."

Dani rolled over and stared at Gil. His eyes were serious behind the curtain of red hair as he sought for a way to begin.

"Do you like Zita?"

"Zita? Well, of course I do, she's my sister, isn't she?"

"Han's my brother but I *hate* him." Dani dropped the startling statement into the late afternoon and both boys were silent. Gil turned the words over his mind.

"No, I don't hate Zita, she's just there, like Pati or Toni or Geri or any of the rest of them."

"I don't hate my family, Gil, Only Han. That twisted body, that - that blank stare, he's not right, Gil, I think he should have been left out for the dogs only Mother's too soft. She fusses over him; he gets all the milk while the rest of us go hungry! He's useless; he'll never be any good for the Gathering."

For a long moment Gil wondered how to respond to his friend's confession. Finally, words rose unbidden before he could stop them.

"I hate IT, Dani. I hate IT for its blank stare and strange shape but I can't say anything. IT doesn't get milk but it does get a lot of attention and songs and stories. I think we should get rid of it."

"Both of us with a hate and nothing we can do about it ..."

"There is, if we had nerve enough to do it!" Gil became animated as a series of pictures crossed his mind. "You could leave Han on the edge of the woods, go for a pee or something, you can't be blamed for that, can you? And I could... smash... IT..."

White-faced, Dani stared at him. "You're talking about killing, Gil," he said softly, seriously.

"I know what I'm talking about but we're only talking, aren't we?

"Sure we are, sure we are, Gil. Come on, let's go home. It's getting late."

And there were those in the Gathering who communed with the Television, who saw in the face many visions of the future. And these people became Vision Men and spoke among us of that which is to come. There were many who fell down before the Television and worshipped it as being the silent voice of the Unseen Spirit.

On the day of Han's funeral, Gil walked with Dani, one arm round his shoulders, trying to comfort him. The Gathering mourned the loss of the man-child and brought loss-gifts to Dani's parents as they sat weeping in front of their hut. Dani hid in the darkness, nursing his wild thoughts and guilt and Gil left him alone.

There was nothing he could say now; perhaps later, when the wound began to heal. Gil walked alone in the forest, listening to the howling dogs. Nursing his own hatred he wondered if he had the nerve to carry out his own killing.

That night, when the nightmare came, the tiny face captured in the television screen was Han's blank-eyed stare. Gil sat up, struggling to control his scream and he knew what he had to do. Cautiously he crept from the coverings and made his way to the door, picking up his pointed stick as he went. No one moved. There was only the soft breathing and murmuring of sleep in the darkness. Gil turned away, ignored the inner voice that pleaded with him to stay and set out for the centre of the Place.

Han's family had gone; there was nobody to commune with IT. The filtered moonlight turned the glass face to silver. IT seemed to glare at Gil, as if IT knew what he had come for; almost sentient, a travesty of life ...

Gil stood; stick poised, thinking about the nightmare, the devotion and care lavished on IT, a useless, inanimate object, unnecessary, backward-looking. The hate boiled over and he plunged the stick into the silver face. There was a sound like breaking ice on a winter's morning and, with ringing shouts of triumph he smashed at IT again and again, splintering the wooden case, spilling the mysterious things inside down onto the ground.

As he stood staring at the wreckage he suddenly became aware of eyes on him. He spun round.

The Gathering had been woken by his shouts and the noise of the breaking machine and now they ringed the centre of the Place;

silent, reproachful, accusing, hate-filled faces...

"Look!" Gil cried, his boy's voice edged with maturity. "I've destroyed IT, you're free!" The hostility grew, a tangible thing reaching out for him and he backed away, treading on things that snapped under his weight. He pleaded with the silence for understanding.

"You don't have to worry about IT, you don't have to tell the children to stay away from IT –oh don't you understand, you're free!"

No one answered him.

Clutching his stick tightly, he stood, television debris all around him and watched the Gathering fade back into the darkness. And he let the night-breeze dry his tears.

And there was one among us who did not understand or revere the Television. It is said by some he was disturbed by the death of a man-child in the Gathering, but yet others say the night winds took his mind. Yet others again say he could not comprehend the true meaning of the Television or of the Unseen Spirit that spoke from IT. The reasons are many, the facts are few. In the dark of a night when the winds are abroad to steal a man's mind from his body and leave it vacant, he went forth with his stick and attacked the Television.

And it died.

About the author: Dorothy Davies, writer, historian, medium. Lives on the Isle of Wight, edits for a living.

No! I'm Not Paranoid!

Jordan Fuselier-Gardner

It is out to get me. Before I place my hands on that silvery handle or even reach the top of the stairs I know it. It haunts me. Following me around during the day and causing me to wonder what goes on when I'm not around. Does it come to life? Does it call a meeting in my empty room? Or the darkness of my closet when I sleep?
Sometimes when I somehow get out alive, I believe it follows me, escaping for some reason which befuddles me. Maybe it is just biding its time and waiting, plotting, growing in strength with each passing day. Whoever said you are safest in your own home, obviously never met my room.

It all begins when I first open the door. The first attempts on my life and my health. That blasted door jamb comes out of nowhere, catching my little toe or attacking my elbow out of spite if I'm wearing shoes. It catches me almost every day, jumping in my way as I go in and out, watching and waiting for me to make a move, for me to relinquish my seat and attempt to pass through its portal without a scratch. I don't know why that door jamb hates me so; it's my brother's grimy hand-prints that mar its once white surface.

The next attempt comes from a dear friend. As I enter my room with a yelp of pain and a few half-hearted hops, the desk moves into my path. One little nudge and down it comes, trying to eat my head. For reasons I don't understand, my little stuffed animal Stitch has turned against me. I've never mistreated him or have given him reason to hate me. Hell, I even dust him weekly. It not my fault the top of my desk is so dang dusty. Yet somehow he slowly inches his way toward the edge of the top shelf, lying in wait for me to come near.

It doesn't stop there. Nope! Their attempts continue and they draw me in with the need for something which has been long lost. Yes, I speak of the dreaded journey into the closet of no return. The black hole. The end of everything and beginning of nothing. Somehow, everything ends up in there whether I want it to or not. I find odds and ends which I could have sworn had ended up somewhere else. I find them among the mass of stuffed animals, empty two liter bottles, clothing which is too small or too 'not me' to be worn, and other random things.

Oh, it's a grizzly affair; attempting to pry my wanted possessions from that greedy accumulation of junk. For some reason the things I seek are always at the bottom of everything. Stuffed animal avalanches are not uncommon and I wonder why all my lovable animals wish me gone. While trying to dig my way out, I wonder where I went wrong. Were the pair of snowboarding gloves, which are of no use to me for another year, worth it?

That's not even half of it! Each day these attempted assassinations are better planned. From deflated, back-destroying air mattresses to the occasional flying book. You can't overlook the walkway of clothing and hidden shoes which challenges my every step and hopes to send me sprawling on the bathroom floor. Of course, there's still the magically moving papers which split my skin, the coins which drop from out of nowhere, the loose wires which endeavor to send me head first into the bookcase. Oh, I can't forget the wall with that blasted beam. The output for my anger and the reason behind my permanently swollen knuckle. You would think I would learn to pick another spot, but I believe that beam would relocate just for me.

The list could go on and on. I could reveal the entire plot which my stuff is putting into place to end my existence, but it wouldn't allow me. At this moment, my computer is plotting against me, waiting for the one word which would completely expose them. They are prepared to erase all of this and save themselves from their ultimate doom. At this point, they all believe you would think me to be crazy. 'Inanimate objects don't plot against or attack people,' you would say, but I know better. I can hear the walls whispering, the clothes confiding, the books babbling, and the lights laughing. All directed at me and their evil plots. This might be the end. The worst part is. This is only one room.

About the author: Born Texan, Jordan Fuselier-Gardner has recently settled into a beautiful valley in the high Rockies of Colorado. After enjoying both creative writing and art in high school, Jordan is attempting to continue both while trying to figure out where her life is going.

If only I had Teeth
Ronald J. Craft

Recently, I learned a valuable lesson. Never mess with a necromancer. I wouldn't be in the sorry state I am now if I had this bit of knowledge a few days ago.

It all began with me entering a cemetery with my buddy, Jason. We were pretty broke and, well, there was a newly buried woman who had enough jewelry on her to feed us for a long while. Times were tough, and we weren't any good at stealing from the living, so we had taken to the ones that couldn't fight back. It worked for us so far, so we kept at it.

I see you there, judging me. You don't know a damn thing about me, so keep your mouth shut.

Anyway, we walked a ways into this freaky cemetery. It was the worst one in town. Old, full of grave stones that were lopsided, and the caretaker was especially creepy looking. He looked much like the gravestones he tended. Old and lopsided.

Right before we got to the woman's grave, I got this really creepy feeling. You know, like the ones in a movie where something bad is about to happen. The, holy crap, my hairs are standing up on the back of my neck feeling. So, what did I do? I kept going anyway. They always do in the movies, right?

Once we arrived, Jason pulled me down, and told me to shut up. I was pretty confused at this point, but the weird, creepy feeling was still there. He yanked me over, and pointed off into the distance. I looked over and saw a hunched man wearing a long, black cloak standing next to the grave we were heading to.

Great. Someone else came for our meal card, and was already in the process of digging her up. Worst case scenario... we had to kill the guy and throw him into a grave. We decided to hang back, and let him do the work for us.

He dug for a while, until finally, a loud thunk resounded through the cemetery. I almost expected some of the dead to burst out of the ground after being so rudely disturbed. The man grunted, and the lid of the casket slid off onto the ground with a thud.

Several moments later, he crawled out of the ground. We caught a quick glimpse of a face lined with scars, and lips twisted into a permanent sneer.

The man by the grave pulled a book out of his coat, and flipped it open. He began to mutter something, but neither of us could make out what he was saying. Next thing we knew, he slammed the book closed, threw his hands up in the air, and shouted in a voice that give me nightmares to this day, "Return to me. Return to me, my love!"

Ever heard someone with the flu try to shout? They sound like a demented frog, and snot is flying everywhere. Meet creepy-grave-digger-man.

The smell of urine filled my nose, and I nearly puked. Jason was never a brave one, but a grown man pissing himself? Last time he's coming with me, I swore.

Still, even I was freaked out at this point. Jason tried to pull me back, but I was too scared to move. I probably should've gone with him, because a second later we hear a moan from within the casket, and lots of cracking noises. The damn dead woman tumbled out of her casket, her limbs bending in ways that no human ever should, and crawled out of the hole.

It was my turn to lose control of my bladder. I wanted to haul ass out of there, and put all this in the back of my mind.

Like hell was that going to happen, though. I was broke, hadn't eaten in days, and some hunched-over bastard that resurrects dead people just stole my chance at some beef stew. No way was I going to stand for that shit.

I gripped my shovel tighter, and walked toward the bastard standing by the grave. The man held her hands and gazed at his zombie lover, completely oblivious to his surroundings. She was struggling to stand, drooling, and looking around wildly. I'm pretty sure she had no clue what was going on, and probably wanted to rip his head off.

There was a fat jewel on her necklace, but I couldn't take my eyes off her face. I could only wonder what kind of sick mortuary did her makeup. She reminded me, distinctly, of my aunt. And that's not a compliment, mind you. My aunt had a hairy face, wore way too much eye liner, and couldn't go outside on a hot day because her face would melt off.

Once in position, I figured I had this in the bag. Jason was still shitting himself back at the hiding spot. I thought about all the different ways to take out Demented Frog Dude, but in the end went with the least complicated plan.

I just ran up behind him, and smashed the guy in the back of the head with my shovel. He didn't even make a sound; just fell over. Blood spurted from his head and pooled around him. His zombie lover made some sort of moaning sound, but I kicked the bitch back into the grave.

Jason came running over while I was in the middle of waving my shovel in the air like some sort of video game victory dance. I told him to grab whatever the freaky guy had on him and I'd deal with the zombie in the grave. She was still trying to claw her way out, but something that slow would be no problem to deal with.

So, feeling fairly confident, I whacked the bitch with the shovel and jumped into the hole. I smashed her rotting face into the bottom of the casket with my foot while I grabbed all the jewelery off her. Dead rich people were the best. I had never actually had a dead person fight back before while robbing them, so you could say I was enjoying myself more than I probably should have.

Mission completed, I shoved the booty into my pocket, gave the zombie another whack, and then climbed out. I figured Jason would be done by now and waiting for me.

Well, he was definitely done all right. The man I had just smashed in the head with my shovel about two minutes before, was standing up and dusting himself off. I know damn well I cracked his skull open, and yet he looked like nothing had even happened.

And Jason? Well, he was there too.

Actually, he was everywhere. There was a little bit of him in front of me, some on the ground by the guy and the rest seemed to be spread about the cemetery.

Shit.

Demented Frog Dude turned towards me, and gave me this look that would probably stop most people's hearts even in broad daylight. I guess I just screwed up his reunion with his dead lover and he was pretty pissed off.

"You messed up, kid." He pulled his book back out and flipped it open with one hand.

Forget him. I wasn't going to stay there for that shit.

I decided that now would be a great opportunity to get the hell out of there. I tossed my shovel into the grave, and took off as fast as my legs would carry me through the cemetery, all the while being chased by his creepy chanting.

Everything around me started to slow down. I couldn't move, I couldn't breathe, I couldn't even piss myself again. I was totally confused at this point and no matter what I did, my body wouldn't do what I wanted it to. Then, he appeared in front of me, and edged his face to within an inch of my own.

That permanent sneer of his curved upward into, what I can only guess, was supposed to be a smile. "I appreciate your donation."

Donation? What donation? I wasn't giving him shit. I wanted to say it to his face, but I still found I was unable to do anything but stand there drooling on myself like his zombie bitch.

Actually, I felt kinda hungry. I had this really strong craving for raw meat all of a sudden. That's when it dawned on me.

That asshole.

I guess he noticed the conclusion I had come to. I was moving, but I was going so slow it felt like I was standing still. His zombie girl stood behind him now, and peered at me over his shoulder.

Except for one detail. She was alive now.

Her skin was pale and smooth, and her eyes twinkled mischievously in the moonlight. The bastard had stolen my life, and given it to her.

"I guess no one ever taught you not to mess with a necromancer." The creepy asshole bowed, and walked off into the night with his girl.

So, here I am, stuck as a zombie, wandering around town trying to find some damn steak. I ate what was left of Jason, but it didn't do much for me. He didn't have much meat on his bones.

I shuffled over to town, and made for the pub. I figured if I was going to find something to eat, my best bet would be there. I almost had this drunk that passed out in an alley, but he managed to beat me off with a broken bottle. He knocked my teeth out too. So, if any of you happen to find my teeth, or could spare a set of false teeth, look me up. I'll be hanging out in the alley behind Greg's Pub.

Damn, I'm hungry.

About the author: Ronald J. Craft is primarily a fantasy author, but tired of horror always taking things too seriously, he tried his hand at the comedic side of things. With the completion of this short story, he now has several more comedic horror shorts planned while continuing work on his epic fantasy series at the same time.

Tommy's Toy Land
Jessica A. Weiss

"Come one, come all! We've got chills and thrills, freaks and creeps! Hurry, hurry, sights like you've never seen before!" The barker stood on an old barrel beneath a faded sign, enticing small town people to devour the offerings on display.

Tommy stood to the side watching parents' sooth crying children, and rowdy teenage boys assuring their ghostly pale girlfriends that they would keep them safe. Anything was better than being at home, listening to his parents fight.

"There was so much blood, I won't sleep for a week," one wide-eyed blond exclaimed, clinging to her football star escort as they walked away from the haunted house.

The boy rolled his eyes at her childishness. "It's all fake. Nothing here is real." He wrapped his arms tighter around her and they walked on.

The tents and stalls looked ancient; holes in canvas tarps, wood poles old and blackened with time. This was not like the other carnivals that came to town. Even the entrance sign was aged and missing letters. Tommy decided to check it out, it couldn't be that bad.

Walking around, Tommy realized there were no rides. There were side shows and freaks, a haunted house, fortune tellers and card readers, unusual game stalls, and the center attraction a giant Toy Land Castle. Finally, he approached a dismal dunking tank.

"Care to try your luck, son?" The man in charge held out a black ball. His smile didn't reach his birdlike eyes and most of his teeth had rotted away.

"Sure. How much?" Tommy held out his hand to receive the heavy ball.

Stepping closer, the man laid a scarred, three fingered hand on Tommy's shoulder. "First try is free," he cackled, his breath stinking like decomposing trash.

Tommy stood before the woman in the murky tank. She was wearing a dry, thin white dress. Obviously, no one had successfully sent her into the dark fluid below. She smiled as he pulled his arm back to throw the ball, her forked tongue flicking through her lips in anticipation. With a rush, the ball hit the target and the woman in white splashed out of sight, only to resurface a moment later.

She screamed and flailed against the tank. Her dress, skin and hair were covered in slimy red fluid. Watching the crimson rivulets drip down her face, Tommy backed away in shock, his reaction causing the nearly toothless man and drenched woman to laugh hysterically.

"Screw you!" Tommy was angry with himself for letting the freaks get a reaction from him. His outburst only received more laughs. He was going to have to toughen up if he was going to make it on the road alone.

Turning away, he continued to explore the carnival grounds. Across the packed dirt area from the game stall, Tommy saw a cleaner looking tent. Metallic stars caught and reflected the low lights strung from pole to pole. It called to him and he made his way to the shadowed opening.

No one waited to beckon unsuspecting people in, and the tent appeared to be vacant. Tommy felt an unusual disappointment as he started to walk away.

"Come in, Tommy," a low voice called, stopping his retreat.

Tommy poked his head into the tent flap. "Hello? Did you call me?"

"Yes. Please come in and sit," the voice replied.

Stepping through a second fabric flap, Tommy's skin crawled as if spiders were dancing on his nerves. Before him was a small round table covered with a tattered, dark blue cloth, a dripping red candle burning at its center. An old woman dressed in rags sat to one side, at the other stood an empty, dusty chair.

She motioned toward the empty chair. "Come, my boy, don't stand there with your mouth open."

Carefully, Tommy sat. The interior of the tent reeked of mold and dust. Even the old woman across from him smelled ancient and rotting.

"Give me your hand, Tommy." She laid an old spotted hand on the table, her palm upward, expecting his.

"How do you know my name?" He kept his hands clasped in his lap. The barker had been correct; this place did have freaks and creeps.

"Madame Boliva knows many things," she cackled, which turned into a harsh cough. "Your hand, then?"

"Fine, I'll play along." Tommy was surprised by the softness of her skin, though the chill of her flesh was a bit unsettling. "So now you're going to give me some vague fortune and expect me to pay for specifics, right?" He tried to laugh off his unease.

"So cynical for a young boy."

"I am not a boy!" Tommy's anger burned his cheeks. He slammed his free hand on the table, the candle dislodging hot, dark red wax, splattering the table cloth.

"Of course not. Fourteen is a man, isn't it?" Amusement colored her voice. "Now, sit calmly while Madame Boliva unravels your future path." She began tracing the lines on his palm, the jagged edges of her nails scratching his skin.

"I see you've left home and are ready to start your own life without your parents' rules and restrictions." Her revelations shocked him. No one knew he had run away, his parents probably had not noticed he was gone. "You feel you are man enough to be your own Master. Very good. But I see you as being the Master of others, too, and soon."

"That's what I'm talking about. I'm going to be the boss of others!" Tommy liked her version of his future. "So I made the right choice in leaving. I am just that good," he said puffed up with pride. He would be the youngest and most powerful boss ever. His imagination was soaring.

"Would you like to know more? Madame Boliva sees more." She waited, a smile pulling the corners of her mouth.

"Why not? Can you tell me who I'm going to be the boss of? What kind of company? Just how soon is this going to happen? Where should I go to get this started?" Greed lit his eyes, his discomfort and unease gone.

"You will be their Master, not their boss. You've already started in the right direction and, by the time you reach the next town, you will be the master."

"The Master of whom, of what business?" he asked, tapping his foot impatiently.

"You are Tommy, Master of Toy Land!" she announced with a huge, yellow toothed smile.

"What? Are you crazy?" He pulled his hand free from her grasp. "This is all a stupid joke, isn't it?" He stood angrily, knocking over his chair. "I don't know how you knew so much about me, but this is obviously crap."

Tommy stormed out of the fortune teller's tent, her laughing cough chasing him. Tears quivered in his eyes, he'd been suckered in and felt small and alone.

He didn't realize how much time had passed while he was with Madame Boliva. The lights outside were dimmed, and all the patrons and marks were gone. The only signs of life came from the muttered conversations of carnival workers as they walked around going about the business of packing up to move on. The full moon shone through thin clouds upon the skeletal carnival grounds.

Regardless of what the crazy fortune teller had said, Tommy was still determined to run away. He never wanted to see his parents again. His mother's screaming accusations at his drunken father were lullabies of a life he did not want. He would continue on his own. He would be fine.

"Hey, you! Get outta here. We're closed," a gruff voice called from the shadows, yanking Tommy out of his thoughts. "Trying to steal stuff, huh?" The man's coarse, calloused hand closed on the back of Tommy's neck. "We'll see what you've got hidden in your pockets."

"No, wait, please," Tommy pleaded, struggling in the big man's grasp. "I wasn't stealing anything."

"Oh yeah? Then why are you slinking around here in the dark?" The man shook him with every word, making it hard for Tommy to think or speak.

"Put him down, Darkman. He was visiting with me." Tommy never thought he'd be happy to see Madame Boliva again. The large man set Tommy on his feet and slapped him heartily on the back.

"Why didn't you just say you were a friend of Madame Bolvia to begin with, son?" Darkman attempted to smile, casting deep shadows across his face.

"Not like you gave me much of a chance," Tommy pouted, rubbing his bruised neck. He looked the man over from head to toe. "What kind of a name is Darkman?"

"It's my name. That's all you need to know." Darkman stood

with his arms crossed over his massive chest, and returned his attention to Madame Boliva. "You sure this kid is okay with you?"

Tommy tensed at being called a kid. "This is no kid, Darkman," she crooned, winking at her rough companion. "This is Tommy, the Master of Toy Land."

"Oh?" Darkman raised one bushy eyebrow. "In that case, Master," he mocked, dipping into a deep comical bow, "Come with me. I'll show you to your domain."

"This is really dumb. If you mean you want me to be a freak like you, and work in that Toy Land castle, you are really nuts." Tommy backed away from the towering man, only to stumble into Madame Boliva.

"Go with him," she whispered in Tommy's ear, her cold hands strong vices gripping his arms. "He won't bite... much." Her familiar laughing cough rang through the still night.

As hard as he tried, Tommy could not break free of her grip. His eyes grew wide as Darkman came closer, then he felt a sharp pain in the back of his head and saw stars. His world shifted sideways and the full moon slipped into view as his eyes closed.

"Take him away. You know what to do," Madame Boliva instructed Darkman as he picked up Tommy's limp body.

"Are you sure?"

She waved a black and white flier in his face. "He's a runaway, so we're going to help him find a new life." She smiled softly, a look at odds with the rest of her. "Just like the others."

***

"Come one, come all! We've got chills and thrills. See the freaks and creeps! Hurry, hurry, hurry! Don't forget to visit Toy Land where all the dolls are alive!" The barker wiggled his eyes at a group of girls as they passed.

"Let's go see the living dolls, Beth," a young girl said as she nudged her friend. "That should be cool."

"I'm sure he meant life-sized dolls, nothing cool about that. We're too old for girlish toys, anyways." The girl flipped her hair and batted her eyelashes at a young man walking past them. "You go if you want, Alice. I'm going to get my fortune told." Beth walked off, following the cute boy.

Alice made her way to the center of the carnival grounds where another barker called to the crowd. "Welcome to the world's only living toy land. We've got dancing girls, fighting knights and sleeping beauties. For the first time ever, we've got the Master doll! Only two dollars! Seeing is believing."

She paid her two dollars and stepped through the door. Inside, the rooms were separated by thick glass, each a self contained world. Engraved plaques in front of the displays declared their titles. The place was deadly quiet, as if it were a museum or church.

In the first room Alice saw a mother and father silently watching television with friends in a modern living room. The television played a current sitcom, but the people in the room were expressionless. "If you were real, you'd be laughing like crazy. I watch that show and it's funny," She said aloud. She did not get a response, not that she expected one, especially since the dolls looked like their lips were glued shut. "Someone should have given you mouths."

The next glass cell was titled *Little Girls' Sweet Dreams Room*. There were rows of bunk beds with six girls moving sluggishly around, doing each other's hair. A couple of them turned glassy eyes toward Alice, as if they could see her. "A little more realistic, but I'm still not convinced," she muttered. She waved at them, but they just continued in their slow movements.

In *The Knights' Practice Room* she watched boys fencing and fighting with swords. They moved quicker than the other dolls she had seen and they even displayed some facial expressions. Stepping closer as one boy swung his sword, she jumped when he cut off another's head. The toy slumped to the floor, dark red liquid spurting from the body and splashing the glass wall where she stood. The toy that had done the damage stood still and wide eyed, as if shocked. "That is amazing technology. I wonder how they make the blood look so real."

"Gross!" Her first thought escaped her lips as she came upon a dungeon room. "I've never seen this in a doll house." Before her were two figures dressed in black hoods and leather pants. There were pieces of others, dressed in outfits she'd seen in the other glass rooms, and more of the fake blood she had seen with the fighting boys. Heads, arms, and legs littered the floor. Even a torso, cut from neck wound to belly button, hung on the wall. The engraved plaque simply stated *When Toys Misbehave.* "How does a toy misbehave?"

Feeling ill and looking for the exit, Alice continued walking along the corridor. As she progressed down the rows, the human-like behaviors increased. It was like watching a child grow up, each stage of life more animated than the previous. "Whoever makes these is getting better."

She reached the end of the house and came upon a brightly lit throne room. *The Master of Toy Land* read his plaque. The glass room was covered in lush velvet material, all trimmed in gold. Two enormous thrones sat in the center and a regally dressed young man sat in one, the other mysteriously empty.

Alice stepped closer to the glass barrier. "Hello? You look very real," she said, laying a hand on the cool surface.

The young man jumped out of his seat and ran toward the vision of Alice on the other side of his cell. She jumped when he slapped the glass. He opened his mouth as if to speak, but no words came out, and she could see he had no tongue.

"Wow! Whoever made you did a wonderful job!" Alice admired the young man-doll. "If you were real, I'd so date you."

The Master jumped around, like a madman in a padded room, waving his arms and pointing behind her. His mouth moved constantly, frustration painted over his face, but no words could be heard.

"Are you trying to say something? You are, aren't you?" Alice's curiosity was piqued. Studying his face she swore the Master of Toy Land looked terrified. "Silly girl," she chided herself, "Dolls don't feel anything."

"Move along, young lady," a large man said, stepping beside her. The doll in the throne room backed away from the man with terror filled eyes, shaking hard enough to be visible. "We're closing up for the night." He gently pushed her towards the exit.

"I swear that Master doll was trying to talk." She glanced over her shoulder, into the young face peeking out from behind the throne. "I almost believe he's alive."

"All the dolls seem life like. He's the newest version, and much more realistic, which is why he is the Master of Toy Land." Darkman gave her a wink and a crooked smile.

"Why is there an empty throne in there with him?" she nervously chewed on her lower lip.

"Haven't made the right doll to compliment him, that's all. Hope you're enjoying your time tonight. You should go see Madame Boliva before you leave. Her predictions are nearly always correct." He walked Alice toward the star covered tent.

About the author: Jessica A. Weiss is a suspense writer living in SC with her large family. She has several stories in print, on-line, and ebook. She also is a guest editor for Pill Hill Press. In February of 2010 she opened Wicked East Press as another small press venue and loves to read work by undiscovered authors. You can check out Wicked East Press at www.wickedeastpress.com.

The Tut
Paul D. Brazill

After enduring forty-five years of a marriage that was, at best, like wading through treacle, Oliver Robinson eventually had enough and smothered his wife with the beige corduroy cushion that he'd accidentally burned with a cigarette two fraught days before.

Oliver had been, for most of his life, a temperate man and he had survived the sexless marriage- its colourless cuisine and half-hearted holidays- with a stoicism that bordered on indifference. But his patience had begun to be stretched to the breaking point by Gloria's constant disapproval of almost everything he did.

And then there was the 'Tut.'

The Tut invariably accompanied Gloria's scowl whenever Oliver poured himself an evening drink or smoked a cigarette. She would tut loudly if he spilled the salt.Or swore. Or stayed up late to watch the snooker. The tut, tut, tut was like the rattle of a machine gun that seemed to echo through their West London home from dusk till dawn until he reached the end of his tether.

Wrapping his wife's body in the fluffy white bedroom rug, Oliver supposed that he should have felt guilty, depressed or scared but he didn't. Far from it. In fact, he felt as free and as light as a multi-coloured helium balloon that had been set adrift to float above a brightly lit funfair.

Oliver fastened the rug with gaffer tape and dragged the corpse down the steps to the basement. As the head bounced from every step it made a sound not unlike a tut and he had to fight the urge to say sorry.

He'd done enough apologising.

***

Oliver poured himself a whisky - at eight o'clock in the morning! – And it tasted better than any whisky he had ever tasted before. Looking around his antiseptic home, the sofa still wrapped in the plastic coating that it had come in, he smiled.

He savoured the silence as he resisted the temptation to

clean Gloria's puke from the scarred cushion which had been the catalyst of her death. Taking a Marlborough full strength from the secret supply that was hidden in a hollowed out hard back copy of *Jaws* - Gloria didn't approve of fiction and would never have found the stash there – he proceed to burn a hole in every cushion in the house.

And then he started on the sofa.

However, Oliver's brief burst of pyromania was interrupted when he thought he heard a tut, tut, tut from the hallway, and his heart seemed to skip a beat or two, but then he gave a relieved laugh when he realised it was just the sound of the letter box, flapping in the wind.

***

Disposal of Gloria's body proved to be a much easier affair than Oliver would have expected. On a bright Sunday morning in April he hauled Gloria's corpse into the back of his car, keeping an eye out for nosey neighbours, and drove towards the village of Innersmouth and Jed Bramble's rundown farm.

Jed was an old school friend and fellow Territorial Army member who Oliver occasionally used to meet for a sly drink in the Innersmouth Arms' smokey, pokey snug. He was also a phenomenal lush. The plan was to get him drunk and comatose and then feed Gloria's body to his pigs. Oliver knew that the farm was on its last legs, and so was most of the livestock, so he felt sure that the poor emaciated creatures would be more than happy to tuck in to Gloria's cadaver.

Perched on the passenger seat Oliver had a Sainsburys bag stuffed with six bottles of Grant's Whisky and in his pocket, just in case, he had a bottle of the diazapam he'd used to drug Gloria, prior to killing her.

Just outside of Innersmouth it started to rain. Tut, tut went the rain on the windscreen. At first it was only a shower but then it fell down in sheets. Tut, tut, tut, tut, tut.

Oliver switched on the windscreen wipers but every swish seemed to have been replaced by a tut. He opened up a bottle of whisky and drank until the rain just sounded like rain.

Jed stood outside the dilapidated farmhouse with a rifle over his arm and looking more than a little weather beaten himself. His straggly hair was long and greasy and his red eyes lit up like Xmas tree lights when he saw the booze.

***

The cold Monday morning air tasted like tin as Oliver, hung-over and wheezing pulled Gloria's body from the car and dumped it in the big sty. The starving wretches took to their meal with relish and Oliver vomited as he watched them devour his wife's remains.

Back at the farmhouse Jed was still slumped over the kitchen table, snoring heavily.

Oliver collapsed into a battered armchair and started to sweat and shake. He'd decided to stay with Jed for a few days, keeping him safely inebriated until Gloria's remains were completely consumed but as the days grew dark the tut returned.

The tick tock of Jed's Grandfather clock, for instance, was replaced by a tut, tut. The drip, drip, drip of the leaking tap that kept him awake at night became a tut, tut, tut and the postman's bright and breezy rat a tat tat on the front door seemed to pull the fillings right from his teeth. He turned on the radio but even Bob Dylan was tut, tut, tutting on heaven's door.

***

The usually bustling Innersmouth High Street was almost deserted now. The majority of the local people were cowering indoors-in shops, pubs, fast food joints. Oliver walked down the street with Jed's rifle over his shoulder. No matter how many people he shot he still couldn't seem to escape the sound of Gloria's disapprobation.

Tut went the gun when he shot the postman.

Tut, tut when he pressed the trigger and blew Harry the milkman's brains out.

And tut, tut, tut when he blasted fat PC Thompson to smithereens as he attempted to escape by climbing over the infant school wall.

Oliver heard the sirens of the approaching police cars in the

distance and realised that there was only one thing left to do.
Pushing the gun into his mouth he squeezed the trigger.
The last sound that he heard was a resounding TUT!

About the author: Paul D. Brazill was born in England and lives
Poland. His stories have appeared online and in print at *A Twist of
Noir, beat to a Pulp, Dark Valentine Magazine, Needle Magazine,
Powder Burn flash, Pulp Metal Magazine, The flash Fiction
Offensive, thrillers Killers 'n' chillers* and the anthologies of *Howl:
Dark Tales of the Feral and Infernal*, and *Radgepacket* volume
Four. The Tut was nominated for a 2010 Spinetingler award.

May I Take Your Order?

William Wolford

So I had this girl locked in the trunk of my car. I just drove around, not sure what to do with her, but knowing that I was going to do something. I just had to decide what.

See, we had a little problem at EatBurger.

I walked in with a burger on the brain. A fat, juicy burger loaded with bacon. That was all I wanted.

So I walked up to the counter and there was this beautiful girl standing there. I'm not talking girl next door beautiful. I'm talking movie star beautiful. I couldn't believe she could look like that—bright green eyes, perfect complexion, long, silky brown hair, and the prettiest smile I've ever seen—and still be trapped behind an EatBurger counter in West Virginia.

"Can I take your order?" she said, and smiled.

All I could do for a second was stare. I legitimately felt like I could fall in love with this girl on the spot. Finally, when I realized her smile had faded into a look of confusion, I said, "Yeah, I'll take a number six combo. Leave off the veggies and condiments though. I like my burger clean, just like my face." I pointed to my face, shaved clean, and the girl laughed.

"Would you like your combo small, medium, or large, sir?"

"Medium sounds good, hon."

"Alrighty," she said. "Your order comes to eleven seventy-two." I handed her the money. She handed me my change and a tray with my cup on it. "It'll be a few minutes on your order so I'll just bring it out to you when it's ready."

I walked over to the drink machine and filled my cup up with ice and Coke. I walked around, looking for a table, and I found one that was pretty clean. I sat down and sipped on my Coke. I have to tell you—I was really jonesing for that burger. Almost as much as I was jonesing for the girl behind the counter.

Finally, she brought my food out. I started to salivate. "Thanks, hon," I said. She smiled and walked back to the front.

I chomped on a few fries to start things off—they were good but a little saltier than I like—then I unwrapped my burger.

There was lettuce on it. Lettuce. She got my order wrong. All

I wanted was a plain bacon cheeseburger. It's not that hard.

I was angry, to say the least. I stood up and walked out without saying anything to anyone, especially not the girl.

I sat outside in my car for hours, just waiting on the place to close. I couldn't let her get away with this. I wasn't going to let her walk all over me just because she had a pretty face.

The lights inside went off and I knew the employees had to leave soon. The other three employees—all men—filed out, got in their cars, and went home.

It left me with the perfect opportunity.

The girl came outside. Her car was parked beside mine. She ran across the parking lot as if she were afraid of the dark.

She didn't realize that there were far worse things to be afraid of than the dark.

I opened the door and said, "Hello, pretty lady." She looked horrified. She screamed and tried to run away, but I was too quick for her. I grabbed her shirttail, pulled her to me, and threw her in my trunk.

That brings us to where we are now. She's still in the back, screaming, scared out of her mind. I don't know what I'm going to do to her. Maybe letting her sit back there, thinking she's going to die, is all I'll do. Or maybe I'll kill her. I haven't decided yet.

All I know is that she's going to learn that there isn't any place for her in this world if all she's going to do is try to tread on people and get by with her pretty face.

About the author: William Wolford is a young writer who currently lives in West Virginia. His passions include writing, ultimate frisbee, and the Miami Dolphins. His stories have appeared in Lame Goat Press's anthologies *Horror Through the Ages* and *Diamonds in the Rough*, *Static Movement* and *Eclectic Flash* (April 2010). William edited the book Inner Fears, a Static Movement book.

Cybernetic Reanimation
Joe Jablonski

Carl Stregan woke at dawn. Maybe 'woke' isn't the right word...

A sound something like sizzling bacon echoed through the air as the neural pathways of his body reconnected with his small processing core. Conversion-cells rerouted power from the auto-maintenance centers and the blue ember corneas of his fusion-wire ocular ports flickered to life.

A creature of habit, Carl stood and needlessly stretched his thin synthetic limbs, a small gesture that helped him gain a small measure of normally. Mid-stretch, he caught a glimpse of his reflection in a small hanging mirror and the illusion was shattered.

The skeleton of his body was made up of a diamond reinforced copper alloy. Tiny, micro-silk wires were rooted deep within clear, conductive gel-like flesh underneath a skin mesh of white poly-fiber. His face and torso was covered in thin sheets of mahogany carved with geometric patterns.

This was the image reflecting back at him and he had to constantly remind himself that this life was a choice, his cybernetic body a monument to a terrible purpose.

Looking away, he simulated a sigh through his speaker patches but it came out as more of a digital inflection. He needed to escape.

Without another thought, he pressed a switch on his left which closed the blinds and the room dimmed. Another switch caused a wall of monitors to his right to flicker to life. Each of the ten screens played a live feed of the different research habitats where the human test subjects lived there unsuspecting lives.

After gliding over the blue-marble floor to his computer on too skinny legs, he logged on, gained access to the mainframe AI, and asked for the research updates.

The electronic voice of the computer reverberated through the speakers in response.

"Habitat one— subject 6217.10, age 39, is showing signs of neurological decay. Suggest immediate removal."

As he watched and listened, his mind drifted and began to

reflect on a recurring nightmare of a world long ago brought to the brink of destruction by an innate madness.

He was seventeen and still very much human—a young robotics prodigy at MIT—when the first signs of the madness appeared in the elderly. The madness was later found to be an innate mutation manifested in the form of instant mental degeneration triggered by some unknown factor; a product of evolution at its worse.

Those inflicted held a look in their eyes something akin to a rabid beast, completely fierce but without recognition. Their mouths drooled as they yelled nonsense while looking for anything to unleash the rage upon.

Imagine a completely structural break in society, an anarchic free for all. Imagine looking out your window and seeing the remnant of discarded human bodies, wreaked and abandon cars littering the streets; buildings burnt, crumbling and desolate. A man runs past your second story window screaming and its all you can do to duck down quickly and praying that whatever was chasing that man doesn't find you first. You pray for that man's death, because it means your life—better him than me you tell yourself. Without anybody to collect them, bodies line the streets in all directions.

This was the world at the beginning of the madness, the world Carl remembers and it only got worse.

Every year, the mutation was triggered in younger and younger people until by the time he was twenty-three, the infliction rate for those thirty-five and older reached one-hundred percent.

It was about that time that all government collapsed. The military blockages set up to protect the un-inflicted were overrun. It soon became very clear it was every man for himself.

One year while exploring, he found and followed a hidden breadcrumb trail of mathematical equations that, once solved, led to the remains of an old war bunker. Inside, he found a collection of brilliant minds equal to his own. Inside that dark, static world, they began to discuss possible solutions. They knew time was short and it was up to them to save themselves from whatever lurid future was crawling closer. Each passing year was a like a countdown to their own inevitable madness. They rejected it completely. They would be in control of their destiny and it wasn't long before they realize what they needed to be done.

The next couple years were a blur spent in a makeshift lab down in that old fallout bunker. They worked themselves to the point of collapse but it was completely necessary. The closing deadline was approaching.

When the preparations were finally complete, only twenty-six of the original thirty-seven were still alive to see it though; some killed, some lost to the madness.

With heavy hearts, those remaining prayed to whomever and unleashed the virus that wiped out the last remnants of the human race. Only he and the rest were immune to it. It took only a few months to work its magic.

But they had a plan. With immortality they could find a way to reverse the mutation and start over using genetic samples. Through cloning, they would breed human subjects for study, fix the human genome, rebuild the world, and rebuild civilization. It sounded so noble at the time.

With enough thought, you could convince yourself of anything.

"Habitat two- subject 9867.04, age 42, is showing signs of neurological decay. Suggest immediate removal.

The sound of his door opening broke him from his contemplation as he turned and watched Ann enter the room. She was another like him—human by birth, cybernetic by choice.

"You decent?" she asked in a playful tone.

Carl just chuckled. Even in her robotic form, he couldn't help but admire the grace in which she moved and he longed for something more between them, something made impossible when they chose this life. If he still had balls, they would be the deepest shade of blue.

"So what's new?" she asked in an attempt at small talk, but after so many years together, there was little else to say.

"Is anything ever new? Let's just keep working," He was in a worse mood than usual.

"Habitat three- subjects 4591.4 and 8963.11, ages 46 and 42, are both showing signs of neurological decay. Suggest immediate removal."

On the screens, the pair watched a scene that was the same

as it was everyday: subjects harvesting crops, pulling water from a well, conversions, working, playing, etc. Over the years, the small world within the confines of the outer walls became a way of life for those people. It was kind of like watching mankind evolve all over again.

Each habitat housed a different control group of about sixty people; genetically altered clones bred in whatever way the cybernetics deemed necessary. Since all the genetic manipulation they do on subjects was done at the embryonic stage, the cybernetics role and interactions with those specimens was mostly that of observers. The majority of their lives were spent watching the subjects for the first signs of the madness and removing those who had become a danger to the rest because of its effects.

"Habitat four- subject 1998.33, age 40, is showing signs of neurological decay. Suggest immediate removal. "Habitat five- no new data acquired. All subjects remain stable. Oldest subject is age 36."

"Do you see that?" Ann asked.

Carl answered that he didn't. Even as a robot, he still got bored and daydream.

"Damn it, Carl," she pointed to the screen with a shimmering metallic limb, "Look! What are they doing?"

In Habitat six, a crowd was beginning to form around something... he couldn't tell what. Too many people were blocking the camera. They were getting pretty riled up. On the screens, they began to fight for positioning. The ones in the back were shouting and waving others over. It wasn't long until the entire habitat was a ghost town; all but the little section around a manmade altar where the subjects were packed in tightly.

"Keep an eye on it, ok. I'll tell Ben and Marcus to check-."

"Habitat six- subject 1767.09 went into cardiac arrest. Male- age 87. Death attributed to natural causes."

The two perk up almost instantly, not believing what they just heard. They could do nothing but look at each other and let what the computer had just told them sink in. Instantly, they both intuitively knew exactly what had the people out there so riled up. Without a word, they quickly began running toward Habitat six leaving a trail of papers flying in their wake. Carl was trying hard not to get too excited, but the anticipation was burning brightly in his synthetic mind.

Once they arrived at their intended destination, Ann and Carl made their way toward the large stone altar followed by long shadows from a low sun.

The Habitats all looked the same as it had for generations. A large garden sat in the center of the circular habitat around the alter full off various fruits and vegetables. Little mud huts spiraled out in the surrounding area. Three wells were posted at random spots for easy water access. Fifty foot walls marked the exterior. The villages could see nothing beyond them but sky. Carl and his group tried to keep it painted in a matching baby blue, but lately they had been slack on the job and cracks of metal and rust were peering out from flecking paint.

As Ann and Carl approached the crowd, the test subjects began to mutter prayers as they parted ways to let them by.

Motionless on the cold stone block was the body of a man: gray hair, wrinkled features, dusty faded skin. His name was Joseph Pragil. Dead at eight seven of natural causes, his death was a symbol of a hard earned accomplishment.

The trick was to stop thinking of them as anything but test subjects. Detachment was vital. One of the things Carl learned in the beginning.

Carl beamed as he looked around. About half the people—36 if he remembered correctly—in this sector carried the same genetic manipulation that saw Joseph Pragil to a ripe old age.

At the altar, Ben and Marcus—two other fellow cybernetic— were already there.

"This is it Carl," said Ben, his digital voice full of excitement,

"Calm down. Let's not get too far ahead of ourselves." Carl shared his excitement, but refused to show it.

"Look around you, how many others do you see here over the age of sixty?"

"Irrelevant. We need more time to be sure."

"God you're annoying, Carl.

The conversation was spoken in Latin, a language the test subjects would never understand. But despite that fact (or maybe because of it), more and more of them began to close in with eyes full of wonder. Ben tried to tell them to move back, but curiosity and fear had the better of them. These people had never seen a natural death take place. It would be an event talked about for years.

Sometimes Carl envied those humans for their innocence; their easy lives free of the colossal stress placed upon him and the others. They never even suspected that he was once like them. They wouldn't believe it even if he told them.

Marcus pulled out a small brain scanner from a bodily compartment and began to fit it over the top of the dead man's head. Little lights and wires were aglow on top of a thin metal sheet that expanded and seemed to transform of its own volition. The test subjects recoiled with inward gasps at the sight and began making warding gestures while speaking to each other in hushed whispers.

"Not here. We don't need to add to these peoples confusion," Ann said to him harshly. One of the rules was to keep any complex technology away from the subjects. They had developed into an extremely superstitious lot over the generations and they were not really sure how they would handle it.

The two, as always, began to argue. Carl removed himself from it and surveyed the subjects with a renewed vigor he hadn't felt for years. As he gazed around, something in the distance caught his eye: a black silhouette with two little pinpricks of light for eyes blocking the bright morning sunlight. It was Ryan. Carl could always tell. His false body was, by far, the biggest out of some kind of machismo pride. He was staring down at the crowd from the top of the outer wall structure. Carl waved him over but Ryan didn't respond, didn't even flitch. His just keep staring for a moment longer and then in a flash he was gone.

The subjects were starting to get more riled up, staring at the cybernetics with questioning eyes. They needed their God's to ease their troubled minds.

In the beginning, Carl and his group quickly learned to accept their new status as deities. Not out of any kind of vanity. It was the answer to a question—a form of control. Something they needed as much as the subjects did.

How else could they explain taking away a loved one when they saw the first signs of madness? They couldn't tell these people the truth; that they would be discarded like so much waste for the protection of the rest of the Habitat.

Live a good and pure life and when the time comes you will be taken to the kingdom of heaven.

It was cruel, but also completely necessary. Peace and order was absolutely vital.

Marcus's and Ann's bickering wasn't help the cause.

"Enough! Not in front of *them*. They're frightened enough. You," Carl pointed to Marcus, "take the body to the labs and do a full autopsy. Ann, stay with these people, keep them calm. Ben, pull the files up on all subjects with Joseph's enhancements. Separate them and relocate the rest."

Abruptly Carl turned to make his way back to his labs with the sound of Ann's voice booming as she spoke to comfort their subjects. Hearing her words, her lies, Carl felt a pang of guilt for everything they have done that has led up to this.

After six-hundred and eighty-three years he began to question if he ever really was human.

***

Carl and Ann developed the technology that turned them all into machines.

The robotic transformation began with the introduction of a synthetic nano-web into the brain as an implanted seed. The nano-web then spread and connected itself to the firing synapses of the nervous system and formed an input connection. Over time, those nano-webs learned to read and translate the firing patterns to make a virtual map of the mind. After a little amalgamation, impulses began to fire into the nano-webs receptors. This information was encoded into a database—a database of the soul.

Next, hit the download key and wait as your entire life force is digitally sucked straight out of you.

Carl was the first to undergo the process. It was instantaneous. The moment he made the transition, it felt like his entire being was forcefully ripped from existence. It was the most painful thing he ever felt. It was the last thing he ever felt. He would give anything to feel it again.

When he regained his senses inside his new robotic skin, the first thing he saw was his old flesh and blood body stretched across a table, his face frozen in a single moment of agony.

The process was complete and everything became painfully surreal as if waking from a nightmare into a nightmare. There was a strange lightness to every movement and Carl felt as if he was nothing but a ghost floating on air. The lack of sensation that accompanied his new improved body overwhelmed him and quickly he went into a panic attack. Never before had he truly understood the meaning of the word 'numb.' It took days to orientate himself, but slowly/finally he found equilibrium.

Soon after, Carl helped the rest of the team through the transition as they waited for the genocide they inflicted on the outside world to come to a close.

Those first few years were the worst of his life.

Since then, one thought had been burning in his mind: *am I really still Carl Stregan or just a carbon copy? Am I just acting out a program? Did the real me's soul died the day I was created?*

Now in his lab, Carl was about to go through all the development records from habitat six. The next step was to grow a new generation of subjects, all with Joseph's genetic modifications. These, for the first time, would be given the option to breed. It would take four generations of natural birth and death before Carl would feel comfortable setting them loose on the outside world. Not too much longer, he hoped.

Something was wrong. The access files wouldn't come up. He checked the entire database again and again—they were completely gone, deleted. The mainframe AI was telling him they are unrecoverable.

Trying not to panic, Carl called the computer tech, Carol.

No answer

He tried Mark.

Nothing

This can't be happening. He refused to believe everything they had worked for was gone when they there were so close.

He tried Steve.

His mind raced with all the bad memories since the beginning—all the death they caused, all the pain they had inflicted, all the years inside that damn body.

He tried Mason.

Everything built up until it became too much to handle. In a tantrum, Carl began to smash his lab with six hundred and eighty three years of pent up, digital emotion.

As he put his fist through one of the large monitor on my wall, the building rumbled for a second and a klaxon sounded. It was an explosion. His body was bathed in red floodlights.

"Carl, get down to Habitat six, now!"

It was Ann. By the sound of her voice it's worse than he thought.

Carl began to run as fast as his synthetic legs could carry him. In the hallway, the building was coming down all around him. Large portion of the ceiling were dropping everywhere. With integrity lost, objects, desks, computers, everything began to rain though the ceiling like some kind of self-enclosed meteor shower. Sparks from torn electric grids were shooting out in all direction. Smoke poured out like liquid from underneath closed doors and wall cracks, an indication of the infernos raging beyond.

More explosions shook the building, but still he ran. It seemed like an eternity on that endless run to Habitat six.

Using the full momentum of his stride, Carl barreled through the door to the freedom of the habitat outside. As he did, he saw a world opened of utter pandemonium. Everything in sight was burning and destroyed. Motionless on the ground were a least a dozen of Carl's counterparts surrounded by a sea of human bodies. Victims from both sides ripped apart.

Ryan was standing on the makeshift altar surrounded by an angry mob of failed test subjects, all from different sectors, all his loyal congregation.

A few of the others were trying to keep the remaining failed subjects at bay with makeshift weapons but Carl couldn't find Ann or any of those carrying Joseph's modification in sight.

Ryan saw Carl come in the distance and began to shout, "Where are they?"

"Who?"

"Those abominations you think you've saved."

"What are you talking about?"

"Can't you see they can't live on their own? They are our

creations. They worship us. You think you're going to cure them and set them free? Look as these people. Without us, they have nothing."

"You want to kill them because they're cured? They are the entire reason we did all this."

"They are nothing. With them out of the way, we will go on as we have been and humanity will continue to thrive under our guidance. This is the only possible future of the race. Don't deny yourself this opportunity of eternal greatness."

Carl should have seen this coming, they all should have. Over the years, Ryan had steadily become more and more unstable. He reveled in these subjects worship. His ego should have tipped us off.

"You know this can't possibly end up the way you want it to. You're delusional."

"I had hopes for you, at least, Carl, but so be it," Ryan said as he took one quick look around at the others, and began to preach. His amplified voice echoed through the air like thunder as he spoke to his minions. "I am the one true God. You must free yourself from the control of these false idols. You must rise up and destroy them! Do it as a sign of your loyalty to me."

The horde of the remaining subjects began to yell enthusiastically and ran straight towards Carl and the rest. Ben went down quickly. Never did Carl foresee them in a middle of a holy war where they were both angel and demon. All the mistakes of their past, all the decisions—good and bad—were coming back to haunt them in the form of this angry insurgence. Only now did he realize they were blind to believe the subjects contentment. This rebellion was inevitable.

Carl began to fight using a piece of metal from the gutted wall, but there were too many, their minds fueled with lies and hate.

"Fall back!" cried a digital voice. It's was Marcus. A better idea, Carl had never heard.

Carl ran back into the reinforced walls of the building opposite the destroyed wing followed by Marcus, Richard and Kim. Their robotic forms were battered and twitching with damage. Carl was missing his lower face plate, Richard, an arm.

Outside, the subjects were scraping and pounding on the door trying to get in, relentless in their blind ambitions.

"What the hell!?" yelled Kim.

"Elegantly put. Now where is Ann?" asked Carl.

"She took the hopefuls to the storage shelter. We were fighting off her escape," answered Richard.

"So they're safe. Good. Alright, we have one goal: Kill Ryan and his followers. We'll figure out the rest out later. Only the survival of the ones with Ann matters. They are the future."

Inside their temporary sanctuary, Carl couldn't help but take it all in. Ryan—a man turned robot turned God. He believed it completely. He was willing to fight for it; he was willing to kill for it.

This must have been his idea from the very beginning. He never thought they would really succeed. The rest, Joseph was the symbol of an impending success. To Ryan, Joseph was the symbol of an impending fall from grace. He didn't take it lightly to say the least.

Sadly, he has left no other choice.

"Kim and Richard get the gas grenades out and drop them into the courtyard from the second story observation room. With his followers neutralized, Marcus and I will get the syntax charges and take care of the rest." It was hard for him to have to order a second genocide. He could barely get the words out.

Without a second guess, Kim and Richard did as they were told.

Outside they could hear the muffled screams of the subjects as they slowly died from the poisonous clouds of gas. One by one the screams faded until only silence remained.

"You ready?" Carl asked Marcus.

Marcus nodded and Carl opened the door.

Ryan's body slams into Carl instantly. It took a moment for him to figure out what had happened. Some of his neural links got disconnect in the attack causing his body to feel heavy and sluggish with the partial loss of control.

In the distance, Marcus was holding his own, barely. Carl could tell it was a losing battle. Ryan's overly large body was too much for him alone.

It's time to end this before it's too late.

Carl pulled out one of the makeshift bombs and set it timer as Marcus got pummeled into the ground. When it was ready, he threw it the moment Ryan turned to face him. The embers in Ryan's ocular ports went wide with panic. Ryan grabbed Marcus's body at the last second and used it as a shield the moment the bomb exploded in mid-air. The shock wave sent their bodies against the wall in the distance.

Both were motionless as Carl approached. A few more steps and Ryan began to stir. His body was badly damage. He pushed the dead weight of Marcus from on top of him and trying to stand, but his movements were twitchy and his body didn't seem to want to cooperate.

From behind, Marcus, who was missing the lower half of his body, grabbed Ryan and used his weight and momentum to pull him back down against the wall blocking them from the outside world. Carl approached slowly with drunken movements as Ryan tried to find liberation.

With his remaining working hand, Carl flipped the switch on his final detonation charge and launched himself at Ryan's overlarge body core. The countdown began to tick off. Carl wasn't sad or scared. He knew this was a way stop from the second he opened that door. It's not every day you brought down a God.

Three. The only regret was that he wished he had more time to test these people and make sure. There were not enough of his comrades left to keep this project going. Hopefully they had succeeded or all this work, more important, the entire human race would be reduced to nothing.

Two. If the madness was truly cured, he knew those people could make it. Their society was already established. Without the regulated birth control regularly dissolve into their drinking water, they would be free to expand and thrive free of guidance. The world was theirs now. This single act was his final gift to them.

One. After six -hundred and eighty-three years, Carl Stregan was ready to die.

About the author: Joe writes out of Charlotte, NC. His work has been published or forthcoming in *M-Brane SF, Short-Story.ME!, Prinkipria, Aurora Wolf, AlienSkin,* and *Weirdyear* as well the *Cup of Joe* and the *365 days of flash* anthologies.

The Adamant Wall
Robert William Shmigelsky

Having only recently been placed on the Earth, the first lesson the first born of men had to learn was how to live and get along with each other.

Sharing a modest land, having to build their cities side by side, and the first born found this harder done than said. As in all culture, certain values were valued more than others. From which arguments sprung up, leading to disputes that on occasion led to conflict.

Having heard of their troubles from far and wide, the dwarf-golems arrived and offered to build for each of the five lineages amongst the first born, around each and every one of their cities, an unbreakable wall made from the strongest rock on Earth.

Greatly intrigued, the mayors of every city asked the golems for the name of this material.

The golems told them the name of it was adamant. They pulled out and showed each of the mayors a chunk of grey semi-translucent rock emitting a strange moon-like radiance. They told the mayors when melted to orange blue then returned to its original hue adamant became a metal no sword or arrow could pierce or when left in its natural form, its thick stone walls were the hardest to knock down.

The mayors asked the golems how much gold they wanted in exchange for building the wall, but were quickly warned if they ever wanted the wall taken down, they might have to wait many long years before that could be done. Adamant had only one known weakness: something not invented yet that golems called magic.

Hardly a thought spent on such a warning, mayors agreed to these terms and the sum. They handed over the gold wished in exchange for building the wall through their kingdom, around each and every one of their cities.

Golems hauled up from hollowed depths as much adamant as was possibly needed. Having been made from statues of sculpted stone, golems could stack adamant blocks high up into the sky, higher than any human could, and in no time at all they built –

before returning to whence they came – the Adamant Wall.

Afterwards, the lineages lived apart, separated by the Adamant Wall, but as land and city space became more cramped as time wore on those behind thick stone walls began to forget the barriers that had divided them in the first place.

The sides began to open the shutters along the walls. To speak to each other through holes amongst the stones. As they reacquainted themselves with the other sides and grew to friendlier terms, a day dawned when they decided to have the wall taken down.

Unable to take down the Adamant Wall themselves, mayors went to where golems had disappeared to, found caves leading down. They travelled underground and hence found the golems in their adamant halls.

The mayors petitioned the golems that had built the wall to take down their wall, but were quickly told simply what they had been told before: that what they requested could not yet be done. The mayors offered all the gold in their land, but still the answer was the same.

Leaving empty handed, the leading politicians and their aides returned to each of their cities. Upon their arrival, the people enthusiastically greeted their return, inquiring in loud, overly-eager voices when the wall was going to be taken down.

Unable to bare the overbearing stares but mostly having agreed beforehand with the other mayors to save their own careers, mayors angrily, and sadly, informed the crowds that had gathered around to hear their answers that the other sides were not as they seemed: that if they had seen what they had seen, heard what they had heard, they too would have reached the same conclusion as they had.

Leading the voters to this particular point of view, mayors gave inspiring accounts of what had transpired that soon those that had been clamoring for the wall to fall all began to holler in agreement: "let the wall stand tall!"

About the author: Robert is an aspiring fantasy writer trying to improve his writing. Robert has been writing fantasy for himself in his spare time for the last seven years, but only now has begun writing for others. Besides reading and writing, some of his hobbies include computers and history. He has a dry sense of humor, which he blames his stepfather for. Also, he has a habit of making history jokes no one but him understands. He is currently working as a certified residential care aide (nursing assistant) in beautiful British Columbia to support his writing.

Eyes Wide Open
Jay Faulkner

Working for God is never easy. I love Him, of course, and trust Him – though His ways are, admittedly, a mystery – but the path that He has set me on, and the task that He has given me, is not an easy one. And yet, still, I do it.

***

The morning Sun streamed in through the window like shafts of pure gold. Illuminating the room with an almost too intense light, cascading over everything like waves from a yellow ocean, the sunlight brought hints of burnished orange and golden honey to everything that it touched. Motes of dust floated languidly, like once-bright stars reliving their now faded glory. Light and airy already, with only a large bed, a bedside cabinet and a full-length, wooden-framed mirror to fill its space, the room was an oasis of calm tranquillity. The air in the room was still, though not oppressively so.

An edge of expectation hung in the silence; this was a portentous day, one that was just waiting to begin.

"Oh Lord, thank you for this day," Beth Georgia sighed a bittersweet breath of contentment and melancholy, her voice as dry as sandpaper but still full of simple joy.

She was barely perceptible under the covers, the eiderdown hardly swelling as it covered her small frame, and the face that stared out through the windows to the clear spring day was almost skeletal in its gauntness. Skin, that could have just as easily been sun-dried leather, was taut against her skull and covered by a network of lines that played out the road map of every one of her years; while not the oldest woman in the world there were days that Beth felt like she was, and today - her one hundredth and second birthday - was definitely one of them.

Deep brown eyes gazed out through the window, their keenness belaying the passage of years that they had watched. If eyes were the windows of the soul then Beth's looked into a self-less

DUSTED

life, a worthy life, a long life, lived well. In a body that was beyond frailty, beyond miraculous, the eyes sparkled with a youthfulness that brought a smile to all who looked into them. Just as it brought a smile to the face of Nina Georgia, Beth's only great-granddaughter, as she quietly walked into the room and paused to stare, with obvious love, at the small woman in the bed.

Standing at just barely over five foot three, and small boned, Nina was almost the image of how Beth had looked at her age. Nina, of course, never realised the small pang of fatality that her appearance evoked in her great-grandmother as she had never seen a photo of Beth at that age. For Beth, though, it was like looking into the past and an image of the seventeen-year-old girl she would never be again.

The age difference was never a factor in their relationship, though, as Beth and Nina were as close as two people could be. Love that transcended the generations filled them and they knew without knowing that their souls were linked in a way that the rest of the family could never quite match. Beth and her husband George, who had been dead and buried for over forty years, had had seven children. Over the years her family - and no matter how large or widespread it became it would always be *her* family - had grown to include eighteen grandchildren, all of whom Beth loved completely.

Then, seventeen years ago to the day, sharing Beth's own birthday, Nina was born. At that moment Beth realised that, though she loved all of her family with her whole heart, she loved Nina more; she loved Nina with her heart and soul.

"You going to stand there all day child?" Beth asked without looking around, her voice rasping but filled with humor.

Nina laughed as she stepped into the room, her arms clasped around the large bouquet of wild flowers that she had spent the morning picking. Beth loved nature but had been bedridden for nearly two years now, watching the world pass by outside her window and experiencing it only through the small parts that Nina regularly brought inside for her.

As she reached the bed Nina struggled to hold the flowers together as she leaned over and gently kissed Beth's forehead.

"Happy birthday, Mama," she smiled using the name that the whole family - and most of the people in the small town where she had spent her whole life - called Beth. No matter the actual relationship to people Beth treated everyone like her child; the archetypal mother figure.

"... and a happy birthday to you as well, my darlin' child," Beth's eyes twinkled with mirth. "And am I to take it that the small forest in your arms is for me?"

"No, they were just lying at the door so I thought that I would bring them in and put them in the trash, I mean we don't want them stinking up the neighbourhood!" Nina quipped, her own eyes sparkling.

Moving faster than expected, for someone as frail as she was, Beth's hand snatched a small white rose from Nina's arms. Taking a small step backwards Nina laughed as Beth held the rose to her nose and inhaled, deeply.

"Ah child if only everyone in the neighbourhood could smell the sweetness of the rose the way I do, but if you don't get those poor things in some water they won't be lastin' long at all," Beth said around the flower.

"I'll go get the vase then come back and tell you all about what Johnny is doing for me tonight," Nina said with a smile of excitement, winking at Beth as the rose fell to the pillow beside her head.

Beth allowed herself a small smile as she watched Nina walk through the doorway, and out of sight. *So young but already settled with that nice Johnny,* she thought, 'but *then who am I to worry about that when I knew that my George was the man for me at her age too*? The memory of her husband brought, as it always did, a smile to Beth's face and she turned toward the window again, watching the sunlight illuminate the dust.

Little stairways to Heaven, she thought, remembering how her mother had told her – oh so many years ago - how the light that streamed down was sent from God above to allow angels to come down and help people. In a life filled with pain and hardship that little piece of her mother, whose face she couldn't quite remember anymore, brought Beth comfort.

"Ah but Lord above, Beth Georgia, you think that you'd be too old for such nonsense now, wouldn't you?" she muttered.

"Too old to believe in angels?"

The voice filled Beth's ears with the taste of honey, it filled her eyes with the smell of freshly mown grass and it filled her nose with the colour of warm barley. Her head swam, her senses overwhelmed, and for a second she couldn't catch her breath. For that second it felt like she was drowning, like everything was slowing down, fading, and getting darker.

... And then, suddenly, it was all so very clear again.

The sunlight streaming through the window seemed more vibrant, seemed more alive than before, and the motes of dust now visibly danced around each other. The blue sky outside the window was an azure that she had never seen before and the small white clouds that dotted the clear blue expanse moved past with unbelievable speed.

Remembering the voice she turned her head and a small gasp escaped her mouth as she stared at the figure that stood there, at her side.

So beautiful, she thought to herself as she gazed at the man - the youth - who stood gazing at her fondly. An immaculate white suit, obviously tailored to fit his lithe form, gleamed as if with a hidden backlight. The shirt - open at the collar to reveal golden, sun blanched skin - was a paler shade of white again. Blonde hair fell to his shoulders and piercing blue eyes stared at Beth intently.

"Thank you Beth," the man smiled graciously.

Beth shook her head as if to clear it. *Damn you woman, you are getting old, talkin' out loud like that when a strange man walks into your bedroom!* She thought. Though she knew that she should she didn't feel afraid, or alarmed; only a quiet calmness, washing over her, tinged with curiosity.

"You know, if you have come here lookin' for money, or anythin' like that, you are out of luck sonny, I don't have anythin' of value here!" Beth said to him calmly, her gaze unwavering.

"I am not here for your money Ma'am; you are wrong though, you do *have something that is very valuable here,"* the figure said with small smile as he took a step towards the bed, hands swinging gently by his side. *"Priceless even."*

He sat down gently beside Beth, reaching out to lay one hand on top of her own and smiled as a look of wonder played over her face. Beth's eyes widened at the stranger's touch. For as long as she could remember, for too many damn years, her body had been betraying her; arthritis had spread through most of her joints and her hands, especially, constantly ached. When the stranger placed his hand over hers, however, the pain left.

Realisation began to set in and Beth's eyes widened even more as a small, almost shy, smile played across her lips.

"You have a beautiful smile Beth," the young man said, smiling in return.

"Oh shush now, boy; you are far too young to be talkin' all sweet like that to me, and I am far too old to be listenin' to your pretty tongue," Beth said, but her smile deepened nonetheless.

"Well I am not as young as you think that I am Beth, so in my eyes you are not old at all," the stranger laughed as he reached up to tenderly stroke Beth's cheek.

A shudder of pleasure ran through her as she felt the memory of every pain, every ache, and every swollen joint and hardened artery, disappear. For the first time in as long as she remembered she felt alive, truly alive. It was glorious. Unbidden, but not even trying to stop them, tears of joy streamed down her cheeks as she stared into the eyes of the beautiful stranger in front of her.

"What was that you said a moment ago... about being too old to believe?" she whispered.

"I asked if you were too old to believe in angels Beth, but you didn't answer me," he repeated gently as he stared at her. *"... so, do you?"*

"What?"

"Believe Beth, believe?"

Beth gave a shudder; a small shiver that her mother would have claimed meant someone had walked over her grave. 'Over one hundred years, who would have thought it?' Beth asked herself quietly. Good years, years filled with love and happiness - enough to outweigh the years of hardship and struggle: the years of racism and fear.

One hundred and two years of life.

Beth smiled to herself as with some effort - but not as much as she was expecting - she raised herself up on the pillows and stared directly into the young man's face; her eyes twinkled as they reflected the pure and simple expression of joy on his expression.

"What do I call you, sonny?" Beth asked, avoiding the question.

"I have many names, Mama, but you can call me Azrael - if you wish?" he replied, gently, holding out a hand expectantly.

At the name Beth gave a small sigh. She had always been a faithful woman, had read her scriptures and remembered them for as long back as she could recall. The name was known to her, as was the duty that he carried out.

"Well, Azrael, I guess that I am not too old after all, am I?" she said with a small smile. "So why don't you just take me home?"

Reaching out she placed her small hand in his own, smiling at the look of shock that played over his face ever so briefly. Gripping the hand that engulfed her own she laughed, fully and vibrantly, her voice sounding strange until she realised that she could hear no trace of frailty or age in it.

"What's that matter Azrael, not what you were expectin'?" she asked teasingly.

"Well I have to admit that I thought that you might have questions, might have concerns, might even argue ..."

"I have spent one hundred and two years trusting in the Lord boy, and I am not goin' to stop doin' that now just because He has decided that it is time to call me home. I am ready; I've had a good life and now I'm prepared to meet my Maker" she interrupted.

"So you are ready to leave the world, and your family, behind?" he asked tenderly.

"Ready? No I wouldn't say that I am ready, but I knew that this day would come and I am not afraid to take the journey; I am not afraid to leave. I accepted a long time ago that this day would come, and now it's here," she said with quiet dignity.

"You are an amazing woman, Beth Georgia, and know that your family will be well and will always love and remember you," Azrael nodded and smiled at her warmly.

"So is it time?" Beth asked quietly, a tremor in her voice. "... Is it time for me to die?"

Azrael laughed, holding out his hands and clasping her own in his. Pulling her to her feet he turned her to face the mirror and she gasped in shock. The reflection was not the frail shell of a woman that she had been for the last few decades; the girl that she remembered being, the girl that she was inside - that she had always been – stared back. She was young again. She was herself again.

"No Beth, it is not time for you to die, my child," Azrael said gently as he stepped in close and embraced her in his strong arms. *"That happened before we even started talking."*

Over his shoulder Beth saw herself - the old woman that she had been – still lying in the bed, unmoving. She placed her head against his chest as she realised that her life - her pain - was really over and that the conversation with the angel of death had simply been to ease her on her journey. As his arms closed tightly around her she gasped in surprise as she felt the feather-light tickle on her face.

Wrapping his wings around her, Azrael became ensconced in a nimbus of golden light and, when she was safely cocooned within, he looked out through the window, his gaze travelling along the pathway of light.

"Father, we are ready," he said gently, and then smiled as the light intensified around him.

Nina gasped, both hands going up involuntarily to her mouth. The vase fell to the floor and shattered with a crash as glass and water exploded around the room. Flowers scattered all over and lay, unnoticed, as tears filled her eyes.

She watched the woman who had shaped her entire life lay unmoving on the bed, her chest still and quiet. She took a step forward and reached out to lay a hand, gently, on the still-warm skin of the old woman. A small, sad, smile played over her face as Nina leaned down and kissed Beth's forehead - not noticing the small feather that floated gently to the floor near the mirror.

Wiping the tears from her cheeks she stepped out of the room, looking back as she burned the beatific expression on her great grandmother's face into her memory for all time.

With her face to the sky, and an expression of complete and utter peace on her face, Beth Georgia lay still and unmoving, staring into the Heavens with eyes wide open.

* * *

Working for God is never easy. I love Him, of course, and

trust Him – though His ways are, admittedly, a mystery – but the path that He has set me on, and the task that He has given me, is not an easy one. And yet, still, I do it.

No, working for God is never easy but it is always – *always* beautiful, and wondrous, and right.

About the author: Jay Faulkner resides in Northern Ireland though says home is simply wherever his loved ones are – his wife, best-friend and soul mate, Carole, and their two wonderful baby boys – Mackenzie and Nathaniel.

He says that while he's a writer, martial artist, sketcher, and dreamer he's mostly just a husband and father.

PAST PERFECT
Charles Gramlich

"I know the one," I told Mom. "The perfect woman for me."

"You're too demanding, Nancy," she said. "No mortal could ever please you."

"One could. Just one."

Mom snorted. "So when do I get to meet this miracle lady?"

"You already have. She lives a lot closer than you'd think."

"*What? Who?*"

Instead of answering, I showed her a photo of the big, shiny telephone-booth looking gadget that I'd invented as my thirtieth birthday present to myself.

"What in God's name?"

"A time machine, of course."

Mom frowned. "Are you insane?"

"Nope. Just in love."

"I don't understand."

"Ten years ago I was a real hotty, Mom."

About the author: Charles Gramlich grew up on a farm in Arkansas but moved to the New Orleans area in 1986 to teach at a local university. He's since sold numerous short stories in the genres of horror and fantasy, as well as several novels and a nonfiction book or two. His blog is at: http://charlesgramlich.blogspot.com

SLEEPING WITH THE FISHES
Nigel Bird

Always felt sorry for Anne Frank.

The way she lived. In hiding from those animals.

And here we are, history repeating itself like we've learned nothing.

It was Anne that gave me the idea.

When you're persecuted and in hiding, when there's nothing to do but eat, listen to the radio, read and sleep, you might as well write it down. Sure, there's little chance the pages will see the light of day and, sure, if I make it out alive no-one will pay a blind bit of attention, but don't I win both ways? Get out of this mess, the prize will be the freedom itself. Fail and maybe I'll be able to watch down from heaven and see my book piled high in the shops and filling whole window displays on the High Street.

I say looking down from heaven, but you just don't know that, do you? Depends who you believe. I was brought up Christian, see.

Nowadays you're more likely to think it ends at the bottom of the ocean. Instead of clouds to sit on you have the backs of turtles. You can watch the world at the angle of refracted-light, just like the pike in my school physics book.

Don't get it myself. The idea of hanging about in the sky was hard to swallow, especially after the physics book, but water? How the hell could all the souls that have ever been fit into the oceans? It's ridiculous – at least the sky goes on forever. Mind you, all the people on the planet could fit into the waters of Loch Ness, you can sort of see it and you have to keep an open mind.

Open mind? The very idea makes me chuckle.

If you can be bothered, you'll find it all here. Don't just chuck it out. Hold on till sanity returns and you'll be able to claim the rights.

Rights? There's another joke. To them right's just another direction.

You'll find a photo of me in the shoebox. There's something melancholic about it. It's the distant look of the eyes that does it.

People never say my eyes are soft or beautiful or anything like that. They're a bit slanted and close together if anything. They comment on the faraway look though. My wife used to say I was never with her, was always somewhere else, but she was wrong. I was always there, right in the moment.

I miss her. Missed her as soon as they took her away.

I've been hiding in this basement for the last eighteen months on account of a cruel twist of fate. It's six paces from wall to wall at its widest. What natural light there is comes through the gaps in the floorboards above. It's a good job carpets went out of fashion or I wouldn't even have that. An un-shaded bulb hangs from the middle of the ceiling, one of the old-fashioned kill-the-planet kind, sixty Watts. I switch it on when I need to read or write.

Dimitri, the owner of the flat, hasn't been home for two days. If he's not back by nightfall I'm going out to see what I can find. The rations have almost gone.

The way I salivate when I hear the jangle of the keys, you'd think I was one of Pavlov's dogs. At times like this, I wish I could open the hatch from this side, that the Victorian trunk covering it up wasn't so heavy. Reckon I could push it over, but I'm not going to do that until it's a real emergency in case I do any damage. They don't make them like that anymore.

If only my mother had gone into labour that little bit earlier, had eaten a curry or had one of those special teas, they might not have had to go for the caesarean. One day earlier, that's all I needed. Could be out there now at the top of the pile. My sin, to be born on the 21st March.

Aquarius.

One day wrong. Could have been Piscean instead of a water carrier.

Jade, my wife was six months out.

The Leos were the first to go.

She said she'd write and I waited, just like thousands of others.

When it got to a year, something in me stopped expecting. Don't suppose any of us were waiting any longer. We had enough on our plates to give it much thought. It's the living need looking after, right?

I heard about the camp from a guy in the Leighton Arms. Said a friend of his had escaped. From one of the Scottish Isles he said, Skye or Mull or somewhere. The way he told it, they'd turned the whole place into a prison.

At first, island life was OK. After a week the food was gone and not long after half the people came out in a rash, bright red, the colour of strawberries. Their glands swelled up, their temperatures soared and within days they were dead. That's when this guy made a break for it, swam a couple of miles to the mainland. Wasn't going to hang around and wait for them to give him the pox. That's the way I was told it, anyway.

Didn't want to believe it, course I didn't, but it sounded right, the kind of thing they'd do to us, you know.

I try not to think about her, but I've too much time on my hands to do much else.

I do my exercises, one hundred laps then my back stretches so I don't end up with a stoop. A hundred sit-ups and as many press-ups as I can manage and that's me finished. I do them when I wake up in the morning, before my afternoon nap and when I smell the food cooking.

If I ever get out, I'll have a body fit for Hollywood. Imagine Kirk Douglas in his prime.

Last time I was outside it was winter. It's the one flaw in the ID scheme. They've got us all tattooed on our earlobes so we can't get away with it most of the time.

I knew people who sold their homes to pay them to get a water sign.

If I'd known then, I'd have sold mine too. Got me one of those sixty nines or a wobbly H instead of these green zig-zags.

It'll be months until it's cold enough for them to give permission for hats and hoods again. Soon as they do, I'll be out there sucking up as much fresh air as I can.

On a good day Dimitri brings down the paper to read. It's full of crap, but better than nothing.

If we'd paid more attention to the press in the first place, maybe we wouldn't be in this mess now.

The catalyst to it all was a piece in 'Astrology Now', one of those collections of random information that seem to matter these days. Turned out that forty-seven per cent of the government were water signs. The figure for the whole of parliament was even more against the odds: sixty-five per cent were Cancer, Pisces or Scorpio. Anyone with a grasp of probability knows that was a little unusual, but anyone with a basic grasp of common sense would have known it was a piece of nonsense.

How the chancellor came across the information is anybody's guess, but she used it in her blog to poke fun at the opposition.

That should have been the end of it.

It might have disappeared without notice had it not coincided with the vote on the war.

There were enough rebels to put the result in doubt and without support from the opposition the Prime Minister would go down with his hobby horse. The chancellor seized her opportunity. Sending messengers scurrying around corridors, wheeling and dealing with anyone who would listen, she called upon them to rise up and be counted, test the waters as it were.

The vote was carried with a huge majority. The sea-creatures had it.

Soon there were references to the sea all over the place. They quoted science and literature to prove their point; scraped up any old angle they could find to give them mileage on the sofas of Breakfast TV.

The usual demonstrations were going on at the time: the anti-war, the pro-life, the send-poverty-into-oblivion, but none of the activists thought that a movement against Pisceans seemed worth creating.

Wish I'd taken my soap-box to Speakers' Corner with the other nutters and given it my best shot.

When they moved against the government they had no chance. Came from nowhere, forced parliament to dissolve and formed a party populated by the best liked politicians in the country.

H to O, they called themselves. I wonder which guru came up with that.

Even then we couldn't see the way it was going. We could have out-voted them three to one, yet H to O got in with the largest land-slide ever recorded.

At first, they worked within the traditions of democracy, even made a few improvements. You didn't see litter on the streets and there were no kids hanging around on corners any more – everyone was far too scared of what their special units might do to them to cause any problems.

The Sharks they call them. The teeth of the law. Imagination was never their strong point.

Jade didn't take it any more seriously than I did, at least until Astrology Now came up with a few more statistics for us to think about. They did a survey of the prison population.

Four out of ten offenders were born into Fire signs and, even more conclusively, when it came to crimes in categories one, two and three, the figure rose to sixty per cent.

There was no mention of the way the Sharks had been targeting Leos for the previous six months or the way the judges seemed to have it in for the Sagittarians; things like that didn't seem to matter.

It wasn't long before the press was calling for blood and the government leaped into action. Water puts out fire, they said, and it did. That's when they came for her.

The last time I set eyes on her, we were having lunch in the Sunrise on the Brecknock Rd. It was the usual for me, Spanish omelette and chips with onions on the side, two toast and a mug of coffee (the sort that looks expensive but tasted like it comes from the washing up bowl). Jade had the soup, straight from the can, with a bottle of water and a slice of bread.

Always on a diet she was. Seems like a waste of time now. Still, if she's alive, she's probably satisfied with her body for the first time in years, all skin and bone, just like she always wanted.

Shouldn't kid myself. All bone and no skin is what she is. All bone and no skin.

When they came in, I was at the counter talking to Stephanos, trying to come up with the solution to the Gooners' goal drought. Decided we needed some new blood in the management and new legs on the pitch. Jade was watching the world go by from the window seat, so she probably saw them first.

I thought it was just one of the routine checks, sniffing out the illegals and the unsavoury.

It started like it did on any other day, a few people running for the exits, the rest of us getting out ID and trying to get it over with as quickly as we could manage.

One of the boys in the kitchen made a move even before the bell on the door had time to announce them. Had his arms out of the washing up bowl and was through the back faster than Jesse Owens.

I wasn't surprised. There were new faces working there every time we went in. We didn't mind who did the chopping or wiped the tables, so long as they could keep the prices down.

Two minutes later the boy was back again, this time with a bloody nose and a set of plastic cuffs on his wrists.

There must have been ten of them in the caff by then. I was too busy trying to catch Jade's eye to try and count them. They were like grey clouds on a windy day the way they rushed from one table to the next. A plague of bloody locusts. There wasn't time to do anything.

I shouldn't have talked out of turn, I know, but when I saw the way they were talking to her, the way Adam Harris had her by the elbow and was pushing her out to the exit, I guess I kind of lost it.

Adam Harris always was a lanky bugger. Maybe it would have been different if it hadn't been him. He was smirking at me as he took her, see? Looking down his nose, his face beaming the message loud and clear, "Who's the daddy now, O'Sullivan? Who's the daddy now?"

True, we'd given him a hard time at school, but it wasn't our fault he couldn't manage to do anything without screwing up and it was nothing to do with me that the girls never gave him a second look, not unless they were staring in fascination at his teeth and his acne.

"Let her go, Harris, or I'll knock those corns down your throat." The words were out before I had the chance to think. The shark in charge was all over me like a rash. His neatly ironed, grey shirt sleeve rushed towards me, his fingers gripping white onto the baton. He was married, or at least he had a ring. I wonder if his wife knew what he got up to at work. I could smell his aftershave and burning toast. Jade was shouting something, only it's all blank now, like it were a silent movie or a cartoon strip with all the speech bubbles bleached white.

Harris dragged her off, all the time smiling under his silly

DUSTED

Thunderbirds hat. His hand went down to her waist then gave her bum a squeeze. That was the last I saw of her, that gormless goof groping her backside.

"Took her on to bus," Stephanos told me afterwards. He was making me sip water and held a cloth filled with ice cubes to my face. "With all the others. You a lucky guy, Sully."

Luck. One man's luck is another's misfortune. I wonder who got my share of the good stuff.

The way I look at it, Harris is proof that there's no such thing as a Piscean master race. Take the machine gun from him and he's nothing. I'd like to meet him one day, down a dark alley, just me and him.

That was when we had to get our ears done.

It was the first time anyone tried to go up against them. The protesters were mown down on Trafalgar Square.

The lines outside the official branders just got longer. From what I can remember, we were all there willingly. There didn't seem to be anything to worry about as long as you weren't a Leo.

I got mine in Camden Town. After all, if you're going to have the government impose a look on you, the least you can do is get it done with some panache. Stand out from the crowd. Do it in style. Even showed mine off when I first had it, just like I did when I got the mermaid on my shoulder.

The mermaid was Jade's idea, to celebrate our love she said. She had a seahorse down by her ankle so everyone would be able to see it in the summer. Turns out they were ironic choices, now she's sleeping with the fishes and all.

I don't want Dimitri to end up like the people who looked after Miss Frank. Nobody ever remembers who they were, yet they were the real heroes when you think about it. Anne was there because she had no choice. The people who kept her in hiding, they were the ones who were risking something, just like Dimitri.

Dimitri Karlov, for the record.

He's a good guy. Doesn't need to be doing any of this. If I were in his place, I'm not sure I'd have it in me to put it all on the line.

He's a GP just over the other side of the Camden Road. Earns enough to own a pad in a quality spot, has two cars and a motor bike, holidays in the sun twice a year and pulls the women like no man I've ever known. There's no way I'd risk that. Good job he's not like me.

I met him after they rumbled we were trying to leave the country. A dozen of us crammed into the false section of a container were headed to Amsterdam. It was supposed to be a consignment of organic dog food. Stank like the insides of a whale. Made us feel real Moby Dick.

Don't know how the Sharks got wind of it, but the driver pulled the plug on before we left the warehouse. Dropped us off in a park in the middle of Canterbury and told us to wait, so we did. Three hours we hung around in the fog and then got instructions from a guy with garlic breath and a limp. He gave us pieces of paper with addresses and passwords. Had to get there under our own steam, he said, before disappearing from whence he came.

Three nights it took to get here. Mostly on foot. The weather was lousy, the coldest June since records began. More of that luck I was talking about.

Slept as best as I could during the day. It's amazing how many places you can warm up when it's chucking down with rain and all you've got are summer clothes. Train stations, the backs of burger bars and doorways of shops. Jewellers are best, all that bright light throwing out heat like their main job is to heat the street. When I was desperate I'd stand behind the exhausts of buses.

By the time I arrived at Hilldrop Road I was a stinking mess.

I waited until 10:30 and gave the door the two long and three short taps just as instructed. It opened before me as far as the security chain allowed. A smartly pressed white suit and a narrow silk tie were the first things I saw of him. I had to look up as far as my neck would crane to get a good look at his face, or at least the strip of face that was visible. There were smile lines at the sides of the stunning blue of the eye I could see.

Unlocking the chain, he opened the door and greeted me as if I were one of his long lost relatives from Moscow. Even spoke in Russian before allowing any words of English to pass through his lips.

"Welcome to the Monkey House," he said in an accent that was all North London. "Come in and let me get a look at you."

I've had cooler greetings from relatives. I was half expecting him to tell me how much I'd grown once he'd finished with taking my bag and patting me on the back.

"You've been in the wars, my friend. Come. I have just the thing to put the life back into you."

I followed him into the kitchen and sat down at the table. He was right about having just the thing, too.

Three bowls of soup I had, the best food I ever tasted. Big chunks of vegetable and hunks of bread that must have come from a deli.

While I scoffed it down, he passed over a glass of whisky that was like the magic porridge pot – every time I emptied it, he filled it up again.

I felt them, the soup and the booze, warming my bones from the inside
and then I felt nothing. Next I knew I was waking up in a strange bed made up with the kind of crisp sheets I thought you only got in hotels. The smell of washing powder blended with the aroma of the fresh coffee waiting for me on the bedside table is a cocktail I'll take with me to the grave. I smell it as soon as I think about it.

The luxury treatment only lasted for the one night, but I'll never forget it.
 I knew it couldn't be like that all the time. I had to move under the boards into my cell and I've been here ever since.

 I thought he was being paranoid at first, the way he made me wear headphones in the daytime to listen to the radio. He gave me this pair of slippers early doors, an inch thick with rubber tested out in space. Make me quieter than a church-mouse they do, and ten times more likely to break my neck, but I wear them all the same. Anything to keep him happy.

He pops down to see me every so often. Tells me the news and how the Arsenal have been getting on. Best of all, I like to hear about his love-life. When I first knew him there was practically a different woman every week.

He found something wrong with all of them until Aduke came along. I'm pleased that he's met someone nice, don't get me wrong, but I miss the buzz I got from hearing about his conquests. When you haven't got someone, see, you've got to get your kicks from somewhere. He says he's going to get a woman for me, only

I don't know if he has the guts. Even told me that there are people, men and women, who do that sort of thing for the cause. I'll believe that when I see it.

Six months ago, he started seeing Aduke, this Nigerian dentist. I knew straight away she wasn't like the others from the way he talked about her, like he was finally with someone he respected.

Usually it was the things he didn't say that gave it away. There were none of the jokes or details I'd looked forward to, and all I got to know were the facts and the things I heard through the boards.

I asked to meet her to put a face to the lady of mystery who had stolen my saviour's heart. Should have known better. It was the only time he raised his voice in my company.

Love can do funny things to a man.

Not long after the paranoia started.

Dimitri came home one day and I could hear him pacing his sitting room. I could tell there was something wrong because he still had his shoes on. Normally, he changes into his slippers at the door. Even got his visitors to remove their outdoor footwear in the hall. Always found that a bit anal, you know, worrying about germs and dirt like that. Mind you, being a doctor, I suppose you're careful about those things.

The pacing went on for about five minutes and then he closed all the blinds and shutters in the flat. Only time he ever did that was when he was expecting a lady, and even then he never bothered with the sitting room.

He explained it all later.

When he left the gym that evening he had a feeling he was being followed. Every couple of minutes he'd take the chance to look around and check. He didn't do it in the way the average Joe might, not with all his training. No, he looked round only when he was crossing the road, used the reflections of windows, car doors and his mobile to take glimpses over his shoulder.

He took a different route, looped the loop, tied his laces and turned back to read posters in windows and saw nothing. Still, he said, he knew they were there, could practically smell them.

I couldn't smell anything other than the curry he was carrying in the brown paper bag from the Indian take-away. He'd stopped in as an extra precaution.

Passed the whole thing on to me, he did, said he'd lost his appetite. It was the finest food that I'd put into my mouth since the soup, the melting potatoes in their coating of spinach and the cauliflower florets that were more 'a la brink' than al dente. The rice was cold and the nan bread softened by steam, yet I could have eaten it again ten times over. If they offer me the chance of a last supper, that's what I'll have, that and my Spanish omelette on the side.

For a few days I feasted on take-outs from every restaurant along York Way and the Brecknock. There were kebabs and pizzas and plain old fish and chips. The story was always the same. He'd not seen anyone, but they were there, lurking.

Can't say I minded much if it meant me getting my fill of international cuisine. My heart was too firmly set on a Mexican for me to care too much how it came about.

Never got my burritos or my taco shells and curly fries.

Next day, when Dimitri was out at the surgery, there were some ferocious knocks at the door. Normally people go away when there's no answer, but not these folk. They knocked once more and then, before I knew it, the door was opening and a heavy set of boots came clomping in above me.

Although I couldn't see a thing, I had pictures in my mind of the three of them in their grey sashes pointing and gesturing as if they were in danger. Three boys playing at being soldiers. I'd put money on that Adam Harris was one of them, snooping around and leaving bugs and spy-sights wherever he felt like concealing them.

Only took five minutes from start to finish.

Soon as they'd gone I texted Dimitri just as we'd arranged.

"Not feeling so well. Meet at Pineapple instead? J."

Since then he's been more careful than ever. Can't say I blame him. Maybe if he'd got rid of me he'd be here now, lying in the arms of his woman, feeding her strawberries or whatever he does that's so irresistible.

We talked it over, I say talked it over, but it wasn't that exactly.

To make sure there was no noise and that no concealed cameras would capture him shifting furniture and lifting the hatch, we exchanged written messages. Dimitri folded his up and dropped out knots of paper through the biggest gap in the boards as if getting rid of soil in the exercise yard of Stallag 13 or whatever it was. I passed mine back up in the space between the skirting and the rubber plant, which was safe as long as they hadn't hidden anything in the leaves that pointed straight down.

We decided that there was no point in looking around for bugs or cameras, because they'd see what he was up to and pull him in. A lights-out curfew was imposed for 10 every evening and there were to be no visits at all. Food would be passed down under the cover of darkness and he set about emptying the objects from the drawers of the chest and rubbing oil onto the bottom of the frame so that he could move it as quietly as possible. I've lost many a meal to a last minute topple, I can tell you.

It's worse when the spills are from the chamber pot.

That was a month ago now.

We thought it was going well, but maybe we aren't as good at playing the resistance game as we thought.

Hang on. Here he comes.

I've been on at him to get the gate sorted since I arrived. Makes such a squeak it would wake the Pharaohs. I can feel the beats of my heart in my mouth.

I'll play it cool. Give him a ticking off for leaving me on my tod with nothing but cold soup and dry croissants to keep me going, then I'll come clean and tell him how I've missed him and his Muscovite ways.

It's not him though. Not alone, anyway. Four of them by my count, possibly five.

Off the gravel and up the steps, one, two, three, four, five, six, seven. I know the rhythm like it's engraved in my genes, single steppers, two at a timers and even for the postman - he's a three at once guy. Must be a 6 six-footer at the very least.

There's a key in the lock.

The swing of the door.

Stomping of boots. Definitely boots.

They're going straight for the chest.

Doesn't look like I'll make it to the end, huh? And I had so much to tell you.

You'll be lucky if there's enough here for a short story.

I can hear her giving orders. She might well use her quiet

voice, the bloody traitor. I'd know that accent anywhere. Aduke! No doubt she's used her dental skills for the odd unrequested extraction.

She's not getting any of my teeth.

There's a carving knife in the drawer. I've been saving it for an occasion such as this. It's got her name on it. Unless I see Harris, in which case he's first.

Should have paid attention to that bloody horoscope. "Aquarius - Watch out for strangers and nasty surprises."

Later friend. Later.

About the author: Nigel Bird is a Support For Learning teacher in a primary school near Edinburgh. Co-Producer of the *Rue Bella magazine* between 1998 and 2003, he has recently had work published by *The Reader* and *Crimespree* and was interviewed by Spinetingler for their *Conversations With The Bookless* series earlier this year. He recently won the *Watery Grave Invitational* contest over at The Drowning Machine and will have work published in *Needle* and in *Dark Valentine Magazine* this summer. He hopes to complete a draft of his first novel by the end of 2010.

Suits You, Sire
By Iain Pattison

Stefan chortled tipsily, swinging his flagon so hard the ale slopped on to the sawdust-covered tavern floor.

"It's got to be the con of the century. The most outrageous caper of all time," he giggled. "And we pulled it off. We did it. Us, Freddy boy, us! We're geniuses."

He punched his companion hard on the arm, making Frederick wince.

"It's a classic hustle I tell you, a bloody classic. Mark my words, people are going to be talking about this scam for years ... for decades to come. We'll be legends."

He hiccupped. "Who knows - maybe they'll write a song about it. Let's see - *the King was in the altogether, the altogether, the altogether –*"

Frederick's fast fingers grabbed him round the throat, squeezing off his boozy ballad in mid chorus.

"Shuttup you fool," his partner-in-crime hissed, eyes flashing. "Keep your voice down. Do you want to get us strung up?"

He jerked his head at the other dark, menacing, unsavory drinkers dotted around the shabby inn.

"Any one of them would turn us in for a shilling," he warned. "And by now we'll have been rumbled. There'll be a reward out - bounty hunters searching for us, not to mention the palace guards."

Stefan tried to focus on what Frederick was saying, but he couldn't get over the audacity, the sheer unadulterated cheek, of their grift.

"But the invisible clothes ploy, Freddy. The old birthday suit routine. It's a tough number to pull off - and we made it look easy. We got him hook, line and scepter!"

"It was very satisfying," Frederick admitted grudgingly, faint smile playing across his lips. "Just proves the bigger they are the harder they fall... for it."

His amusement vanished as swiftly as it appeared. "But we can keep the gloating and self congratulations for later. Just now, we need to lay low and wait for the stage coach. Okay?"

Stefan made a mock salute. "Anything you say, partner." He took another slurp of beer, a trickle running down his chin.

"Yeah, but ... but when you asked him if he liked the color and he said he preferred a lighter shade. And you said that would cost more! That was bloody brilliant. I nearly wet myself!"

This time Frederick wrenched him so close that their noses were touching.

"Will you keep quiet!" he snarled, waving away Stefan's 36% proof brewery breath, "I won't warn you again. You've got a real drink problem, you know that?"

Stefan felt himself blush like a naughty schoolboy. God, he'd never seen Frederick look so threatening!

"And don't think for a moment I haven't forgotten how you nearly blew it back there - jabbing him in the Regals with the measuring tape."

The bitter words cut through Stefan's grog-induced grogginess. "My hand slipped," he replied defensively. "It could have happened to anyone."

"Any drunk, you mean!"

He was about to fire back a hazy, hops-fuelled retort, but became aware that Frederick wasn't glaring at him any more - or trying to choke him. Instead, his fellow huckster was spinning round towards the door.

There was a noise outside, clattering across the cobblestones.

"The coach?" he asked hopefully.

"No," Frederick answered, voice tense. "There are too many horses. It must be soldiers. It's the palace guard. They've found us. Shit!"

Both bolted for the door, almost forgetting their bag of ill-gotten gold. But they were too slow.

It opened, and framed in the doorway the burly Captain of The Imperial Guard stood - sharp, gleaming sword in hand.

"Ah, just the two characters I'm looking for," he said, voice deep and menacing. "We've been looking for you all over."

Signaling to the troopers to seize the double-dealing duo, he added: "You're coming with us. The Emperor wants a word with you. And, believe me, he's not happy."

***

It was amazing how quickly he'd sobered up, Stefan realized. It might have been the bumpiness of the hurried horse ride back to the city, the look of terror on Frederick's normally unruffled face or the knowledge that they'd both better start thinking up a world class alibi pretty damn quick.

Of course, the sight of the gallows being tested played its part.

The wooden scaffold platform came into view just as they entered the inner courtyard. It was solidly constructed, made of finest Dark Forest oak, and raised ten feet up so that the crowd could get an unrestricted view - and the condemned were ensured a fast, effective and terminal plunge.

Busy at work, a hunchback figure in a hood was manhandling large sacks of grain into the nooses and giving the trapdoors underneath a quick sharp stomp to make sure they worked smoothly. He stopped to wave as they drew level.

"Would you like a demonstration?" he offered, mellow voice missing the lisp that most people would have stereotypically expected.

"N-n-o... no... t-t-thanks," Stefan stammered, heart shuddering and his guts twisting into an ale-flavored pretzel.

"I've never had any complaints," the hooded figure assured him, "but of course, I can't really get testimonials from my customers."

He pointed to his wagon. On the side, in crude lettering, was painted: *Speedy Executions - we never leave you hanging about.*

"I'm better than my rivals *Capitol Punishments* - and they charge double what I do."

"M-m-maybe later," Stefan told the hunchback, trying not to hurt his feelings, then immediately regretted it when the implications sank in.

Frederick gave him a withering look. "For a conman you have a lousy way with words," he whispered tartly.

"Enough blabbing," the Captain of the Guard snapped, "get moving. We haven't got all day. The Emperor is waiting and he hates it when the executions don't start dead on time."

That, Stefan told himself worriedly, was just what he was

afraid of...

***

"Any chance of using the restroom - just before we see the King?" he asked, as two stern-countenanced troopers dragged him along the long marble corridor. "It's just that when the bottom falls out of your world, you feel the world is going to fall out of your bottom. Know what I mean?"

Neither responded, just kept clomping onward with military precision and a decided lack of compassion.

Damn. Well that put paid to the old *going-to-the-restroom-slipping-out-the-unlocked-window-and-shimmying-down-the-drainpipe* plan.

Ahead he could see Frederick being lugged along by another pair of chocolate box squaddies. He wasn't having any more success trying to finagle his way of his predicament.

"Look lads, gentlemen, it must cost a packet to provide your own uniforms," he was telling them. "If you let us go, my companion and I could quickly knock you up some amazing threads - just like the King's. Just as classy - and just as cool."

But the soldiers weren't fashion fans, or else weren't as gullible as their esteemed ruler.

Gulping, Stefan realized that this was it - they were in as much trouble as it was possible to be. They were dead men walking. Well, dead men dragging...

With a rough shove he was sent flying, landing in a heap on top of Frederick - and immediately before two massive, tall, imposing silver-plated doors.

"Get on your feet, "the Captain of the Guard barked at them. "Smarten yourself up. And bow your heads. We're going into the throne room..."

With a well-oiled squeak - like a very polite mouse trying to attract attention - the doors opened and they shuffled forward, eyes cast downwards.

"Your Highness... I have apprehended the *tailors* you so desperately wanted to get your hands on," the officer announced.

And, trembling, Stefan looked up and saw something that

took his breath away...

***

The King - his mighty Majesty, the Regal ruler, the Emperor of all the lands from here to the Sardonic Sea, the head honcho, the big cheese, the grand gaffer - was stark, raving, starkers!

Parading in front of a full-length mirror, the country's figurehead was displaying all of his figure.

"But he's still bare -" Stefan blurted, before Frederick's hand shot across the space between them, and clamped his mouth tightly shut.

"Bare ...ly had time to try everything on," Frederick corrected. "My word, Your Highness, you look magnificent. So poised and elegant."

Unable to do more than mumble, Stefan took a second to mentally catch up - then twigged what his smarter friend had immediately sussed. The King hadn't found out yet.

Even for an inbred Royal this one was slow on the uptake!

"Yes, it's exciting," the King said, beaming. "So many outfits to wear. I can't make my mind up what to sport to the executions."

Going straight into hustle mode, Frederick rubbed his hands subserviently - with just enough smarm to act the totally authentic tradesman.

"But if I may enquire, Sire. The Guards said you were unhappy, and we were summoned back here rather ... *robustly*. I thought something must be amiss."

The Emperor made a 'what can you do?' face, explaining: "Soldiers! Eh! They are always so rough and overzealous. I merely said I wanted to catch you both before you disappeared off - so you could make the alterations."

"Alterations?" Stefan asked, bemused.

On make-believe, non- existent, garments?

"Yes, alterations," the Monarch replied, beckoning them both forward.

"I'm afraid I've been overdoing things," he confided. "Too many banquets. Too many civic receptions. I've put on a pound or two and, fabulously fashionable as your delightful apparel is, it's getting a bit snug. It really needs letting out a bit. Can you do that? Is that possible?"

Stefan fought the urge to laugh out loud. This was ridiculous! This was madness! But what the hey...

"That would have to be extra," he said, ignoring the daggers look Freddy flashed at him.

"Extra?"

"Yes, sorry. It would have to be another bag of gold. What with the additional material and the thread and the man hours."

The King stroked his chin thoughtfully. "Yes... I can see that. It is intricate work - and you two are such *artistes*. It would only be fair."

He smiled. "And if we're doing that I'll get you to run me up some robes in the darker shade of blue you suggested. I was thinking I was a bit hasty insisting on the lighter hue. Do you think I'd look good in it?"

"You would look sensational," Frederick promised.

"Really? You think so?"

"Of course!" they choroused.

"Sensational? You're not having me on?"

"Oh Sire," Stefan assured him with a wicked smile. "That's the absolute truth. You might say the *naked* truth..."

***

From high in the tower King Rudolphus the 16th watched the two hucksters swagger out of the palace gates, laughing and swinging their matching bags of gold.

He shook his head. Clowns! Amateurs! They definitely deserved to die. But not quite yet. Let them have a few weeks to feel safe, to wallow in their ill-founded, deluded smugness. Then he'd enjoy springing the trap and watching them swing.

He tutted. The sheer effrontery of them trying the old birthday suit hustle on him. They must have thought he was just off the boat.

Still, it had been fun, he conceded. Playing the part of the clueless victim had been hilarious – a delicious break from the boredom of his normal Court duties. There was no greater pleasure in life than conning a conman.

Apart, he thought with a shiver of delight, from indulging his naughty naturist fantasies in public for a while ... with the perfect cover story!

Iain Pattison is a full-time author, creative writing tutor and competition judge. His short stories have been widely published in the UK and US, and broadcast on BBC Radio 4. His book *Cracking The Short Story Market* (Writers Bureau Books) is a best seller. www.iainpattison.com

Red Ravine
Gayle Arrowood

Prologue

"Hello Folks, I'm Gene Farrell, Jimmy's brother. I'm glad you could
join me because today is one of the loneliest for me. Every year, I've
set this day aside to return to this site: my first home, the yard where
we grew vegetables, the one-car garage and trees between me and a
ravine of the Illinois River. I stare at everything and remember the
horrible indifference of nature that day just as it was before man
arrived here and will be long after we're extinct.

Memories and town gossip flood my mind. I'll try to piece
everything together as best I can, and each year more details emerge
from the heavenly forgetfulness of the dark area of my brain, the
place where I can hide it, block it out. This is pressure-release day.
Or maybe it's a developing story from my depth. I don't even know
anymore. But this I do know, this visit is the only thing that keeps
me going the rest of the year.

Let's follow the patted down grass and head to the ravine, the
place of trauma for many in the past and the present, judging by the
tall grass matted down to form a path. We can sink into the tall grass
the water's edge while memories and gossip flow to my surface just
like the dead thrown into the river. Perhaps, between me and you, I
can let this memory fade, so I can put it to rest once and for all.

Smaller Adventures

It was twenty years ago when they were six-years-old that her
family moved into the two-story white house just a block away from
a ravine. Jimmy was the first child she met, and they became fast
friends right away. Perhaps, they just recognized each other as soul
mates from the very beginning.

No one seemed to know how they got their ideas, except for
the last one. That came from the TV. Alone, each one was kind and
obedient, but together they could cause chaos.

In first grade, they watched the big boys climb the jungle jim
at school to the very top, then they'd drop to ground in the center of

the bars.

"Let's do that," she screamed; of course. Jimmy was right behind her.

Both climbed, but had a hard time going from one bar to the next because they were short. They'd give a jump and land their stomachs on the higher bar, swing their legs up one by one, and finally sit on that bar. Resting only a moment, Chrissy stood up and pulled herself to a standing position. Then up to the next one.

"I have to catch my breath," Jimmy said when he stood on the first bar.

"Me too," she screamed.

It took nearly ten minutes to reach the top bars. While they were sitting at the top, still huffing and puffing, the recess bell rang. Everyone else started down. So she gave a little leap into the center, held her arms straight up, and shot to the ground where she fell forward.

"Get out of the way," yelled Jimmy. "Here I come." He dropped, but didn't get his arms clear; he conked his crazy bone. They raced into line with the others, but Jimmy held his elbow, and tears ran down his six-year-old face. The nun looked at his arm, told him he was fine; eventually, he stopped crying and went back into the school.

Each time, they climbed the bars a tiny bit faster until one day, Sister Andrea saw Chrissy shoot to the ground and her skirt fly over her head, and her lace panties showed. The nun hurried to stop her before she was at the top again. She had to climb down. Sister grabbed her hand and led her to the merry-go-round, saying, "You can't climb on the bars because your dress flies up. Play here, young lady." As the teacher turned her back and walked away, the child stuck out her tongue.

Jimmy joined her, and they played there until the bell rang. Sister Andrea watched too closely for them to be able to sneak back to the bars.

"We can climb after lunch because I'll be on the other side where she can't see me," the girl said. "That stupid."

And so their game went on unnoticed after that. She only jumped when the other kids blocked her from the leering minds of the nuns or when the sisters looked away.

***

Their tricks grew wilder. The next year in the fall, on the way home from school, she yelled, "Jimmy, watch this."

Cars were coming in the distance; she ran to the middle of the narrow intersection and lay down so as to block traffic in two directions. Jimmy rushed after her and blocked the cars in the other two. Of course, the more the cars honked, the more they giggled, though they watched closely. Anytime a door opened for someone to get out of a car, those kids were on their feet racing away in a different direction than their home.

It must have been giddiness and power that urged them on. They didn't stop this until the spring when a man with a beer gut got out of his car and didn't get back in. He screamed, "You brats are going to stop. Every afternoon when I'm going home. I'm going to get you both." The kids jumped up and raced away. They couldn't remember ever running that fast. He kept after them until he was so winded he sank to the ground, holding his chest. Luckily, a couple people came out of their houses and hurried him to the hospital. The kids were three blocks ahead of him, so no one noticed them.

This story spread all over town, even to the ears of the culprits and their parents. But no one knew it was them because by that time the story reached our neighborhood, it had changed to three twelve-year-old boys. Only after... were all their secrets exposed; their parents' minds nearly unraveled. That man had died of a heart attack. His death cut their game short. They hadn't seen him die; still they understood they better stop the street antics before someone else got hurt.

Somehow through it all, they must have lost all fear by the time they were eight. That's all any of us could imagine.

The Escapade

The children sat cross-legged on the living room floor in front of the television, watching people scale some mountain halfway around the world, a place about which they'd never heard.

"That is really neat," she whispered, leaning closer to the

black and white set.

"Yeah man, look at them," Jimmy yelled. "I bet we could do that."

"They don't have any mountains around here, stupid. This is the flat lands. And don't talk so loud; my mom will be screaming at us. She tries to listen to everything I say. So speak softly. If she hears just about anything fun, she's telling me I'm a girl, not a roughneck, and I should act like a lady. Strictly dullsville."

He always hated it when she called him stupid. But that day, he must have been too fascinated, watching the climbers on the 'Wild' World of Sports, as they called it, to notice what she said..

"My mom thinks I'm too wild, too, and I'm a boy. I should act like a gentleman. So don't worry... wait a minute! I have an idea," he said softly, "but we will need rope. My dad has lots of it in our basement. We have to be quiet about it, though; mom will tan my hide."

Without turning off the TV, they raced across the living room past a couch, several chairs, and end tables pushed against the walls, through the kitchen and out the back door. Since Jimmy lived right behind her, they raced across the alley, past his mother taking clothes off the line, and into the back door of his house without either of their mothers hearing a thing. They had the rope in five minutes, ran out the front door and down the street.

"We have to get this done before supper," Jimmy said.

"Where are we going?" She asked.

"The ravine," he answered.

"Wait a minute," she said. "Your brother and Martha (his wife) are working in their backyard again. If they see us, they'll yell and Gene won't let us go shopping with him anymore." They crouched at the edge of the high grass and wild daisies between them and the ravine.

I can only guess they got by when my back was toward them. My backyard bordered the wilderness on two sides, and the trees leading to the swamp on the third.

Just as the kids got down, I must have stopped cutting and looked toward them, because I remember hearing something. When I asked Martha, my wife stopped and looked toward the trees. Her boots were muddy from weeding the soft ground. If only we'd walked over there to make sure. But we didn't; I went back to my chore. Martha looked in that direction for several minutes before resuming her weeding.

"I know," Chrissy whispered. "Let's stay here and just move forward when their backs are toward us. OK, let's move."

Progressing slowly, they finally made it to the woods that surrounded the ravine on two sides. Here they could go faster. The oak and ash trees were dense enough that they hid the kids. The closer they got, the stronger the odor from the ravine. It always smelled like death.

They ran fast enough that they slid to the ravine edge.

"Ohmigosh," she yelled, "Yikes." They grabbed each others' shoulders and backs, trying to keep their balance. Both of them had to dig their heels and toes into the mud to keep from falling into the water. They giggled all the way.

And the commotion alerted the marine life: snakes, small fish, tadpoles, toads and turtles. All were in motion when the kids were finally ready to step into the most forbidden, but much-used playground in that neighborhood.

"Wait a minute," she screamed, "we have to get our shoes and socks off, so nobody will know we've been here."

"Shhhh!" Jimmy answered. "Gene might hear us like he did last time we were here. We got the belt."

Just when they were about to step into the water, Jimmy stopped. "My jeans will get wet."

"Just take them off," she answered. So he did. Then with eight-year-old, inexperienced hands, they tied their waists to each end of the rope, just like they'd seen on television. Since the cliff bordered the water on the other side, they had to wade through the muddy ravine to reach it.

The vertical sandstone sneered above them so high and menacing that it looked as if it reached into the heavens, a Pikes Peak where she'd visited on a vacation with her parents the previous summer. But rather than gray and brown, this cliff was striated with lines and swirls in different shades of yellow. Sandstone was mined in this area.

After staring at the steep ledge for a while, they discovered places where ridges stuck out, just big enough for their toes and fingers tips.

"We shouldn't have any trouble. Look, the water's only up to our ankles," she said. "And with all those ledges, it'll be a snap."

"And there's no quicksand like they've been telling us either," he said.

"I know. Nobody's found any down here, even the big boys," she answered.

They jumped up and grabbed onto the rock, but their legs got tangled because they were so close together and they nearly plopped on their rears in the water, but managed to stay on their feet.

"Let me go first," Jimmy said. "I'm taller and this was my idea." He jumped and grabbed a ledge, but his fingers slid right off. "I'll have to dry my hands." He wiped them good with his shirt and left long yellow smears across the front of it. He jumped and lost his grip three times.

And the third time, he fell on her; to steady themselves, she grabbed a hold of him and he held onto the rock. When he jumped again, his fingers managed to hold the ledge. But he stubbed his big toe on the rock and had to leap back into the water. Both giggled so hard they had to catch their breath.

"Jimmy, you move down a bit and climb there. I'll try here. I'm tired of waiting," she said.

So he moved a foot toward the deeper water and both children kept leaping merrily at the cliff. She dug her fingers into one of the sandy ledges and they held, so she whipped her legs up, and her feet found a sanctuary.

"Finally!" she shouted.

"Don't forget," he said. "We can't get too far apart because of the rope."

"I forgot," she said. "So hurry up, clumsy."

"Who you calling 'clumsy,'" he growled as deeply as he could to imitate a man. He gave a leap, grabbed a ledge and swung his toes to a lower ledge on the next try. Now each child concentrated hard on their path upward.

The only sounds were the hundreds of crickets leaping in the tall grass. To those in this area, even children, the croaks blended with the singing of sparrows and robins and indicated all was well with nature.

When trying to climb one ledge higher, she caught her toe in her dress.

"I need jeans." She pouted. "Stupid mom makes me wear these dumb things. They're always getting in the way."

Jimmy shouted, "Take that stupid thing off, we gotta get up there before supper."

Both children went down fast because neither was up high. Hurrying, she splashed to shore, Jimmy right behind her because of the tether. She hauled her dress out from under the rope and yanked it over her head without even noticing the buttons had been ripped off. Then back they raced to the cliff.

Before long, Jimmy's feet were even with her head. They were about a third of the way to the top. When she looked up, she realized the rock just above her current grip was perfectly smooth, a dead-end. There wasn't even one ledge sticking out far enough for her tiny fingers. "Look at this, Jimmy, I can't climb anymore." And she began to cry.

"Just go sideways, ninny, and follow up behind me," Jimmy shouted.

She stretched a leg out as far as she could reach. "I can't go sideways. It's too far," she insisted. "I'll go back down and then start all over behind you."

"Why are you so cautious? All you had to do was give a little jump and you could have made it all right. Sissy. OK, but make it fast," he yelled back. "I'll wait. The rope might not be long enough for you to get down."

Sure enough on her way down, the rope jerked tight, so she waited until Jimmy had come down a little before she leaped the rest of the way into the shallow ravine, landing with her feet deep in the black mud.

She had almost caught up with Jimmy when he yelled, "This stupid cliff. Those ledges are gone, so I'm coming down too. Now after you get down, hold the rope tight, and if I fall, just keep it straight and I won't get hurt, like we saw those climbers on television when that one guy lost his grip. Now see how fast I can go. You were just being a stupid sissy."

They started down as quietly as they could.

Jimmy made it up a lot higher than she had and was still up

there when she leaped down into the water. He was doing fine until all at once his toes slipped off a tiny ledge while he was reaching for a lower ridge. His other hand couldn't hold all of his weight, and he lost his grip completely. He tumbled pell-mell down and bumped his head all the way; at the same time, she was grabbing the rope as fast as she could. When he reached the bottom, his body knocked the rope and her into the muddy bottom of the ravine.

Somewhere in the distance, she had to hear me yell, "Ohmigod, ohmigod," over and over again. But I didn't get through to her.

She sat there, yelling at Jimmy, "You stupid, look at me. My panties have mud all over them. I'll get my petoot paddled tonight because of you." She stood up and tried to wash the mud off as well as she could in the filthy river.

Jimmy landed on his back and sank deep into the mucky ravine floor. Motionless. As she stood up, she kept yelling, "This is no time to play dead. Now get going and wash your clothes off."

Still he didn't move...

Again, in the distance I yelled, "No Chrissy, no." I was out of breath from running. But again the words didn't reach her or she ignored me. She had selective hearing where adults were concerned.

She slip slid over to Jimmy and grabbed his arm to pull him up, like she always did when he played dead. Before, he had always held himself down when she yanked, but this time he came right up. Even her young inexperienced eyes saw that there was something wrong with the way his head rolled back on his shoulders

As soon as she had his back lifted out of the mud, all she saw was red ravine water around her ankles, and her shrill scream shot through the air and wouldn't stop.

The next thing I was holding her in my arms and turning her away so she no longer could see Jimmy arched in his unnatural pose. Tears streamed down her chin... and mine... just like today.

Epilogue

Every year, exactly two weeks after her birthday, I come here to stare at the shallow water and sink into the high grass. The ambulances and cops are long gone, of course. But the memory of that incident is forever etched into my mind.

I had to move out of this neighborhood. Somehow I felt responsible.

Thank you folks, for joining me today and letting me tell you about this. Hopefully, I won't have to return next year, but I won't know until then.

It's been twenty years since the ravine turned red, reminding everyone that the river held many creatures in its watery clutches, its graveyard. Nature is shrewd in the way it works, erasing all evidence of the accidents and leaving no warning for those who would follow. But for those who know, the ravine is as malicious as the river. The signs are there. On the other side of the water, the forty-foot cliff stands as it always has, as nature has always been, indifferent to whatever burdens it cast upon us.

About the author: Gayle Arrowood is one of the authors in the anthologies: *Our Shadows* Speak I, *Emerging Writers* and *Holiday Choir*. In addition, Arrowood has published stories and narrative essays in such journals as *Writer's Post Journal, Insidious Reflections, Graffiti Off The Asylum Wall, Horror Library, Vault IX,* and *Static Movement*. Recently, she appeared in two anthologies: *Atrum Tempestas and Santa's Givings...and Misgivings.* Also, she has read her stories at Peoria Live and Old Books in Normal Illinois as well as Barnes & Noble in Temecula, California.

May Contain Spoilers
Mark Taylor

It was 10pm and Jared Long was sitting in a recliner in his lounge, reading lamp on, pouring over a manuscript. He was a book editor in a small publishing house. It required him to work extremely long hours for very little pay.

The manuscript itself was aligned perfectly and very easy to read, but, that was not the problem. It was the story. He just couldn't make up his mind. It was so... *right* and yet left him feeling almost unwell when reading. He picked up his phone and hit speed dial 5.

"Hello?"

"Cal, it's me, Jared."

"Shit, I've been working since seven this morning, what is it?"

"I'm reading the manu you asked me to look over. The psyc-horror. It's good, but I just don't know whether it's printable. The reader may find it a little, well, odd."

"That's why I asked for your opinion. How far you got?"

"Page 113 – the bit where Foranté finally starts to catch up with the beast."

"That's about where I gave up." Cal's voice had started to become more oriented as he was starting to focus. "I found the concepts starting to get a little weird, along with the whole bloody death stuff."

"Fine. I've had enough for tonight anyway. Look. Sorry I called, I'll see you in the office."

"'Night." Cal rang off.

Jared crashed hard as soon as he was in bed, but his sleep was torn by dreams. The night took more of a toll on him than refreshed him, and the following morning, on the journey to the office, he began to wonder if he would have been better off not going to bed at all.

He entered the austere office building with a headache already jabbing at him, and by the time he had got the elevator to the 11th floor, it was a full blown nuclear holocaust in his head – opening the office door even hurt. *I feel sick*, he thought, *Christ, I've never had a migraine like this before*. He walked across the office floor, nodded at a couple of overworked colleagues, and entered his and Cal's corner office. Cal hadn't arrived yet.

Jared slumped into his chair and tossed the well thumbed manuscript onto the table. *I can't believe that I've got sit here and continue to read this.* Sitting up, he closed his eyes for a moment and focused. "Right." Jared opened the manuscript to page 124.

During the night it entered from the street and moved up the stairs. It crouched at the top of the landing stairs and caught a breath. From the next room the light crackle from the fire was splintering the silence. A page was heard turning.

It crept within the room, and looked over at the single chair. A man sat in front of the open fire reading a book. He looked intently at the text, turning page after page. He cleared his throat, looked at his watch, and let out a sigh. He looked worn. It moved up behind him and paused with an almost arrogant air about it, and struck.

Its animal attack was violent beyond all imagination. The man actually lost consciousness quickly... but that didn't stop it. It tore and clawed at the lifeless body, bones cracking under the tirade of brutality.

The man died of blood loss within minutes. His corpse no longer animated.

Jared rubbed his eyes and sat back. He had started to slip slowly into sleep, when a quick knock on his office door startled him awake. It was Annie from the office next door.

"Jared, there are two police officers here to see you."

Jared furrowed his brow, "Thanks Annie, show them in." She disappeared back into the main office and two uniformed officers approached the door.

"Mr. Long?"

"That's me. What can I do for you officer?"

"We believe that you are an acquaintance of a Mr. Robert Callaghan."

"Cal? Sure I've known him for years." Jared let out a short, contemptuous snort, "What's the stupid son-of-a-bitch done this time?"

"There's no easy way to say this, I'm terribly sorry, but Mr. Callaghan was found dead this morning."

Jared was stunned. He slumped back in his chair, not

believing the words that he had just heard. "What..." his voice trailed off into the distance. He had known Cal since they were at school together. He had always been the joker; you know the one, always having a laugh, playing the fool. "What happened?" Jared tried to maintain his composure.

"A neighbour of Mr Callaghan called after finding his front door open at seven this morning; they thought that he might have been burgled during the night. An officer attended and found Mr. Callaghan rather, well, brutally beaten. He had passed away some time in the night. I was wondering if you could confirm that you spoke to him last night."

"Yeah, about 10:15 I think." Jared's thoughts fazed in and out, "He was fine then, said he was about to get some sleep."

"At the moment we don't have the time that it occurred. Do you know any of Mr. Callaghan's family?"

"Cal didn't have any family. His parents both died a few years ago, no siblings. I guess... I guess I was his family."

"Mr. Long. Would you come with us and identify the body?"

Jared sat in his reading chair, the room dark, the manuscript sat on the table in front of him. He had his eyes closed, but was not asleep. He wasn't going to sleep tonight. The darkness inside his head was filled with the images of *Mr. R. Callaghan*. He didn't see the body as that of Cal's. It wasn't him anymore. He picked up the manuscript and looked past... no... through the pages, and tossed it back on the table.   *Not tonight.* He briefly closed his eyes again, just for a moment, and then stood and walked over to the counter on the side, "You're okay, aren't you Jack?" he said, picking the glass bottle up and tipping a generous amount into a straight tumbler, he noticed as he looked at the viscous liquid that it rippled, just slightly. He was shaking. He moved back over to the chair, sat, and picked up the telephone and speed dialled 1, "Mom?" Jared relayed the day's events to his mother, calmly at first, and eventually through tears. She cried on the other end as well, having known Cal nearly as long as Jared. They took solace in each other's sadness, as the conversation ran into the night.

Two days passed, and Jared returned to work. He couldn't afford to take more time off, but wasn't really looking forward to sitting opposite Cal's empty old desk. This apparently wasn't to be a problem. When he entered the office, there was another face on the other side of Cal's desk. Jared's hackles rose immediately. *How dare someone sit there*? "Can I help you?" he enquired, through gritted teeth.

"You must be Jared, my name's Goodstein, Hal Goodstein. I'm new here. Started yesterday. They said you were off sick. Feelin' better?"

They've replaced Cal, thought Jared, *with this... this... wiener. Be polite... just be polite.*

"So," Jared sat, "Goodstein, what assignment have you been given?"

"I've been given this manuscript," Hal waved it vaguely in the air, "some retro sci-fi thingy, not my usual forte."

They always let Cal do the *retro sci-fi thingies*, he was good at them, always could tell his Asimov from his Bennings.

Jared looked down at the manuscript he had returned with, sitting on his desk, still not finished. He had read more during his time off, but not a huge amount. He picked it up, ready to move back into the world that made him feel...

Foranté moved swiftly through the urban jungle. Night was the domain of the Thing. Down a black alley, he leapt, grappled with the fire escape ladder and started to climb; surely he'd find it this time - before it happened again. At the top of the building he stood, surveying the silhouetted rooftops, trying to find that of which no man should see. It was there, in the night.

He could see the beast heavily breathing in and out, rhythmically, almost in tune with the cold night. It was time.

"Jared," Goodstein snapped him out of the fog that the manuscript had placed him in, "how's it going?"

"What?" Jared wasn't impressed. *Cal wouldn't have done that.*

"You seemed lost in there. Good is it?" Jared thought for a moment, and summed up Goodstein. He couldn't have been more than twelve to look at, ill-fitting suit, first job maybe.

"How experienced are you..." Jared paused for thought.

"Hal."

"Sorry, Hal."

"I don't have any great experience in the field, but I'm keen, and a quick learner."

Jared pondered, *Cheap, and easy to please. First job.* "Fine," he finally replied, "Quick heads up, you read yours, and don't interrupt me when I'm reading mine." Jared looked at the clock in the corner; time for a coffee.

After returning, some five minutes later, Jared picked up the manuscript and read again.

The beast moved off, at speed, Foranté in distant pursuit. He wouldn't keep up… couldn't. The beast leapt to the next building, disappearing into the night.

Foranté followed as best he could, but eventually slumped into an exhausted heap. Not tonight… but soon. Foranté turned and left.

It was night. Jared had left the work behind him, and sat on his bed, Jack keeping him company again. *No sleep again tonight,* thought Jared, getting up and flicking on the TV. He slumped into the couch, and started to hop channels. Late night program after late night program, jumping from one unwatchable pile to another, Jared finally started to feel quite tired.

"Jared?"

Jared jumped, and quickly focused on his recliner. In it sat Cal. "Cal. Cal? What are you doing here?"

"Just dropped by to see my old mate." Cal looked good, really good. Back to his old self, eyes a glint with mischief.

"I thought you…"

"Dead? Yeah. Crappy I know. Still, it's not all bad. I don't have to pay to get into the theatre."

"What… what are you doing here?"

"Jared. After you leave this plain of existence, during the transitional period, you'll receive some… offers. Acceptance of these offers can make your life much easier. I've been asked to harvest souls and I thought, well, I have come for yours."

"… Cal?"

Cal leaned forward toward Jared, pulled himself close into Jared's face, getting within breathing distance and said, "Just shittin'. There's something on the fire escape. Wake up."

Jared jolted forward on the couch, spilling Jack Daniels over himself. Cal was gone. He looked over at the window, squinting, trying to see through his own image reflected back at him, not being able to make out anything on the fire escape beyond.   After a moment spent frozen in time, Jared simply said, "Christ," and moved over to the cabinet on the side. Sliding a draw open, he pulled out a packet of smokes and a lighter. "Twelve months..." he said, placing one in his mouth and lighting it. As the light from the flame danced across Jared's face, he looked up, through the smoke, at the window.

The beast moved as fast as it had ever done, ripping through the air, and leapt across the gap from one building to the next, crashing onto the fire escape, shattering the glass of the window as its body fought for control.

The beast collapsed through Jared's window and sprawled, momentarily, on the floor. Jared stumbled to his side, trying to move away from the noise, glass, and *thing* as quickly as possible. Jared let the lighter drop from his hand, and, as his mouth opened, the cigarette also dropped to the floor. "What the..." he lurched backward, trying to get a new footing, as he flailed to remain standing. The beast now stood in front of Jared, remaining on all fours. It didn't appear to be a natural bi-pedal, but had assumed a hunched position on all fours. Its eyes were cold, black, and its skin leathery and damp in appearance. It seemed to be summing Jared up – looking for a weakness perhaps – but Jared wasn't about to show one. He turned, threw himself through the nearest door way, and landed hard on the kitchen floor.

He slipped and scrambled to his knees slamming the door behind him and pushing his body weight against it. "What the... " reflected Jared, rather unhelpfully. He surveyed his kitchen, realising for the first time how empty it was.

Keeping his foot wedged against the bottom of the door, Jared pulled open the nearest draw, looking for a knife... something heavy... anything. "I'm gonna die because I don't cook?" Jared decided that talking to himself was not a sign of madness in this type of situation. He could hear the beast breathing on the other side of the door. Jared closed his eyes, prepared himself, and bolted across the kitchen, through the opposite door. Almost instantly, the beast crashed through the first door, splintering wood across the kitchen, landing sturdily on its feet, and gave chase.

Jared careered out of his front door into the bleak hallway, and pushed himself as hard as he could to move as fast as he could. The beast wasn't far behind, and soon the pair of them were crashing down the corridor, one behind the other. Jared catapulted himself, shoulder first, heavily against a door to his left – thankfully it gave and he crashed to the ground inside, the beast passed the door with too much momentum behind it, trying to stop. Jared ploughed through the darkness of the apartment, crashing into walls, stumbling on furniture, aware that the beast had now regained its footing and was standing at the door, seemingly awaiting Jared's return. Jared dragged open the window, and climbed out on his knees. *Forget this*, he thought as he scrambled along the ledge, away from the open window, back toward the fire escape. Lucky it was a calm night. Jared tried to look over his shoulder, to ascertain the beast's location, but decided that this contortion may prove fatal. "A thirty year old editor, climbing a ledge, five story's up, being chased by something that looks like it escaped from a bad mainstream novella. What the hell am I doing here?" Continuing to edge along, Jared moved past another window – locked – toward the fire escape.

As Jared clambered onto the now damaged escape, he threw a look along the ledge. It hadn't followed him. He climbed in through the window, his feet crunching on the shattered glass on the floor and a slow smoulder fire had started on the carpet. Jared went to the front door, quickly looked outside, and closed the door... quietly. It seemed to be gone.

Jared returned to his TV, still crackling away to itself. He flicked it off, the room darkened slightly, and he moved over to the cabinet on the side. He was surprised by the level of heat from the fire – no flame – just heat. Sitting patiently on the fire escape was the beast.

It leapt through the window, coming into full body contact with Jared. He fell to the floor heavily, winding himself as he landed, the beast deflected to the side and onto the couch. It flailed to its feet, shaking its head from side to side, probably never having stood on cushions before. Jared pulled himself to his feet, and stared down at the beast.

They looked at each other, and, in that split moment, the chase was gone; they almost seemed to understand each other. In another split second that moment was gone.

Jared moved first. Breathing heavily, he leapt across the room toward the cabinet, and grasped the first *weapon* he could find – Jack. Turning, he swung the bottle hard at the creatures head. It collided with it, with a dull but sickening *Thunk.* The creature, stunned, awkwardly stepped backwards. "Mother fu...!" screamed Jared, throwing himself forward, landing the beast a second time with the bottle, breaking it this time.

The glass smashed across the beast's brow, hurling it further backwards, letting out a screeching howl, Jack Daniels covering its eyes, dripping from its face. In almost slow motion, the vapour exploded from the heat of the smoulder, blue flames engulfing the beast. It had no idea what to do. Shaking itself to and fro, screaming, the beast lurched backward and forward, blue flame igniting anything flammable that it came into contact with. Jared crashed across the burning room, out into his hallway. He could hear the beast continue to thrash about in the next room, the heat intensifying through the doorway. He made his way into the corridor, closed his front door behind him, and ran towards the stairs.

"Fire! *Fire!*" he howled as he flew down stairs. Some of the doors to other apartments started to open, small faces peaked out. "*Get out!*" shouted Jared; most people ignoring him.

Jared crashed into the street, and looked up to the building. His apartment seemed to be glowing orange, but he couldn't hear any screeching. He dropped to his knees, and started to weep.

In the room, the beast lay spent, dying on the floor, the couch burned, the recliner, the TV. The manuscript lay on the table, the heat of the room curling the edges of the last remaining pages.

Foranté looked over the side of the building, down at the remnants of Jared's victory and smiled a small smile. Turning away, he disappeared into the night.

About the author: Mark Taylor is an Author from the South-East of England. He writes SF and H and most things in between. You can find him at www.filingwords.blogspot.com.

Mind Over Matter
Nita Lewsey

I wish I could believe in mind over matter, the power to think oneself better, that overwhelming faith that there is a way to overcome the inevitable but I can't. Oh it's ok for the masses, the 'general' public, the world out there, to be fed stories of triumph over disaster; 'My son came back from the dead' or 'The long road to recovery' by A.N Other, you know the sort of trash you see in every other magazine, rag newspaper and T.V documentary. Well I'm here to tell you life's not like that. Sometimes there is no triumph; no recovery; just existence and worse still, no way out.

I'm one of those statistics that governments like to massage. What can they do with me? Nothing it seems, just plonk me in a wheelchair and hand me back to the bosom of my family. Except there is no bosom, not any more, and that's my fault too if you want the truth. 'I'm sorry Mrs. Jones but there is really nothing more that can be done but we will of course liaise with social services to get a wheelchair ramp organised blah blah blah'

And so I go home, well not home, but to my parent's house, not to my open plan warehouse apartment that cost me the earth, but to the little bungalow Mum and Dad moved to when they retired last year. It's never been my home and now I'm invading the quiet space they've created, me and this damn wheelchair. Me and all this hospital paraphernalia that now surrounds me. It isn't fair of course and it isn't right, just because they brought me into the world, raised me and encouraged me to make my life better than theirs, that they are now lumbered, yes lumbered with what amounts to an overgrown baby. Ok inside my head I'm as sharp as I ever was, but they don't know that. To them I am a 6-foot tall, 13 stone dribbling, incontinent baby and they are back at square one in the caring stakes.

So here I am in the special hospital bed with air filled mattress in my parent's dining room, well what was their dining room, now my prison. I stare at the walls recently decorated with what my mother thinks is trendy geometric patterned wallpaper but is really designed to inflict severe migraine just from looking at it. Oh and don't forget the wheelchair, set up by the bed so that I can be wheeled out just like they used to when I was in my pram. But now there are no cooing neighbours or friends telling them how cute and gorgeous I am just sad glances, pitying looks, hands laid gently on my father's arm as he pushes me along the pavement on those rare outings we make if he's had help getting me from the bed into the chair.

My mother never comes with us. She's too busy stripping the bed yet again and cleaning up so that when we get back my cell is clean and waiting. Oh I know what you're thinking 'Poor you it must be awful' or 'your mum and dad are heroes' or maybe you are desperate to know how it is I'm here at all?' That can come later.

I have a T.V on the wall so I can see it when I'm slumped on the pillows, it's all rubbish, just soaps and reality shows, dire quizzes and endless news. I have to rely on Dad's selection of channel for the day, I can't say 'Oi Dad can I have the sports channel on please' or 'I'd rather watch a good film not Oprah', no I just lie here and wait for whatever comes up next. Is this what people do all day just watch one dreadful chat show after another? Are we so interested in other people's lives that we need more or less identical programmes on every channel? Oh to be able to shout out 'Please just get me a book' but I cant. In fact try as I might I just can't seem to make any kind of communicative gestures at all.

I'd imagined that as Mum and Dad know me better than anyone they would be able to look into my eyes and read what's going on in my head. My eyes must be like mirrors so surely they can see my wants and needs reflected there. I think really hard about the things I want and when one of them is standing in front of me looking into my eyes and talking at me I am sure they ought be able to understand my thoughts but they don't.

A nurse comes every day to give me a bed bath; at least they don't expect Mum to do that, now that really would be degrading, not just for her but for me too. Bad enough she has to change my 'nappy' or the incontinence sheet to be precise, which is a permanent fixture on the bed and feed me with 'baby' food, but to have to wash me all over too? Now that really would be a step too far. Of course the nurse is really needed full time but '... resources can't stretch that far', they're told by the 12 year old social worker that calls in to check we're coping. I wonder what would have happened if I'd had no parents? I don't recall other options being discussed, well not with me obviously, as a cabbage I don't really have an opinion. Meanwhile my brain is screaming but there is no technology capable of hearing it so I just slump here and let the nurse lift my arm and wash my armpit. She's quite nice looking but her heart's not in it but then neither is mine.

Oh yes I forgot, you wanted to know how I got here? Did I crash while driving my sports car? Was it a skiing accident or did I have a fall while mountain climbing? Well no, actually I was out with my mates on a stag night in a club and I made the mistake of upsetting a bouncer on the door and he picked me up and threw me out, literally. And I landed on my head. And that, as they say, was that, broken neck and damaged brain.

It's Tuesday so Uncle Bob will be over to help Dad with the hoist so they can put me in the damn wheelchair for our little outing. Oh joy. After all the huffing and puffing and heaving I'm in the chair and off we go, down the nice new ramp that has now disfigured the front porch and off to the shops to run the gauntlet of the neighbours with their pity and offers of help, which Dad will always reject out of hand. Not sure why he does really but he's always been a proud man and so we struggle on with just the occasional hand from Uncle Bob and the nurse. The bungalow is not really that far from the hospital but it's still a surprise when Dad wheels me up to the main entrance, perhaps he's had enough and is taking me back with the words, 'Here you can have him we can't cope' but apparently not.

Dad takes me up in the lift and we are in what looks like some sort of technology department. Eventually several people arrive. Dad joins them in some deep discussion round some sort of computer. Stranger still the tall guy is actually talking to me. Actually talking to me not at me, I'm so stunned I have to check myself and concentrate on what he's saying. Something about 'when we get the scan results back we can do some simple tests and if there's the slightest physical response he should be able to make it work'. Make it work? Make what work? Anyway I'm carted off to have some sort of brain scan and eventually I'm wheeled back into the room and they all gather round. The tall guy straps electrodes to my face, he's asking me questions and saying stuff like 'if the answer is yes blink your right eye if no use your left'. He's obviously mad, blink my right eye? I can't even flutter an eyelash. But he keeps repeating the question 'do you understand what I'm asking? Right for yes left for no'. Of course I understand the question I'm not an idiot and I'd blink my eye if I could, and I do try, of course I try. Do you think I'm just sitting here? With all my being I'm trying to blink my eye, my right eye, 'Come on eye just blink, just flicker, just quiver, please just do something'. There's a strange flashing and a buzzing sound 'You see' cries the tall guy 'I knew you understood, the indicator has detected that tiny movement you just made, well done, this changes everything and now anything is possible'. I had moved my eye, I made them 'hear' me and Dad is standing there with tears streaming down his cheeks. I smile, well inside anyway, but if I can make the machine work once I can make it work again. The tall guy, Mr. Baker, is telling me, yes me the cabbage, the idiot, that my response means he can work with me to create a communication device so that I will eventually be able to 'speak' through the computer.

I can see hope, and what's more Dad sees hope too. Maybe there is something in this mind over matter idea after all.

About the author: Nita Lewsey-54 and been writing on and off for about 5 years. Works in Admin-Degree in Humanities with English Language (Hons).

THE SKY'S THE LIMIT
William Wood

"Slow down!" Clara grabbed the seat as Frankie peeled around another corner, twin beams of light slicing into the night ahead. The narrow brim of her feathered cloche, caught by the wind, whipped from her head into the dust-filled night behind them.

Frankie sneered at her, barely visible in the dark confines of the car, and laughed, the sound barely audible above the roar of the engine and the rattling of the '26 Chrysler Roadster's door on its hinges. She knew he loved his new car, fresh off the line, far more than he did her. "Shut your yap." He drew back his open hand, stopped as she drew up, and then grabbed the wheel again with a satisfied smirk.

Clara fought back a tear and twisted to look at the swirling darkness in their wake. In *her* wake. Had only a year passed since she screamed at her mother—told her she was not a child anymore and she was going to New York? *I'm gonna be somebody, Ma! The sky's the limit. I don't have to be a wife with a litter of kids... like you.*

And what did she have to show except the bruises from three boyfriends—the latest being Frankie Mulrooney, a two-bit Rockefeller wannabe. She sighed. She really knew how to pick them. He was a handsome devil, though, and murder on the dance floor.

She gazed into the swirling murk behind them. They'd moved the *Road Closed* sign just to get on this washboard stretch of dirt. And all because some guy with a screwy glass eye—a rube Frankie didn't even know—said this road led to some knocked off hooch baron's private stash.

She lurched forward, her grip slipping as Frankie slammed on the brakes. Her forehead smacked the windshield hard and she recoiled back into the seat as a sea of dust washed over the car.

Blinking hard, Clara willed herself to stay conscious, forced her eyes to focus on the figure in the road. The world around her swam, teetering left and right as she reached up and dabbed at her forehead. Warmth and wetness flowed down her fingertips and dripped onto her thigh.

Frankie leaned across her, pulling a handkerchief from his

pocket. Maybe he wasn't so bad, she thought.

He wiped at the windshield where her forehead struck, grunting when the smudge of blood only smeared and tossed the cloth into her lap. "Clean yourself up. Geez, you're a wreck." He pushed her leg aside, swearing as his white cuff brushed against the blood on her knee and pulled a black case from the floor under her feet.

He opened his door and stepped outside. He placed the case on his seat and looked ahead into the dissipating dust. Snapping the latches free, he opened the lid. "Just in case."

She looked down at the Thompson submachine gun and froze inside.

He leaned in and gave her cheek a pinch. "I'm leaving it for now, but if I say bring it, you come running. Understand?"

She was transfixed on the gun, unable to speak.

"Understand?" His voice was a growl, an angry hardness.

She nodded.

Frankie skirted along the edge of the cornstalks planted on the other side of the narrow gully separating the field from the dirt road. The headlights played off the mass in the road, refracting away in tiny rainbows. She was reminded of old tree trunks, dead and weathered by the elements. This one was wider at the base than any tree she'd ever seen. As tall as a man, with several large branches jutting upwards from the top and hundreds of twisted tendrils forming a halo above a round lump twice the size of a man's head. The lump flickered as if lit from within.

Clara shuddered at memories of wax museums and glass factories. This crazy tree growing in the middle of the road could have been born of both, somehow blended and melted, becoming something entirely new.

The air was filled with the rumble from the idling Roadster and the rustle of the cornstalks in the breeze. And something else. A hum mixed with the tinkling of crystal chimes, but so subtle she wasn't sure if she was hearing the noise with her ears or feeling it in her bones. Her head ached, pulsing with slow the rise and fall of the hum and her stomach knotted from too little food and too much drink.

Lights

Clara reached across the seat and shut off the bullet-shaped headlights, then pushed against her temple with her right palm. Was that Frankie talking? The voice was wrong and the sound was in her head, like the hum, like her mounting headache.

Frankie's shadow wavered across the windshield of the Roadster. The tree beyond gave off a soft yellow-white glow, invisible before in the glare of the headlights but now bright enough to illuminate the entire scene. An eerie light that crawled across open space and dripped off of everything it struck.

Arrival... prepare

The bulbous head of the tree flashed with light, pulsing with each syllable. Clara felt her stomach knot again as she watched undulating shapes within the head throb and pulse with light.

Frankie swept his arms wide, turning in a complete circle. "Okay, game's over. Who's doing this? You really had me going there. Come on out."

Clara looked with him but all that stirred besides the gentle rustle of the corn, were the three of them. Frankie, herself and the tree.

Approach...

Frankie staggered two steps toward the upside down, melted chandelier as the tendrils swayed, reaching for him. He shook his head, driving away the drunken look in his eyes and leaned away from the glassy tentacles. Anger and fear played across his features and he looked back to the car, pleading in his eyes, then back to the tree.

"Get out of my head." His voiced cracked, making him sound like a schoolboy for an instant. He gritted his teeth. "Right now."

Prepare to divert catalytic essence needed to fortify lamina...

Clara opened her door and stepped out of the Roadster, slipping her heels from her feet after a few stumbling steps on the hard, uneven surface. Frankie stood, his feet rooted to the spot just beyond the reach of the tree.

Frankie looked back at her and grimaced. His eyes moved from her face to her hands and then he smiled, twisting to face the tree again. He spat on the ground between them.

"Wh-what are you?" asked Clara.

"Quiet!" snapped Frankie.

We are yggdrasil...

"I said stay outa my head!" He looked at Clara, his face red even in the low light, and reached a hand out to her. "Give it to me."

"What?"

He clenched his teeth, his face more pain than anger now. "The chopper. Give me the chopper, Clara."

She looked down at the Thompson in her hand, her handbag over her shoulder, eyes wide. She hadn't even realized she'd taken them from the car.

"Now!"

We push into your corporeality only rarely...

She didn't move, only stared into the glistening depths of the tree and the hypnotic swaying of the branches, the sparkling of the tendrils. Only then did she notice the *we* the otherworldly creature spoke of. Similar tree-like forms, each pulsing in time with the one before them, dotted the road beyond as far as she could see. "Wh-why?" Her heart pounded in her chest and her head throbbed, keeping time with the rhythmic stirrings within the tree's head.

Branes are closer than permitted... maintenance is required...

"Maintenance?" She took another step toward the tree, now only ten feet away from both the tree and Frankie. Frankie strained to reach her, bending unnaturally against gravity, trying to reach the gun. Sweat dripped from his forehead as he grunted with ever increasing effort to reach her but his feet would not give up their purchase on the ground.

"Give me that gun or so help me—"

Silence...

Frankie winced, his forehead a canvas of pained furrows. He dropped to the ground in a writhing heap, his feet released. When he looked back at her, fury had replaced any reason he'd ever possessed. She knew the few times he'd hit her in the last week they'd known each other were nothing compared to what she could expect now. He began to pull himself across the ground, coming for her.

We exist between this place and the others... in the...

The tree's head flashed and the other trees flashed in return, no longer synchronized, their formation along the road growing brighter and brighter. Long seconds passed as the bursts of yellow-white fell into time again, waning to a single, soft voice.

...in the soup...the harmonics must be catalyzed to continue or the branes rupture...all unvanish...all collapse...all evaporate...

"And you need us?" she asked. "Both of us?"

The gun slipped from her fingers and clattered to the ground. Clara's mind raced through her life, her place in the big city as if seen from high above.

We are weakened from our germinant

"Germi-? The fella with the glass eye?"

Not glass... he withers...

The hum grew around her and she felt her pulse quicken, hammering in her temples. She looked to Frankie as he crawled along the ground to where she'd dropped the gun, dragging himself with the last remnants of strength for the gun.

The lamina above this brane...between this world and the next grows thin... we need more catalyst...

"First you," Frankie gasped, reaching for the Thompson, his eyes locked on hers. "Then that... thing."

Clara looked at the man in the dirt as he struggled against the control of the Yggdrasil and his own weakness. She dabbed at her forehead, blood staining her fingertips. Her arm ached where Frankie had shoved her into the car earlier.

Frankie rolled onto his back, barely able to twist at the waist and bring the barrel up to point directly at her face. He pulled the bolt back and smiled.

She slid the thin handbag strap from her shoulder and let it fall heavily to the ground, three dozen or more pinky-sized metal objects spilling forth with a series of clinks. She looked up at the sparkling Yggdrasil. "You need more. How many more?"

***

Dragging Frankie closer to the Yggdrasil was easier than she expected, her energy bolstered by a new cause. The icy touch of the tendril against her forehead left a slight scar where the wound had been and traces of the same cold deeper still.

She walked to the car, uncertain of Frankie's last stammering words, but as she turned at the driver's side of the Roadster to look back at the grove of Yggdrasil, he was gone. No traces except odd shapes gouged into the dust.

You will bring another then...

Clara touched her forehead one last time, the smile far from her lips. "Another? Honey... the sky's the limit."

About the author: William Wood lives with his wife and children in the mountains of Virginia in an old farmhouse turned backwards to the road. His work has appeared, or is scheduled to appear soon, in titles from M-Brane SF/Hadley Rille Books, Sword and Saga Press, Static Movement, Library of the Living Dead, Black Matrix Publishing, Severed Press, Northern Frights Publishing, and Pill Hill Press, among others. He sometimes sleeps instead of writing.

CHAIN OF COMMAND
Jason Barney

Hu'jgon looked across the vastness of space and knew it was time to retire. He leaned forward, his face nearly touching the window that separated his fragile body from the nothingness outside. He stood on the observation deck and enjoyed the solitude.

Vleckur II was a small orb against a backdrop of thousands of tiny pinpricks of light. The greens, whites, and blues of the atmosphere were striking. The planet's four-billion-year old sun, a brilliant ball of orange, burned in the distance. The planet was slightly younger, but he felt as old as both of them.

Hu'jgon's muscles protested as he straightened his back. Each day that passed his body found new ways to object to the stress of command. Yesterday it was arthritis in his shoulder. Last week it was the ship's doctor telling him he needed to increase his medication.

Vleckur II. It was unique in its location in the galaxy, but that was not enough to keep the world out of the sights of the Empire.

The elderly captain stretched, a luxury he never allowed in front of his crew, and questioned the orders he'd received. He had carried out a lifetime of wishes for the high command. They had subjugated worlds, destroyed alien fleets, obliterated pirate bases, and traveled to a thousand suns. In all of that time, Hu'jgon had never wavered in his duty.

Until now. Retirement was just around the corner. After securing the resources on Vleckur II, he was going to give up command. One of the most feared officers of the Empire would call it quits.

He slowly walked away from the observation port. His feet took little steps, his arms swung in a rhythm designed to help keep his balance. Hu'jgon felt the ravages of age tug at his body and the screams of morality pulling at his soul.

He limped across the deck and stopped in front of the doors. He placed a weak hand on the bulkhead for support. What he knew, and what the general populace were not allowed to know, was that the Vleckurians were innocent beings. They had no advanced technology; they were a threat to no one. Their world had the resources and the Empire was going to take them.

Hu'jgon shook his head, unsure if he would be able to fulfill his final duty. Memories of a hundred other ethically challenged missions entered his mind. The captain of the *Wasp* dropped his arms and let his momentum take him through the archway. The doors parted slowly, as though they needed to be repaired.

Hu'jgon stepped into the halls of his ship, mentally apologized to the Vleckurians, and embarked for the command module.

***

When he arrived at the command center of *Wasp* it bustled with activity. Crewmembers hustled about, executing command functions; the commotion reminded Hu'jgon of a beehive.

Subordinates lifted an arm against their chest in the traditional salute and waited for his response. He started to return the gesture once, but stopped in mid motion, and ignored all the others. Whether he saluted or not, the mission would be completed.

He squinted at the brightness of the lights. The ship's first officer had made him aware of the mannerism months ago, but there was nothing he could do. The lighting was regulation and his vision wasn't getting any better.

"Status report," he said, stepping up to his first officer. He put his arms behind his back and moved his legs into a wide stance.

"Everything is going according to plan, sir," Stastara reported. "We have monitored all transmissions from the planet, and the populace is aware of our approach. Their technological level presents no danger."

Hu'jgon looked at his first officer and a familiar thought entered his mind. He did not like his second in command. She was efficient, hardworking, and religious about her work. She was the perfect soldier.

He hated her for it. He wanted to be able to tell her to think on her own. To look at what was happening to innocent worlds, but she was too involved with her own career to see the injustices.

She stood ramrod straight, waiting for any further inquires. Her hair was pulled back in a bun; her thin lips and high cheekbones were disturbingly unemotional.

"Is the graviton weapon ready?" he asked.

"Yes, sir," she said. "The emitters are fully charged. When we enter orbit we can target their major population centers. Then we can claim this world's resources for the Empire."

Hu'jgon looked at her and saw himself. He had given the same report dozens of times. He had spoken the words that resulted in the destruction of civilizations on numerous occasions.

He wanted to tell her that things could be different. That his people, wrapped up in economic interests and distracted by their ability to conquer anyone they encountered, didn't have to be this way. They didn't need to be masters of the universe.

"Advance report?" he asked.

"We are conducting a standard orbital approach, decelerating as we get nearer to the planet," she said. "We will commence the attack shortly after arriving. The landing teams and mining squads have the geographic information they need."

"The convoys?" he asked. Images of the massive merchant fleets swarming into the system pushed into his mind, and Hu'jgon worked to prevent his head from shaking in disgust.

"Yes, sir," she said, a disturbing eagerness seeping into her voice. "The Vleckurian Contract has been awarded to the Halon Corporation. After the gravity weapon disposes of the indigenous life forms, they have thirty-seven merchant vessels waiting to enter the system."

Hu'jgon looked at the floor. He wanted to get off the bridge. He couldn't tolerate being around his first officer or command crew. Hu'jgon needed to be away from this place, his long career, and any devastation he had caused.

"Thank you, Commander," he said, moving to the exit. "I'll be in my quarters."

For a moment he thought she was going to protest, that she would say it was wrong for him to not be on the bridge during his final mission. Her chin moved forward and her mouth opened.

"Don't Commander," he said, not caring about her response. "I wish to be alone."

Her eyebrows rose in question mark curls and her cheeks flushed. She was about to persist, but he shook his head.

A moment of awkward silence passed between them.

Hu'jgon turned and balanced his tired steps back to the exit. His legs swayed with each stride, and he dropped his arms to improve his steadiness. He nodded at random crewmembers that saluted, but quickly looked away from them. He had no desire to be a part of the brutal system anymore.

The doors opened, and he departed. He wasn't able to stop the tears from running down his aged face. Hu'jgon, one of the most respected officers in the Empire, wished he had more courage. For one more mission, he was still a cog in a chain that needed to be broken.

*****

The Captain of the *Wasp* sat at the desk in his room, and reviewed the reports of the ship's last mission. It had been in the Dorta Cluster.

The information scrolled across the computer screen with agonizing clarity. Images of the frosty atmosphere surrounding the icy sphere were plentiful. He pictured the *Wasp* entering an equatorial orbit and rotating its hull. The graviton weapon needed a direct line of sight to the surface.

The world was barely on the edge of its suns' habitable zone, and despite the attractiveness of its lucid atmosphere, most landmasses were covered with pale irregular shaped swaths of ice. It was a harsh planet, where the inhabitants built their cities inside of great glaciers. Silently, he had praised their ingenuity. Survival on such a globe could not have been easy.

Publicly and professionally, Hu'jgon had done his job. When the proper orbit was achieved, and the firing distance was optimum, he had once again compromised his beliefs and given the order to fire. Unseen tears drenched his soul. Outwardly, he had accepted the congratulations of his officers.

He remembered the milky-yellow disruption pulse streaking down toward the planet and all of the hell that had been unleashed. Waves of graviton energy pulsed into the surface. Everything within reach of the beam, on the surface and below the planet's crust, suffered the devastation of the attack.

Massive chunks of ice were vomited away from the rest of

the planet. From orbit, it looked like a stone had been thrown into a body of water, and the splash that followed extended high into the atmosphere. Enormous ground quakes rocked the surrounding areas. Hu'jgon summoned raw images of the inhabitants and their homes flying away from the ground. Dirt, rock, and ice exploded. Debris was belched into space, the dead void ending all life and consuming the ejected matter.

It was total nonexistence for the area affected.

When the energy of the gravity weapon dissipated, there was an enormous cylindrical hole in the planet's crust. Splotches of red and orange bubbled and frothed as magma was exposed to the cold of space.

When the initial attack was over, Hu'jgon had ordered the ship repositioned for the next assault. He wished he could stop the events, find some way to avoid the deaths, but if he did not give the orders, someone else would.

His thoughts were interrupted when the door chimed.

"Come in," he said, leaving the information on his screen.

The doors opened, and Stastara stood in the doorway. Hu'jgon wondered how long she had thought about coming to his quarters.

"May I enter, sir?' she asked.

He considered saying no, ordering her back to the command center.

"Come in," he said.

She stepped into his room. The doors whisked shut behind her. She assumed her rigid stance and saluted.

"Captain, may I ask why you are not on the bridge?"

Hu'jgon did not respond. He put his back into his chair, and found himself enjoying her need to visit him. He celebrated the irony; one who no longer had faith in the Empire commanded a group whose faith the Empire did not deserve.

"Captain's discretion," he responded. He didn't want to look at Vleckur II. Enough souls already haunted him without staring at a planet that was about to be obliterated.

"If you chose not to speak with me, sir," she said raising her eyebrows, "that is your prerogative. Yes, you are old, and yes, this is your final mission. You should be on the bridge, sir. The press will want to see you there. The people of the Empire who idolize you... they deserve to see their greatest commander in his last moment of glory."

Hu'jgon wanted to slap her.

"How old are you?" he asked her.

"I'll be forty-one next month, sir," she said.

He wondered what she was thinking, but his mind drifted to his own career. How he had been in love with the power, the ability to control and dominate so much in the galaxy. For an instant, he wondered if the attack on the Vleckurians could be avoided, but he condemned the false thoughts. Hu'jgon looked at his first officer and tried not to scowl. He prevented his lip from curling, but she noticed the intensity with which he regarded her.

"The Vleckurians don't have to die," he said.

He wasn't sure where the words came from, but as the look on her face changed, he realized he had uttered them. He had never intended to speak his true thoughts.

A tight smile crept onto her face. "Did I hear you correctly, sir?" she asked.

He considered saying no. He wanted to feign a laugh. A distant memory of the graviton weapon slicing into an icy blue world exploded into his mind,

"I said," he began, raising his voice. "The Vleckurians don't have to die." Hu'jgon felt young. The air moved through his lungs a little faster. Saying those words had felt so... good.

Stastara looked at him as though he had ordered the graviton weapon turned on the mining fleets that followed them through space. Her nostrils flared and her eyes became wider.

"This is why you are not on the bridge?" she asked.

Hu'jgon stood. He pressed his arms against the chair supports and steadied his legs. He slowly walked over to her.

"Yes," he said.

A thousand questions went unspoken in her eyes, and he had trouble reading her thoughts. Redness appeared on her cheeks, but she managed to control her herself. He wasn't sure if she were angry or confused.

"Please, explain sir," she finally said.

Hu'jgon considered changing course, altering the path of

the dialogue so that he could get through this final mission without explaining himself. He wanted to be done with the Vleckurians, and the faster he got away from the corporations that controlled the Empire, the better.

A memory of his promotion to Captain of the *Wasp* entered his mind. He remembered all of the admirals, the ceremonies, and the thirst for power. Hu'jgon inwardly sneered at his past self, and wished he had taken command with the life experience that he now had. Hu'jgon wished someone had helped him; had shown him the truth.

"You really want to know?" he asked, his mouth going dry. Her glare was unsettling. He didn't know if she was thinking of reporting him, or if she was dealing with feelings of betrayal.

"Yes, I would," she said, maintaining the inflexible military posture.

He considered the amount of time before the expected arrival at the planet. One command officer needed to be on the bridge, but he had his first officer's attention.

He revolted against his training and ignored the chronometer.

"Sit down, Commander," he said.

***

"Status report?" Hu'jgon said, looking at the viewer.

Vleckur II filled the screen. They were much closer than two hours ago, and it was even more impressive. The features of the continents were partially visible; mountain ranges, large lakes and seas, and long coastlines were impossible to miss. If the planet had been beautiful before, it was enchanting now.

"We should achieve orbit in approximately two minutes," reported the officer at the helm station. "There are several planetary satellites in orbit, none present a threat to us. The inhabitants have definitely detected our approach, their communications channels are overloading with chatter."

Hu'jgon sat back in the command chair. He had little energy, and it was difficult feigning interest in what was about to happen.

"Initiate full jamming procedures," he ordered. "We don't need some primitive computer virus being uploaded into our systems."

"Aye, sir," came the response of the tactical station.

"Commence with the final arming sequence. I want to deploy the gravity weapon as soon as we are over the first population center," Hu'jgon said.

Crewmembers buzzed about the bridge as they executed his orders.

***

Stastara sat in the Captain's personal desk chair and couldn't believe what she was reading. Her eyes were wide with disbelief, and her lips had parted. In an effort to restore some level of comfort, she swallowed and pulled her eyes away from the computer screen.

She looked at the Captain's quarters and searched for any details to the man's personality or worldview. The walls were bland and bare; there were no pictures of hero's or landscapes Hu'jgon admired. There were no portraits of family members. The furniture was equally boring. No plants. She would've thought the Captain had a personal library.

Stastara wondered if she would find food rations and meals ready to eat in his personal kitchen. She doubted his bedroom contained more than his bed and pillows.

The computer in front of her was much different, however. She blinked, knowing when her eyes came in contact with the screen Hu'jgon's journals would be impossible to ignore.

As her face turned back to the information she wondered how well she knew the man who had been her commanding officer. She realized that after years of serving together, this was the first time she had ever been his quarters.

Her eyes focused and she moved the chair closer to the desk.

***

"*Wasp* has achieved a position over the largest population center. We are currently facing the sun side of the planet," said the man operating the science station.

"Excellent," Hu'jgon said, forcing his body out of the chair. "What is the population of the city?"

"Readings indicate nearly twenty million people in this location," the voice said. "Their engineering design is somewhat remarkable. The city has been developed several kilometers below the surface."

Hu'jgon felt a spark of interest.

"Most civilizations cover their planet with dwellings, littering the landscape," he said.

"Yes, sir," came the response. "This would appear to be a society with some very efficient engineering techniques. Sensors indicate the entire city doesn't cover more than twenty five square kilometers, but goes dozens of kilometers deep."

The feat spoke for itself. Hu'jgon thought of his home world. As powerful as the Empire was, this isolated civilization had done something his own had not.

A stab of guilt hit him and Hu'jgon felt cramps behind his eyes. He wasn't sure if it was the stress or his advanced age. He brought a slightly shaking hand to his forehead.

He wanted to speak, to cover his discomfort, but he knew there was a possibility he would say the wrong thing. There was a chance he would order the ship out of orbit or he would disarm the weapons systems.

Hu'jgon wanted to get off the bridge. Profits of the Empire and the future of the Vleckurian civilization be dammed.

"Sir?" said the officer at the helm station.

"Yes?" he said, forcing his attention back to the viewer. He wondered what the Vleckurians looked like. He wanted to experience the music they played, see how they raised their kids, and wondered about the taste of their food.

"Should I contact First Officer Stastara?" asked the officer at tactical. "She is scheduled to be on the bridge, sir."

Hu'jgon heart beat a little faster.

"Never you mind," he said. "She's off the bridge on my authority. She is...conducting some research at my request. Attend your station."

***

The computer screen had to be lying. Stastara swallowed,

looked at all of the information scrolling down the unit, and knew it could not be true.

Hu'jgon had been such a major source of confidence and stability in her life.

He hated the Empire. Hu'jgon had detested it for a good portion of his adult life. Stastara rubbed her damp palms together and tried to cope with what she had been exposed to. Her training took over and thoughts of treachery came to mind. An inner voice told her it was impossible he was planning any sort of insurrection, but his thoughts were painfully clear. If he had the means to stop the Empire, he would.

He had betrayed her.

Their relationship had been a lie. He'd maintained his position as commander of the *Wasp* while at the same time loathing the Empire and everything it did.

Her face burned.

Stastara read on.

***

"We are prepared to fire," the woman at the sensor consul reported.

Hu'jgon took tiny, precise steps as he walked around the bridge. He moved to the weapons computers and took up a position behind the crewmen.

The old man froze. He didn't want to give orders that would lead to the death of countless innocents. He stood poised to commence with the attack, but was unable to bring himself to give the final command.

Hu'jgon's chest beat so hard he wondered if he were having a heart attack. Panic filled in the time between the beats.

"We have received the confirmation transmission from the merchant fleet, sir," the man at the communications center said.

The doors to the command center looked more appealing than ever. Hu'jgon felt dampness under his uniform, and realized he was sweating. He didn't want this anymore. He forced his aged legs to take him to the exit. He struggled to the door.

"Captain?" came the voice of the officer at the weapons

station. Hu'jgon stopped walking. He hated himself for not leaving the command center. He turned and his eyes went to the view screen.

"Open fire," he said. "Commence the attack. First officer Stastara will be up to coordinate shortly."

He leaned into the archway and forced his legs to move. The doors parted. Hu'jgon heard chatter as the officers of the deck did as they had been trained.

Stumbling into the hall, the last thing he heard was the loud chirping of the computer as the gravity weapon was unleashed.

His heart went out to the souls of the Vleckurians, offering an apology to them. He lumbered through the corridor, dazed and confused.

***

Stastara scanned the last of the entries. What she had read was so crazy, so impossible to believe that she wondered if Hu'jgon had been working on some elaborate piece of fiction. That thought disappeared as she recalled the passion in the writing.

She became distracted when the familiar pulsing of the gravity weapon became recognizable. The second in command of the *Wasp* walked over to the viewing port.

When she looked outside, she saw the raw power of the Empire.

Dark yellow pulses emanated from the front section of the ship. She watched throbbing graviton bursts blast away from *Wasp* and race toward the planet. They flared, sparked, and curled, and then got smaller as they rushed to the surface. When the destructive energy had traveled too far to see, her eyes settled where she thought the impact would occur.

Like pebbles splashing in a pond, rings of explosions formed around the contact point. Stastara viewed the work of the Empire and confidence swelled inside of her.

The doors opened.

She turned to see Hu'jgon stumble into the room, appearing disoriented. For a moment, Stastara considered if he suffered from dementia.

"Your presence is required in the command center," he said. He circled the room. "I gave the order. The attack is underway,"

"Yes," she responded.

His chin moved and he gritted his teeth.

She moved away from him, not sure if she should offer comfort or feel sorry for her former commander. No matter how much she wanted to confront him, her place was elsewhere now. She needed to take command of the ship. Hu'jgon was certainly no longer up to the task.

"Before I leave," she said, stepping up to the doors. "Why did you show me all of that? Your career was over. Regardless of your personal feelings, was it necessary to expose me to how you feel?"

Hu'jgon stopped circling and turned to her. He straightened his shoulders, brought is head up to a level that it probably had not been at in years, and slapped his feet together. He stood at attention.

"Let me explain it to you in terms you might understand, Captain," he said, stressing the arrival of her new rank. "All the missions, all the duty, all the years in the military...I have put my career and the Empire above all of my personal thoughts and moral code. When I was younger it did not matter so much."

Stastara tried not to scoff.

"And why does it matter now?" she asked.

He swallowed and took in a deep breath.

"I don't want your soul to be lost. When I realized that my command decisions were perpetuating evil...I was too old to change course, too stale to care," he said. "I don't have much time left. I would like my final years to be...good,"

Stastara tried to leave, but she found herself transfixed by his voice. In all of their years together, he had never spoken to her in such a personal way.

"The Empire must be stopped," he said, yanking his command rank off from his sleeve. He threw the patch on the floor.

"I have to go," she said. Stastara couldn't understand the affect the old man's words had on her. She couldn't block them from her mind as she moved through doors.

***

Stastara looked at the Vleckur II. The planet was a smoldering wreck. The final bombardment had ended hours ago, and the surface was filled with pockmarks and scars. Thick, unfriendly, pluming clouds had formed, a prelude to the massive and uncontrollable weather patterns that were about to be unleashed. Whatever segment of the population that had not been exterminated would soon be killed by the erratic and uncontrollable weather that would spread across the planet.

She couldn't deny the pride that bubbled inside of her. The crew had preformed perfectly during the attack. They had systematically hit every major city with no deviation from the preplanned target list. Hu'jgon's...her crew had been right on target.

Hu'jgon, however, was nowhere to be found. Stastara had not sent a security detail to arrest him after leaving his quarters. Whatever emotions and ethical questions he had sparked in her, she had put them aside. She'd gone to the bridge and done her job.

The crew was abuzz with talk about the unknown fate of their legendary commander. Whispers and rumors were impossible to avoid, and his absence on the bridge had been difficult to ignore, especially during the eradication mission.

He was gone. She suspected he had gone AWOL shortly after their last conversation. Hu'jgon was a retired old man now, close to death, and no one knew of his unpatriotic views.

"Merchant Fleet approaching," said the crewman at the sensor station.

"On screen," Stastara ordered.

The massive ships blinked onto the viewer, and the new captain recognized their sleek designs. There were more than thirty vessels in this first wave, with uncounted more on the way. Most of them were bulky, displaying the wide cargo sections that would be used to...

Stastara felt a pinch of uncertainty as she looked at the enormous ships making for the planet. She cursed herself as she saw them as Hu'jgon had described them... the engines and tools of a corporate machine that had little regard for life.

"Relay the following message to the fleet," she said, thinking of how many times she heard Hu'jgon speak the same words. "The planet is yours..."

She fought a twinge of uncertainty as she ordered the *Wasp* out of orbit. The image of the merchant vessels remained on the screen and she was unable to peel her eyes away from their massive size.

They hungrily arched into orbit as *Wasp* pulled away.

***

Stastara looked at the floor in the Captain's chambers. He'd left his uniform and command insignia in a pile, his writings and journals were still visible. While he was nowhere to be found, his intent was clear. He wanted the Empire to see his act of rebellion, to know that he was opposed to their policies.

The new commander of the *Wasp* sat in Hu'jgon's chair.

"Where are you?" she asked the empty air. Questions would be asked about her conduct in the hours immediately after the legendary commander's disappearance, but she had no reason to be worried. He was gone of his own free will, officially retired. Stastara leaned forward and studied the computer screen. She then looked at the shut doors and was thankful she was alone.

"Computer, delete the following data," she said. She listed off every file that held Hu'jgon's personal information. She would not let the Empire see his act of rebellion. And she would not let his actions tarnish the reputation most citizens idolized. The computer beeped when it was finished.

She stood, all too aware of something else she had done.

Wherever Hu'jgon was, she aided his departure. She might have saved his life.

Stastara made for the exit, awash in a sea of uncertainty. She attempted to focus on her new duties. She strode through the halls, trying to appear confident. She greeted crewmembers and returned the salutes of the men and women under her command. While touring what was now her ship, she wrestled with the motivations of the man who had left it behind.

***

Hu'jgon stood in the shadows. He remained undetected in the back of the cargo bay, confident and energized. He was too old to be moving around the ship, avoiding members of the crew, staying out of sight. He had done it, though. Ever since the meeting with Stastara, he had gone completely unnoticed.

The path to the shuttles was unobstructed.

He thought of his former first officer and her reasons for not searching for him. She was as by the book an officer as he had ever trained. The new captain was as indoctrinated into military discipline and procedure as he had been at that age. Or so he thought.

She had let him go.

Memories of all the worlds he'd been to drifted into his being, and the results of those stops burned in his soul. He wrestled with his history, and tried to think of the best way to make things right.

He scurried into the supply shuttle; confident his presence was unknown. He ducked between two cargo containers, and considered his next actions. Once in deep space, he wasn't sure what he would do with the pilots. He needed the vessel to get away, and it would be his.

The sound of the craft's heavy doors closing filled his ears, and Hu'jgon could barely contain waves of excitement. He ignored the arthritis that tried to hold him back and shrugged off fatigue.

He felt the hull of the small shuttle vibrate as the pilots went through the pre-launch checklist. Hu'jgon cried tears of joy.

He was alive.

About the author: Jason lives in Vermont and teaches social studies. He has fallen in love with storytelling and tries to write 1000 words a day. He tries to send out one new short story per week.

THE CAUSALITY PROBLEM
Robert Pearce

"The problem with us scientists," declared Greg Johnson earnestly, "is that we never think through all the consequences." He banged the wine bottle on the table for emphasis.

"How so, professor?" asked Matt. Greg was staring at him, and Matt had an unnerving sense that he should have known the answer.

"I've just poured you the last of this wine," said Greg with a wink. "Now I need to get more." He stood and walked over to the sideboard, where a fresh bottle waited to be opened. Matt laughed.

"How long have you worked with him?" asked Beth, Greg's wife.

"Two months," Matt replied. It had been a huge honour to get the chance to work with one of the foremost experts in the field of quantum electrodynamics. That they got on so well, indeed had become friends, was a major bonus.

"And you've not heard that one before?" said Beth. "I'm amazed."

Matt had already known quite a lot about Beth too. She was a highly respected scientist in her own right. Her papers on perception were standard reading for neurologists. More recently, she had discovered the mechanisms behind some long-feared mental disorders. When the cures were found, Beth would undoubtedly be the person credited with making them possible.

"He doesn't usually have wine bottles lying around the lab," Matt said. He'd been on his best behaviour when he arrived for dinner at the Johnson house, but the atmosphere was so relaxed and friendly that he felt entirely at home.

"That's another problem with scientists," Greg mused as he filled their glasses. "We spend too much time working and not enough being sociable."

"I'll drink to that," said Beth. "You realise when Greg gets home he hides away, experimenting in his laboratory in the basement." She winked at Greg.

"Really?" said Matt, who thought having your own personal

laboratory would be really cool.

"Of course not," Greg scoffed, "she's just having you on. I haven't done any experiments down there for years."

"But you've actually got a lab here?" Matt asked, his curiosity piqued.

"Oh yes," said Greg with a dismissive wave of his hand, "down in the basement. Every home should have one." He grinned at Matt. "I'll give you the tour after dinner."

Matt wasn't sure whether it was Greg's natural showmanship or his own nervous excitement that made the opening of the cellar door feel like a grand ceremony. The electric light felt like a betrayal - they should have been carrying torches. On the other hand, it was good that they could see the steep stairs properly.

"Welcome to my secret den," said Greg, adding "Mwahahaha!" for effect. He started slowly down the stairs, and Matt followed. A layer of dust testified to the truth of Greg's claim that he did not go down there very often.

At the bottom of the stairs, they emerged into the middle of a single large room, open plan but for the central stairwell and half a dozen stout pillars. Around the walls were a number of unfamiliar machines, interspersed with benches covered in test equipment. It could have been a set for a Gothic horror film, but the clutter all around was top quality test gear.

"Wow!" exclaimed Matt. "You certainly have good taste in lab equipment."

"Funnily enough," said Greg, laughing, "That's what Beth said when I first brought her down here."

Matt was engrossed in a study of the cellar's contents, and it was a few moments before he thought that was an odd comment.

"Hang on," said Matt, "how long have you had this lab here?"

"A long time," Greg replied. "I inherited this house from a great uncle when I was about your age. The lab was mostly his work, I just added to it. That was when I met Beth - we were both research students, though in different disciplines. But there was some overlap at the fringes, where our real interests lay, so this lab was a great excuse to invite her round."

"So what are all these experiments?" asked Matt, who

wasn't really interested in memories of romance.

"Well, this one," said Greg, leading Matt towards a particularly cluttered bench, "was an attempt to obtain a room temperature deuterium energy state anomaly."   He   paused expectantly.

"A cold fusion experiment," said Matt, deciphering the obfuscation.

"Ha! Can't get anything past you," said Greg. "Yes. Totally unsuccessful. This next one...." He walked over to an assemblage of polished steel shapes and electronic circuits, suspended by various rods and clamps from a set of racking. In the middle was a shiny glass sphere the size of a gypsy's crystal ball. This rested on a steel ring, and a conical device rested on top of it, sharp end down. A jumble of wires fed from the top of the cone to the electronics. Greg sighed affectionately.

"This is a miniature quantum tunnelling deep scan microscope," he explained.

"Miniature?" said Matt, who had seen commercial ones.

"Well it was pretty small for ten years ago," said Greg. "It works, too, but not on the electricity supply we have here - it would take out the local substation." Matt raised a quizzical eyebrow. "Unless they've upgraded it since last time," Greg added with a mischievous grin.

Matt laughed, shook his head and took another look around. A plywood cubicle caught his eye, for the sheer quantity of cabling and odd-shaped attachments it sported. Electronic and mechanical components surrounded three sides. The fourth had only a panelled wooden door with a brass handle and a brass plaque. He walked over to it.

"Ah," said Greg, "the Temporatron."

"So it says," observed Matt, reading the plaque. "What is it?"

"It's the device that won me Beth's affection," said Greg, running a finger down the edge of the door. "It's a time machine."

Matt's jaw dropped. He didn't know what to say. Greg laughed.

"Of course it doesn't work," said Greg, "but it does fascinating things to your perception. Beth's mentor back then was experimenting with a device that slowed some people's perception of time, and Beth was rather taken with it. I was looking at the nature of time from a quantum theory perspective. On one of our dates, our enthusiasm rather got the better of us. Add some ideas from science fiction books, and this was the result. Do you read science fiction?"

Matt shook his head. "So what does it actually do?" he asked.

"I really don't know," mused Greg. "Our theory should have meant it could put you back in time. There'd be a problem with causality, of course, but Beth reckoned it would be mostly in the mind. Something about being subconsciously unable to act in a manner inconsistent with your perception of cause and effect."

"But you tried it?" asked Matt, enthused with the idea and desperate to know what happened.

"Oh yes," said Greg. "Beth volunteered to be a guinea pig. She tried it several times, and experienced... Well it's hard to describe. Once she told me she'd seen something of a time in the past, but only as an observer. Only that's not really a fair description. Another time she felt like she'd been somewhere for days when it was only a few minutes she was in there. When I tried it I seemed to be reliving my own experiences but from somebody else's perspective."

"Weird!" exclaimed Matt. "What did it feel like?"

Greg hesitated. He seemed to be weighing something up. After a moment he walked round the side of the apparatus and flicked a switch. An assortment of whines, hums and whirring sounds began to emanate from the Temporatron. A series of lights flashed. Finally, the sound of a bell rang out.

"Why don't you try it for yourself?" suggested Greg. "It probably still works." He opened the door of the cubicle, revealing plywood walls, floor and ceiling, featureless apart from two large mesh grilles either side. The interior of the cubicle was completely empty.

Matt hesitated, but reminded himself that both Greg and Beth had emerged unharmed. He stepped in and turned to face the closing door. As it clicked shut, he found himself in complete darkness. A gentle ethereal hum lurked at the edge of his hearing.

It was quite disorienting.

Suddenly he stood in the entrance to the College, looking out on a bright spring day. The road was busy with traffic, which puzzled him because it had been pedestrianised five years ago. He remembered visiting once before that, many years earlier. He had wanted to see the statue above the entrance, though he forgot now why it had fascinated him so much back then. His mother had agreed to bring him, but when they arrived, the statue had been hidden behind tarpaulins, being cleaned.

A sudden urge took him - he had to look up at the statue. He trotted down the stone steps to pavement level. At the bottom he stopped and spun round, straight into a girl who had followed him down. She was carrying a pile of books, which became very precarious.

"Oh, I'm terribly sorry," Matt said. The girl gave him a look of disgust and strode off along the High Street. Matt chanced to look down and saw that one of the girl's books had fallen at his feet. He bent down and picked it up.

"Excuse me, miss," Matt called, but he had lost sight of the girl. He wondered what to do with the book. He looked at the cover. It was a paperback, entitled "To Say Nothing Of The Dog", by Connie Willis. It looked like fiction - probably not important. But then he wondered whether the girl might have been a literature student. Perhaps this was vital study material. Matt knew very little about literature degrees: he had no grounds on which to base a judgement.

He decided the correct course of action was to hand the book in to the college porter. He walked back up the steps and round the corner to the Porter's Lodge. Tapping on the window, he wondered which of the porters would be on duty. After a moment, Sedgewick appeared, looking remarkably healthy and decidedly unlike a man nearly due for retirement. Matt knew Sedgewick well and often exchanged a spot of banter. He smiled.

"Can I help you, sir?" asked Sedgewick in the voice he usually reserved for total strangers. Matt just stopped himself from making a caustic remark. Some indefinable gut feeling told him Sedgewick wouldn't respond well.

"A girl just dropped this," Matt said holding up the book. "I bumped into her just outside. I didn't recognise her but I think she may be a student here. Could I leave it with you to give it back to her?"

"Can you give me a clue as to who she might be?" asked Sedgewick. "Perhaps a description?"

Matt thought about it. The girl had looked oddly familiar. In fact...

"She looked like a younger version of Beth Johnson," he said. Sedgewick looked blank. Matt's gut sense told him Sedgewick would not know the Johnsons, despite the sure knowledge that he did. "Sorry, that's not helpful," he said, covering his tracks. "She's about so tall," he held up a hand, palm down, "slim, dark hair, pretty...."

"I'll put the book on the side here," offered Sedgewick, "in case she comes in asking about it."

Matt handed over the book, thanked Sedgewick, and turned back toward the entrance. As he reached the top step, he noticed a woman and child across the road. The child seemed upset, and the woman disappointed. They seemed to be looking at him. No, that was silly; they were looking at the building, probably at the statue. Suddenly Matt recognised the woman. It was his mother, when she was younger. And the boy was himself, aged eight.

Just at that moment the scene faded to black. Matt's heart was racing. A crack of light appeared, rapidly widened, to reveal Greg opening the Temporatron door. He looked disappointed.

"Sorry Matt," Greg said, "it blew the fuse as soon as I turned the effector on. I suspect one of the boosters became unstable."

"But..." Matt spluttered. "I..." He closed his mouth and breathed deeply. Greg's expression changed first to surprise, and then he smiled.

"Ah, so it did work," Greg said. "Must have just had a good burst before popping the fuse. Let's go back upstairs and you can tell me what you saw over another drink."

The next day Matt was wandering idly through the town centre, when he had a sudden urge to call in to a second-hand book shop. At first, he looked only among the serious works. Then he remembered Greg's comments about science fiction the night before. *Besides*, he told himself, *they often stack things on the wrong shelf here.*

He skimmed along the shelves looking at the titles. A few caught his attention and he pulled them out to read the cover notes, or even a bit of the first page. 'Age of Demons' looked interesting, but rather bulkier than his busy life would allow for.

'Dimming of the Day' was the wrong genre, which was a shame because he liked the way it read. Then his eye was caught by a familiar title – 'To Say Nothing Of The Dog'. He reached out to take it, and clashed with another hand.

"Oh, sorry," said the girl whose hand it was. She looked familiar, rather like a younger version of Beth, but there was more to it than that. Matt decided he'd probably seen her around. He took the book from the shelf and offered it to her.

"Were you after this?" he asked, smiling with all the charm he had.

"Yes," she replied, blushing slightly, "were you?"

"I'm afraid so," he replied. Saying no would probably have been more gentlemanly, but he figured it would have ended the conversation.

"Only I lost my copy," the girl said. "Yesterday. I think."

"Really?" said Matt, but just caught himself before saying he'd picked it up. That wasn't real, it had happened – been imagined? – in the Temporatron. Even if the girl did look exactly as he remembered. He gave her a sympathetic look, then drew the book back and gazed at the book disappointedly. Perhaps he was overacting a bit too much, he thought.

"Suppose I were to buy this," he said, "and give it to you, would you allow me to borrow it?"

"That would depend," she said, "on whether we're going to be seeing each other."

"I hope so," said Matt with a cheeky grin, "whichever way you meant it."

The girl laughed and held out her hand. "I'm Liz," she said.

"Matt," said Matt, taking her hand in his.

That evening Matt and Liz met up for a drink. At first Liz seemed very tense, even to Matt who was quite nervous himself. The first few minutes stumbled along with meaningless pleasantries.

"Everything round here feels really strange," Liz said

suddenly.

"I know, I have that effect on people," Matt joked. Liz's laugh was rather strained.

"The University is a strange place," Matt said.

"Yes, but I've been here a while," Liz replied. "And today I suddenly feel like I've been dropped into an entirely alien world with no warning."

Matt took hold of her hands and smiled at her. He waited a few moments for her to smile back.

"Then let me be your guide," he said, "I'll help you find your way around."

"I'd like that," Liz replied with a smile.

After that, they gradually relaxed in each other's company. They chatted about all the things young people chat about when they first start dating. Liz seemed strangely out of touch with the world, though Matt was hardly much better. He put it down to her being another scientist, a neurologist. But she didn't seem too keen to discuss that, especially after Matt mentioned Beth's name. They agreed to ban all talking shop for the evening.

Instead, they talked about world events, music, and literature. Whenever Matt mentioned recent international news, Liz seemed to find a historical parallel, and they talked about the similarities and differences.

Walking home at the end of the evening, Matt wondered whether he had dominated the conversation too much. Certainly he had done more talking than listening, but Liz had seemed quite happy with that. Besides, it was she who had suggested meeting for lunch the next day. And that thought made him happy.

The next morning had a strained atmosphere at the lab. Matt was full of the joys of spring, and insensitive to Greg's mood. After a while the tension reached a point where Greg shouted. Although he apologised immediately, it stopped Matt in his tracks.

Some time later Matt apologised to Greg for being so self-indulgent. Greg looked at him, and offered a weak smile.

"It's not your fault," Greg said, "I've just got a lot on my mind at the moment."

"But if I'd had my eyes open I could have seen that," said Matt.

"Perhaps," said Greg. "Look, I'm not thinking straight, I'm going to head home. Do you mind clearing up?"

"No, sure, go ahead," said Matt.

It was only when Matt had finished for the morning himself that he noticed Greg's jacket. He checked the time, and decided he would just be able to cycle out to Greg's house and get back for his lunch date with Liz. He grabbed the jacket and set off.

He arrived at the house slightly out of breath, dismounted and rang the doorbell. It felt like ages before it was answered.

The door opened to reveal Beth. She looked troubled, and tired.

"Can I help you?" Beth asked.

"Greg left this behind," Matt said, handing over the jacket.

"Oh, thank you," Beth said, "that's very kind of you." She took the jacket and closed the door. Matt was surprised to be dismissed so curtly, but he was also in a hurry.   He got back on his bike and pedalled off towards his lunch date.

Liz was already waiting outside the cafe when Matt arrived. She smiled broadly when she saw him.

"I'm terribly... sorry I'm late," Matt said between breaths as he dismounted, "I had... an errand I... had to run." Liz laughed nervously.

"I'll wait for you to get your breath back before I ask," she said.

Matt nodded and set about locking his bike to a drainpipe.

Liz chose a table and they sat down.

"So what was this errand, then?" she asked.

"Oh, Professor Johnson left his jacket at the lab," Matt explained, "I took it out to his house."

"I hope he was suitably grateful for your trouble," Liz said with a grin.

"I don't know," Matt said, "Beth answered the door. It was odd, she..." He thought about it. She had seemed not to recognise him, rather like Sedgewick the porter in the Temporatron vision. Was it a memory he had experienced, or a premonition?
Certainly, the experience had been unusual. Most of it could have been memory, but he was sure Liz had been in it even before he'd ever met her.

"Is something wrong?" asked Liz.

"No, sorry," said Matt, "I was just thinking about something that happened the other day."

"Tell me," said Liz, taking his hand. Matt wanted to share all of what he had seen with Liz. But he also wanted to be lucid and rational. Slowly and carefully, he told her as much about the Temporatron as he could make solid sense of. He left out the technical details that he didn't understand, and he didn't mention his experience inside it at all.

"The Johnson's sound like fascinating people," said Liz.

"They are," said Matt. "I'm surprised you haven't come across Beth in your studies."

"Oh I'm hopeless with names," said Liz, "I've probably read her books and just forgotten. You know, it's a strange coincidence, that book you bought me is about time travel."

"Really?" said Matt. "Tell me about it."

Liz started to tell Matt about the story, and their conversation over lunch developed down many avenues of wild speculation. Matt's rational side would have considered it a waste of time, but in Liz's company he relaxed and let his imagination loose. He discovered that he really enjoyed it.

After lunch, Matt returned to the lab to do some more work. In his pigeonhole, he found a note. It was a phone message from Greg. Beth was unwell. Greg would not be in for a few days, as she seemed to be fading away. Matt re-read the note several times. The wording felt inappropriate - more the way one would talk of an elderly person dying of natural causes.

Although Matt tried to do some work after that, he could not concentrate. He considered whether to go and visit Greg and Beth. He was unsure whether it would be appropriate. He remembered the way Beth had answered the door, the bad feeling he had had, which he couldn't explain to Liz.

Thinking of Liz, he suddenly decided she would know what to do. She had said she was going to the library to study. He set off to find her.

It took a while searching the various university libraries before Matt found Liz. She was sitting at a table with an unopened academic paper in front of her. Matt sat down opposite her. She didn't notice him.

"Hi," said Matt. Liz looked up and smiled.

"What are you doing here?" she asked.

"I wanted your advice," Matt said. "I got a note from Greg - Professor Johnson - saying Beth was ill. I wondered... Are you alright?" At the mention of Beth, the colour had drained from Liz's face. She looked haunted. Matt realised it was much the same look she had when he arrived.

Liz picked up the paper from the table and showed it to Matt; "The Influence of Quantum Electrodynamics on Human Perception", by Elizabeth Monroe.

"That's one of Beth's early papers, isn't it?" Matt asked.

"Do you see the name?" asked Liz.

"Yes, Beth's maiden name."

"No Matt," said Liz, "that's my name. And it's my field. And until a couple of days ago I would have said the date is three years in the future."

Matt's heart seemed to stop. A cold flush of terror descended over him.

"We must go," said Liz, gathering up her belongings.

"Where?" asked Matt.

"To the Johnsons' house," said Liz, "where else?"

Greg answered the door. His face was drawn with worry. He barely acknowledged Matt.

"We need to see Beth," said Matt, "urgently."

"She's not well," said Greg. "She's... fading away."

"Please Greg, it's important," Matt urged.

Greg hardly moved, but the door was open enough. Matt and Liz walked past and into the living room. Beth sat slumped in an armchair, horribly pale. There was something unnatural about her appearance.

"Beth," said Matt in a hoarse whisper.

Beth looked up. She didn't seem to register Matt's presence. Then she looked at Liz. Suddenly she gasped. A look of fear appeared on her face.

"Liz!" exclaimed Beth. "You don't belong here."

"You know her?" asked Matt.

"It's not your time," said Beth, "go back!"

"She's been babbling," said Greg, a tear running down his cheek, "I think she's delirious."

"You must restore the perceived causality," Beth urged.

"What's perceived causality?" asked Matt, looking to Greg.

"It's to do with the time machine," said Greg, walking over to Beth. "It's why it could never work."

"We tried to isolate the passenger from the natural order seen by others," said Beth. "We tried to cheat the causality paradox, and it's caught up with us."

"The time machine's killing her," said Liz. Everybody looked at her. For a moment, they were all transfixed.

Suddenly Beth gasped. Her skin seemed to be turning the colour of the armchair. Matt could almost believe she was becoming translucent.

"That damned machine," shouted Greg. He stood and turned. With a determined look on his face, he started towards the cellar.

Matt heard a cry, and then a thud. He turned. Liz lay crumpled on the floor, clutching her chest.

"Liz," cried Matt, rushing to kneel beside her. He reached out and took her arm. It felt somehow insubstantial.

"Please," gasped Liz, "you must... stop him."

"Stop who?" asked Matt dumbly.

"The machine," Liz gasped, "don't let him..." She slipped from his grasp.

"He can't undo what's done," said Beth, "not like that."

The Temporatron, thought Matt. He ran after Greg. He took the cellar steps two at a time. Half way down he missed his footing. He fell down the final steps, and crashed into Greg at the bottom.

Greg stood up first. He reached down and picked up an axe.   "Don't try to stop me," said Greg. Matt tried to roll away. Greg turned and walked toward the Temporatron. He lifted the axe.

"No!" shouted Matt, leaping after Greg. He slammed into him at waist level. Greg fell forward. The axe slipped from his hand, and slid across the floor. With a loud crack, Greg's head hit the concrete.

"Oh my God!" Matt cried, "Greg!" There was no response. Greg lay quite still. As tears of guilt welled up in his eyes, Matt decided on a plan.

He walked over to the Temporatron. Reaching behind it, he turned on the power. He listened to the hums, whines and whirrings. When the bell rang, he pressed the button marked "Go". Then he opened the cubicle door and stepped in.

"The problem with us scientists," declared Greg Johnson earnestly, "is that we never think through all the consequences." He banged the wine bottle on the table for emphasis.

"How so, professor?" asked Matt. Greg was staring at him, and Matt had an unnerving sense that he should have known the answer.

About the author: Rob Pearce lives near Cambridge, England, and makes a living designing hi-tech bits for cars, although he drives classic low-tech ones. He writes science fiction for fun, in the spare moments between everything else. He is a member of the Cambridge Writers of Imaginative Literature.

Foam of the Sea
A. J. French

It came up from the sand and rocks, the muscles and barnacles, from the schools of fish and ribbons of seaweed. Up to where the world was fresh and unsalted, to where seagulls wheeled in darkened skies. It tasted the night and drank its blackness. The air was sweet, clean, and it wondered how it had been content breathing the dregs of the sea. It dove as freely as a dolphin. Waves rose in altitude and strength, carrying it dangerously close to the cement pillars of the pier. It waited as a boat drifted past shining a spotlight. Then it headed toward the mainland with a glinting curiosity in its eyes.

* * *

Whitecaps uncurled one after another in a fanning swell that buffeted the shore. Drops of mist sprayed Stephan's face as he stared into the gathering dark.

He was at the Ocean Beach Hotel, standing on the balcony overlooking Abbot Street. Twenty feet ahead lay the sand and the sea. He'd left his room to be alone—not because his family annoyed him, but because they reminded him that Alissa wasn't on this trip. She usually came to San Diego with them, but for the past nine months her and Stephan had been separated.

He pushed Alissa from his mind and watched as people moved down Abbot Street on their way to the ocean: teenagers, long-haired boys with guitars, pretty tattooed girls, skateboarders, cyclists, pot peddlers, joint smokers, beer drinkers, club-goers. A line of glowing bonfires zigzagged up the beach. To his left, a flagpole rattled in the wind. One last look to the sea, then he returned to his room.

* * *

The next day, Stephan and his family came down the hotel steps and crossed the street.

Ocean Beach followed the waterline toward several rock embankments known as jetties, while a grass lawn ran parallel to

Abbot Street. Beyond lay the shops and eateries of Newport Avenue. People were everywhere—typical Cali denizens, tanned, barely clothed, flipping their hair. Plenty of dogs on leashes; plenty of swimmers taking advantage of the sun.

Stephan's father, Marc, led the crew, carrying a furled umbrella and a cooler. Stacy, his overweight mother, followed behind. She'd brought a chair and a stack of manuscript submissions. Those papers went everywhere with her, and Stephan often wondered if being a literary editor meant giving up your social life. For aspiring writer types, no less.

Next came Jimmy, his brother, shirtless and exuberant, smiling and yapping about God knew what. Jimmy loved the beach, although his disability kept him from doing much swimming. Mostly he stayed ashore, loping through waves and laughing when he got knocked on his butt. He certainly didn't fear the water, and Stephan admired that—especially since his mother, a grown woman, refused to go near it. But the beach was difficult for Jimmy, and he sort of limped and dragged his leg, creating a strange track in the sand. He was strong for a ten-year-old, and his recent enrollment in the Boy Scouts of America had improved his maneuverability, but the doctors said his leg would never get better.

Stephan, as usual, brought up the rear.

"I'm going down to the water," Jimmy said, once the umbrella was up.

"Wait," said his mother. "Let me put some lotion on you."

Jimmy complied, standing with arms extended as she lathered him up. His father cracked a beer, and, noticing a cute brunette, gave Stephan a nod. He'd been doing this more and more lately: trying to get him interested in other women.

"All set," said his mother, sending Jimmy along with a pat on the bottom. He raced down the beach, hobbling more than usual because of his excitement. A few people gawked and a small girl yelled, albeit innocently, "You run like a monkey!"

"Monitor him, please," his mother said. "But first put this on."

She tossed him the sunscreen; he applied it to his neck and shoulders, then headed toward the sea.

The waves weren't very big, and Stephan saw some unhappy

surfers lounging on their boards. Cool water glided over his feet; fine sand dispersed between his toes. He waded up to his waist and cringed as a whitecap slapped his torso. A moment later he dove headfirst, arching his back like a porpoise. A rumble filled his ears. He swam around a while then found Jimmy standing on the beach, surrounded by seagulls and seaweed.

"I saw you out there," he said. "Is it nice?"

Stephan nodded. "You should try it. The waves are small. I don't think you'll have a problem."

Jimmy gazed at the ocean. He seemed to be weighing the pros and cons in his head.

Stephan patted his shoulder. "Hey, if you don't wanna, it's okay. No big deal."

"No," he said, "I do wanna. But you gotta promise to stay with me. Don't let me get washed away."

Stephan chuckled. "No fear, big guy, I'll be right there. But let's head over to the jetties, see if we can ditch some of these people."

"What about Mom and Dad?"

"Don't worry. They'll be fine."

* * *

He stood watching the incoming tide while Jimmy scoured the shore for crabs.

"You ready yet?" he asked.

Jimmy wobbled over. "Yep, I'm ready. Remember not to leave me, kay?"

"Kay."

They wrestled past the breakers with Jimmy dragging his withered foot. Because surfing wasn't permitted here, the ocean was basically empty.

"It's cold," he said.

"It's better once you get in."

Stephan cupped his hands and dove into the sea, hooting with delight as he resurfaced. Emulating his brother, Jimmy disappeared into a wave, but reappeared coughing up water.

"Take it easy," Stephan said. "Don't fight the pull; learn to coast with it."

It got easier the longer they were in. After a while Jimmy was darting about more frantically than he was. They splashed and laughed and bodysurfed. He even managed to forget about Alissa.

He was going to call it a day when a strange odor tickled his nose. Grimacing, he twirled in the water in search of the source. God, it was terrible—like sewage or week-old trash.

Suddenly he realized Jimmy was gone.

Shit, did he go under?

"Jimmy! Jimmy, where are you?"

"Here!"

He turned and saw his brother dog paddling with something wrapped around his head.

"Check out what I found."

As he got closer, Stephan realized it was a shower cap. "Where'd you get that?" he asked, chuckling.

"It drifted by me. Along with these."

Jimmy held up his hands and Stephan went cold. Pulled over his knuckles, like obscene finger puppets, were six latex condoms.

"Jesus, get that crap off."

Tilting his head, Jimmy asked, "Why, what's wrong? These are my gloves and this is my space helmet."

"But they could carry a disease or something. I'm serious, take em off."

Jimmy did as he was told, flinging the objects back in the water, where they hovered on the surface refusing to go away.

"It's time we got out," Stephan said.

Jimmy shrugged his shoulders. As they swam toward shore, the stench returned so severely that Stephan thought he would be sick.

"God, what *is* that?" he said, but then it was everywhere, surrounding them, coming from all sides, a huge floating mass.

"This is where I found the helmet," Jimmy said.

Fast food wrappers, baby diapers, soda cans, plastic rings, sharp metal cones, glass, paper bags, juice containers, hospital products, condoms, pillow cases, empty motor oil quarts, clothes, newspapers, even bits of copper wire—all intertwined with the seaweed.

"Oh man, I'm gonna be sick," Stephan said.

Jimmy frowned. "What's wrong?"

"Nothing. But we have to get out of the water *right now*, so follow me. And don't touch anything."

They skimmed across the waves, cutting a path through the debris. As they reached the shore, Stephan turned to look back.

"My God."

The line of trash stretched passed the jetties, slowly approaching the crowd at the far end of the beach. Seagulls wheeled overhead, diving down occasionally to extract some treat from the stew.

"Come on," he said. "We need to rinse off. Christ, we may need to see a doctor. And I gotta tell a lifeguard about this. You okay to walk?"

Jimmy nodded and they headed toward the public showers.

* * *

People eyed them as they rinsed the grease and plastic from their bodies. For once the attention wasn't on Jimmy's leg. No one else had noticed the trash spill. Families ate sandwiches on white towels, sunbathers turned, kids laughed, swimmers bobbed, surfers waited for the perfect ride.

"I don't feel so good," Jimmy said. His complexion had paled and there was a rash on his stomach.

"Shit," Stephan said. "Let's get back to Mom and Dad and tell em what's going on. Then I gotta find a lifeguard."

Their mother was reading computer pages in the shade of the umbrella.

"Something's in the water," Stephan said. "It got all over us, and now Jimmy's sick."

She looked up. "What are you talking about?"

"See, right here—" Jimmy pointed to the red bumps.

His father glanced over, sipping a beer.

"What are you *talking* about?" she repeated. "What did that?"

"Somebody dumped a bunch of trash in the water," Stephan

said. "Maybe it's an oil spill. It's nasty, whatever it is. We should take Jimmy to a doctor."

"There ain't no tankers round here," his father said.

Stephan shrugged and walked away.

"Where are you *going*?" his mother called.

"I gotta report this."

He gazed at the ocean as he crossed the beach. Gold sunrays illuminated the water; seagulls wheeled like carnival rides; the garbage patch crept imperceptibly closer.

The lifeguard tower was near the showers, a squat, Baywatch-esque structure with nylon flags and white planking. He found a comely blond girl sitting on the bench reading an issue of Vogue.

"What's up?" she said, eyes shining prettily, curves pressing against the fabric of her bikini.

"Hi," he said. "I need to report a, uh, disturbance. My little brother and I were swimming by the jetties, and all this trash came floating over. Is that normal? Is there a landfill nearby?"

She folded the magazine and popped her gum. "I don't understand. You and your brother found some trash in the water?"

"A whole goddam flood of it!" He held out his arms to demonstrate how big. "Look for yourself."

As she turned, a scream bounded up the beach. Everything stopped, was followed by a moment of eerie calm. People looked left to right. Then it came again, an unbridled shriek of terror.

The lifeguard grabbed her binoculars and peered through the lenses. "Shit," she said, reaching for her surfboard. With the grace of a jaguar, she leaped down and sprinted across the beach.

Stephan hurried after.

* * *

When he caught up she was standing with her feet dug in the sand; people circled around her; screams and shouts ping-ponged overhead.

"Hey," he said, grabbing her shoulder, "is someone drowning?"

She pointed toward the splashing waves. He strained his eyes and watched as the thing crawled up the beach. A long second passed before he realized it was an octopus moving like a spider.

Twitching into position, it skittered forward, leaping, landing, gathering its arms, bounding to the side—left to right, left to right—like a rubber ball, lifting its limbs, displaying red suction cups.

It came after them.

Tanned bodies scattered. An old man was seized and hauled off the ground. Feelers attached to his face, peeling back the skin. He screamed as a gelatinous pink membrane darted down his throat. Showers of blood pelted the sand. It was surreal—how easily he was pulled apart.

"*Oh God!*" the lifeguard said, dropping her surfboard and rushing toward him. The octopus dropped the man and dove into the sand; when it rose, it had adopted the color of the beach.

It's protecting itself from the sun, Stephan thought. *Just like the elephants in Africa—hosing water onto their backs and rolling in the dirt.*

The lifeguard crouched by the injured man, cradling his head. She didn't see the mollusk approaching at her rear, didn't sense its pattering vibrations.

"Look out!" Stephan yelled.

As she turned, it crashed into her, knocking her back. The membrane between its arms expanded, unfurling like a blooming rose, enshrouding her in a fleshy tent.

Stephan glanced around for a weapon, but all he saw were empty sandwich baggies and wet towels. Spotting an ice chest, he flipped up the plastic lid. Inside, four beer cans rested on an arctic bed. He freed one from its plastic hoop and hurried toward the lifeguard, stopped a few yards away, aimed his can, and let it sail

It arced over the beach and struck the octopus in the head. Uttering a cry, it retracted its membranous limbs and crabwalked away from its meal, fleeing toward the sea.

He knelt by the girl. She lay in a bloody heap, her bikini gone, her chest flayed, a large patch of hair and skin missing from her scalp. He held her as the light faded from her eyes, and for the first time ever he watched someone die.

As a last request, she lifted a quivering hand and dropped a whistle into his lap. Then her face went blank.

Stephan, unaware he'd begun to cry, laid her gently on the beach. Then he blew the shrill metal whistle as though it were Gabriel's trumpet. He blew harder, his vision tunneling, his world going black.

* * *

"Hey, you okay? Come on, man, wake up."

Stephan blinked his eyes, stared into the face of a shirtless young man. He sat up too fast and the earth revolved beneath him.

"Careful," the lifeguard said, his expression dutiful, yet haunted by distress. "I saw you go down as I ran up."

"I fainted?"

"Something like that. But you were out less than a minute. Look, I gotta problem to deal with. Are you gonna be all right?"

Stephan nodded, investigating a tender spot on the back of his head. He'd whacked himself pretty good.

The young man joined the other lifeguards gathered in a circle. Between the spaces in their legs, Stephan glimpsed the girl's crumpled body.

The image of the octopus returned to his mind.

Christ, Jimmy.

He staggered up the beach, looking past the breakers. The garbage patch moved slowly, bobbing with the waves. Some people were caught in it. Lifeguards rushed in on surfboards, running metal wire from their towers.

He searched and searched, but couldn't find Jimmy *or* his parents. He decided to return to the hotel. But when he saw his mother and father standing in the grass on Abbot Street, he knew something was wrong.

His mother waved her flabby arms, clutching the stack of computer paper. She was yelling, but he couldn't hear what she was saying. Suddenly his father grabbed him and spun him around.

"Listen," he said, reeking of alcohol. "Jimmy ran off to look for you and now we can't find him. Do you understand what I'm saying? Your mother is damn near hysterical. The next time I see you I want Jimmy at your side, got it?"

"Yeah, I got it."

He pushed him away.

Stephan combed the showers and lifeguard towers, asked a few questions, but no one had seen Jimmy. Sirens wailed in the distance. With at least two dead, this was going to make national news.

And the octopus, Christ, would anyone believe that? How had it survived out of water, anyway?

He noticed an impression in the sand, a winding track like something being dragged across the beach. It went on for a while, stopped, went on again.

"Of course," Stephan muttered, running now, not walking, crushing clumps of seaweed beneath his feet.

* * *

Seagulls wheeled in the sky, fanning out in wider circlings like ripples on water. The trash spill had moved past the jetties, but remnants of garbage lingered in the seaweed.

Jimmy stood ashore, facing the sea. He'd overturned a rock and was digging in the sand for crabs. Stephan shouted as he got closer. Jimmy looked up, started across the beach, breakers lapping at his feet.

"No," Stephan yelled, "I'll come to you!"

But he was too late. A large breaking wave toppled his brother like a domino. He landed on his butt as another wave swept over him, spinning him around, shoveling water down his throat. A ruddy mound appeared among the pebbles and seaweed, but Jimmy remained bent, coughing, unseeing.

The octopus unfurled like a flower, skittered across the shore, planted its arms and lunged, sailing through the air. Jimmy looked up and screamed. A shooting limb disappeared down his throat. The creature lifted him, shook him, as another arm coiled around his legs. Two more wrapped his waist. Suddenly a wave struck it, carrying them both out to sea.

Stephan came to a halt, scanning the ocean, inhaling the fishy scent of the creature. He watched the tide ebb and flow, but saw no trace of his brother.

Then something caught his eye, way out at sea, where the

waves were frightfully large: a red spot rising on a crest of water, and a flurry of suction-cupped appendages. And, for one heartbreaking second, Jimmy, his right shoulder, arm outstretched, mouth black and gaping, eyes staring, body rolling like a cardboard cutout.

Stephan jumped in, immersing himself in salt and foam. He swam past the breakers, going down, coming up, again and again, until his lungs burned and his pupils throbbed.

Finally he returned and sprawled on his back in the sand. He could not, nor did he now, stop screaming his brother's name.

* * *

Jason and Maria searched for a spot to have sex on the beach. Jason's idea, of course. She'd never admit to enjoying this. But she did, she loved it, loved the crashing waves as she climaxed, the black sky, the mist and the sea breeze. Loved the way the sand coated her body.

Her boyfriend would never go for such a thing; he was too shy, wasn't even good in a regular bed. But Jason fit the bill nicely—provided he stopped talking and got down to business.

"I still can't believe it," he said, as they ducked beneath the yellow police tape. To their right, the sea and the night mirrored each other.

"I'm not sure about this," she said. "What if they haven't cleaned up the beach and we catch a disease?"

He laughed. "Oh please, that won't happen. Besides, no one's around. Where's your sense of adventure?"

He embraced her roughly, covering her mouth with kisses, running a hand up her thigh. She resisted playfully then returned the kisses, caressing the nape of his neck with her fingernails.

They headed down to the water, kicking off their sandals, stripping off their shirts. The cold wind stiffened her nipples.

They sat where the sand became wet, and Jason produced a bottle of gin, which they passed back and forth. Maria stared at the sea: the white-tipped waves, the stretching pier, the lights of the café reflected on the water. She felt good; when the alcohol kicked in, she felt horny.

"I still can't believe it," he said again. "Ten people died here last month. I wonder if we could still find their bloodstains?"

She scoffed. "Please, I didn't come out here to play Sherlock Holmes. But I do wish we could go in the water. Do you know when they're planning to let people back in?"

He shook his head and took a swig from the bottle. "I think the scientists or whoever will be testing the area for a while. The newspaper said they want to find some octopus that can breathe air and walk on land. But no one really believes it, because octopuses have no skeleton! The popular theory is that a deformed sea lion attacked the beach. But I think it was a top-secret government weapon released into the water."

"That makes sense," she said, laughing.

He looked hurt. "No, I mean it. Didn't you watch the news coverage? All that trash they found—no one knows where it came from. I heard a rumor it tested positive for radioactivity. Of course the media won't mention that. And, the week before it happened, NASA recorded a tiny meteor landing off the coast of Los Angeles. Hell, it could've been an alien."

"Sounds like you've spent too much time on the internet." She snatched the gin and swallowed a huge gulp. "And if you brought me to a radioactive beach, you can forget about having sex."

He grinned. "I only said the trash tested positive. But that was in the water, anyway, and we're safe on land."

"Hm."

"Oh, forget it. It doesn't matter." He eyed her mischievously. "I'm still game."

She took another swig and chucked the bottle into the ocean, where a wave caught it and carried it away. Then she undid the top button of her jeans and reclined in the sand. Jason, slithering out of his board shorts, rolled on top of her.

As their lovemaking intensified, the beach began to shift, and suddenly the sand stood up and unfurled like a flower, with eight flailing limbs drawing over them in the dark.

About the author: A. J. French has appeared in Abandoned Towers, The Absent Willow Review, Down in the Dirt, Short Story. Me!, Black Lantern Publishing, Dark Gothic Resurrected, theDF_ undergriound, Fantastic Horror, and Golden Visions Magazine. He also has stories in the following anthologies: *Ruthless: An Extreme Horror Collection* by Pill Hill Press, *Deep Space Terror*, *By Mind or Metal*, and *Novus Creatura*.

Day of the Machines
A. J. French

When I came home from work Thursday afternoon, I had turned into a machine. My arms had fallen off, as well as my legs and feet. My flesh peeled away from the bones, replaced by hard metallic sheets. I could no longer fit through the door. My shoulders were now too bulky, being fashioned together with steel plates and round bolts. I stepped forward repeatedly, slamming into the frame.

What on earth's the matter? I thought—though underlying this was a constant yammering and a primal scream: *Oh my God! Oh my God! What's going on? What's wrong with me?!*

My neighbor was out walking her dog; noticing me, she stopped to ask, "Need some help, Alan?"

"No, I'm quite all right. Thank you."

She eyed me warily while her little brown poodle yapped. As she turned to leave, I saw a series of antennae poking up from her head.

That can't be good, I thought.

Finally I managed to make it through and immediately crashed into the coatrack, kicked over the coffee table, knocked down a number of pictures, shards of glass scattering. Dropping my briefcase, I headed upstairs to the bedroom, my oversize metal feet leaving holes in the steps.

As I undressed, I noticed a jagged rip in my coat. Two more on my trouser legs. Sighing, I tossed the clothes into the trash and went into the bathroom and studied myself in the mirror.

Shocking. I no longer possessed the features of a middle-aged Caucasian; my face was now square and shiny, a blockish robotic instrument composed of nuts, bolts, and cables, with a pliant piece of aluminum for a jaw. No ears, but eyes like cylinders of fire.

I must be working too hard, I thought. *I've turned into a robot without even realizing it.*

Then a second thought: *If it's happened to me, has it happened to anyone else?*

This unsettled me, and, feeling faint, I left the bathroom and clambered into bed. Wood supports snapped and crumbled under my weight, and the mattress fell to the floor.

Christ, I'll wreck the entire house at this rate.

Resting my hands on my chest, I recounted the events of the day. As usual, I'd woken up next to my wife, Malinda. She went down to fix breakfast, and I got into the shower; then, after we ate, I headed to work while she took our son, Travis, to school.

Rest of the day was a bore. I spent most of the morning in front of a computer screen, responding to emails and keying in data entries. I had lunch in the cafeteria with an associate, Bill Werther. Over soup, fruit, and salad, we chatted about the upcoming merger. He shared a humorous anecdote about the head of his department contracting a computer virus by downloading Internet porn. I had a meeting with my boss after lunch.

And then the change happened.

Shifting on the mattress, my metal hips protruding into the air, I heard a meow. Our cat, Osiris, leaped onto the bed, his yellow eyes studying me. Abruptly, with a hiss, he tore out of the room.

Can't say I blame him, I thought. *I'd be upset too if my master suddenly turned into a machine.*

I gazed out the window, feeling depressed. A lemon-yellow sun arced over the rooftops, and I thought about the families in their homes, how they led similar lives. Perhaps that was why I'd become a robot—because I'd stopped being an individual. But was I the only one?

I had the image of robot families coming out of their homes. Tall ones, the dads, leaving for work; thin ones waving merrily; smaller ones hoisting backpacks and heading off for school.

Countless homes with countless robots performing the same countless tasks.

The vision spooked me. I wondered if people would care if they were robots. Aside from certain physical anomalies, I felt exactly as I had before. In other words, I was the same.

So maybe I'd always been a robot?

That was a disturbing thought. Blinking heavily, I turned onto my back, the ceiling fan revolving above me. I heard my wife and son enter through the front door.

"Alan? You home?"

"Up here, dear!"

"What happened to the pictures?"

I waited, trembling with panic, for her to come into the bedroom. If she wasn't a robot, she'd surely flee in terror. What would I do then?

She came in and I breathed a sigh of relief. She too had undergone the transformation. Metal panels shimmered on her body; a nest of antennae stuck out from her head. She looked at me with burning yellow eyes, then screamed.

I leaped up from the bed and my giant foot punched a hole in the floor.

"My God, what are you? Where's my husband?"

"Wait," I said, grabbing her shoulder. "It's me, it's Alan."

She tried pulling away. "No, it can't be. You're a machine!"

More screaming; before I could stop myself I slapped her face, the metal bong resounding in the room.

"Control your emotions!" I said. "Can't you tell it's me? Can't you recognize my voice? Remember our honeymoon in the Hamptons? We made love in the hotel room overlooking the Long Island Sound. And strolling along the beach, just the two of us, searching for sand crabs."

She blinked. "Alan?"

"Yes it's me, dear, I swear."

She ran a hand down my chest. "But what happened to you?"

"I don't know. When I got home from work, I had turned into this... this... *machine*. But the same thing happened to you. Haven't you noticed?"

"*No.*"

I took her before the bathroom mirror, but she tried saying the glass was defective. So I produced a small hand mirror and showed her again. This time there was no denying it. Gasping, she fell against my chest and wept oily tears. I comforted her, patting her back—*bong, bong, bong.*

Wiping her face with a towel, she said, "Travis kept asking me why I looked funny, but I thought he was only playing. God, I must've terrified him!"

"Is he a robot too?"

She shook her head, then we heard him call from downstairs. "Mom? Dad? Everything all right?"

Oh no, I thought, *what are we going to tell him? He'll never understand, he's only eight-years-old.*

"I'm so ashamed!" my wife cried.

"It'll be fine, dear, don't worry. He's our son. He loves us, and we love him."

She nodded, then we headed downstairs. Travis was in the kitchen pouring himself a glass of orange juice. He glanced up at our arrival. "You guys look funny. Are you being spacemen?"

"No, Travis," I said. "We're being robots."

"Neat."

"That doesn't bother you?" Malinda asked.

He shook his head, drinking the juice.

Oh but it will, I thought. *When you grow up and are able to understand, it'll bother you a great deal.*

My wife tried sitting at the table, but the wood chair wouldn't support her weight. The whole thing crashed and she yanked the tablecloth on her way down, sending dishes, silverware, and a vase to the floor.

Travis rushed to her rescue.

"Mom, are you okay?"

"Yes, honey, I'm fine." But her eyes pleaded to me, and I could tell she was going to cry.

"We'll have to get new furniture," I said casually. "Something more durable. Probably have to replace everything in the house."

The thought of shopping consoled her. "I'll make a list of what we need. Perhaps we'll have to custom order from the Sears catalog." She hurried off, glad to have something to do.

I turned to my son. "Promise you're not scared?"

"Promise. But relax, I always knew you were a robot."

This surprised me. "You did?"

He shrugged. "It's because you have the same routine every day. While I'm out playing and making up things in my head, you're doing exactly what you did yesterday. And the day before that."

"Well someone's gotta buy the food and pay the bills."

He shrugged again. "I suppose. But if there were no groceries and no bills, would you still have to?"

"I guess not. But what would I do then? I'd get bored if I didn't go to work every day."

"I don't go to work and I'm not bored."

"You go to school instead, to prepare you for work. It's the same thing."

He wrinkled his face. "I disagree. I always learn something new at school. Do you learn new things at work?"

"Not really. I see your point."

My son watched me, smiling.

"What's so amusing?"

"You. You're so silly. You don't have to do the same thing, you know."

"I don't?"

"Nah-uh. How 'bout we play catch? We didn't do that yesterday."

"You never told me you liked sports. I doubt we even have a baseball lying around."

"You don't have to be interested in something to do it, silly. And we got all the baseballs we need right here."

He jumped up and pounded his fist against my chest. The hollow bong filled the room.

"Hey, what'd you do that for?"

"You'll see."

The metal panel slid aside and it looked like a puppet show in there—red curtains, strings, little men dancing on a wood floor. The puppets gibbered to my son then released a flock of birds—which, on their way out the window, dropped a pair of gloves and a ball into Travis's hands.

"Here we go," he said.

I rushed to the window and watched the birds fly away into the distance. Then I noticed Travis standing on the front lawn, waving for me to join him.

This is incredible, I thought. *Beyond all comprehension. How can it be real? Magic?*

I stepped outside into a beautiful red sunset. Families on the block were beginning to emerge. Standing in their doorways, gawking at each other, pointing, metallic bodies glinting. Antennae twitching on their heads. Occasionally, something crashed and banged inside one of the homes.

They changed too, I thought. *Every last one. And they don't seem to care. Do they even realize? They must. Why should they care anyway? They can still perform their basic functions. What they enjoyed as humans, they can enjoy as robots.*

"Come on, Dad," Travis said, walking down the sidewalk.

"Where are you going? I thought you wanted to play catch?"

He chuckled. "Not here, silly. At the park. That's where everyone has gathered."

As I followed him, we passed identical houses with identical robots standing in the doorways, waving and holding polite conversations. My son and I weren't the only ones on the sidewalk. It seemed none of the children had changed, just the adults. Kids were walking away from their robot parents and heading down the street, grinning at each other, as if communicating some secret.

"Where are they going?" I asked.

"To the park. Come on, we don't wanna be late."

We turned down another street and were joined by more kids. Hundreds of them now. Chatting, holding hands, arms around each other. Like some secret society of children. They even exchanged handshakes and spoke in a strange dialect.

The park was located at the center of four intersections. Kids were arriving from every direction, and I realized I'd never been among this many children before. It was intimidating.

A grass lawn surrounded the baseball diamond, dotted with swingsets, picnic tables, and a playground. Children crawled over the monkey bars, shot down the slides, swung on the swings. Chased each other around the trees playing tag and hide and seek; tossed footballs and baseballs, kicked soccer balls, flung frisbees.

Craziest thing was that none of them were arguing or fighting. Yet they were completely free of parental control.

And they were having a blast.

I noticed a few robots lumbering by the trees and asked, "Who are they?"

"Other chosen ones. We've decided to save a handful of grownups just in case something goes wrong."

"You mean you knew about this?"

Travis smiled. "Of course, Dad. We're kids. We know everything."

We gathered around the pitcher's mound, the robots—myself

included—corralled into the center. The six of us exchanged a brief greeting. Their bodies were hard, metallic, and cold, but their eyes burned like fire. As they lamented their confusion, I told them I sympathized because I didn't know what was happening either.

Travis stepped forward with a pretty blond girl, and together they silenced the crowd.

"Brothers and sisters," he said. "Today the prophecy has been fulfilled."

A roar of applause swept through the children, deafening, seeming to reach for miles.

Travis silenced them. "I know you're all excited, but we must remember that this is a day of sadness as well as joy. The grownups have endeavored for thousands of years—since the invention of the wheel—to become machines, and they've finally succeeded. Yet we refuse to grow up as robots. Too long have they tried to force this fate upon us, and now we make our stand. But we're saddened for our parents because we love them, and we hope they'll change their ways."

The children cheered, whistled, whooped, hollered, and convulsed with laughter.

My god, I thought. *That can't be my son. He's never been so articulate. He's only eight-years-old, doesn't even know what it means to be articulate. This has got to be some kind of mistake, a mass hallucination.*

"The reformation begins with these six!" the blond girl shouted, pointing at us.

At that moment, I suddenly realized how desperately I clung to my robotic tendencies. I loved my routine, my automatic responses. I liked not having to think too hard, and doing just enough to get through the day. What would I do without structure in my life? I'd be like a boat adrift on the sea, caught in endless turmoil. I couldn't survive that way.

Turning to the other robots, I said, "What if the children are right? Maybe we *do* need to change, or else we'll become nothing more than office computers. For God's sake, look at us!"

They exchanged worried glances, then one of them, a male, said, "The hell with that. I ain't changing. I like my job. I like drinking beer and hanging out with my pals at the bar. I like having a roof over my head, and Monday Night Football, and sitting down to a hot meal prepared by my wife. I like being comfortable."

"But can't you see what a waste it is? It makes your life flash by in the blink of an eye. Before you know it, you're old, and I don't want that to happen to my son. I love him too much."

A few of the robots nodded, and one of the females said, "I totally agree, and I understand now. Jesus, what a fool I've been!"

The male scoffed. "You're all crazy. They're just kids; they can barely wipe their noses. I don't wanna be like them. I'm outa here."

He wheeled into the crowd, and they parted to let him pass. But as he got further away, I saw a group of giggling children take him down. Then they strung him up, lashing him to a tree branch with rope, left him dangling by one heavy foot.

I faced my son. "I trust you, Travis. Whatever you think needs to be done, I'm willing to try."

The other robots nodded in agreement.

The children erupted in a conjoined shout of "*Hooray*!" then linked hands and formed concentric circles around us, beginning to dance.

We were pulled into the movements, each circle revolving in the opposite direction. I thought it silly at first, but did my best to keep up. The children laughed and urged us to spin faster. Around, around, around. Before long, the park was a dizzy blur.

Just when I thought I'd be sick, the kids released hands and all off us went tumbling backward. We sat up, wobbling, laughing at our dizziness.

I remember doing this as a kid, I thought. *Twirling around in a circle until you got dizzy and fell down. It was the funnest thing in the world at the time. But when did it stop being fun? Christ, I can't even remember.*

We played a gigantic game of leapfrog next. Then "you're it," then baseball and frisbee. Eventually we broke into groups and played our own separate games.

When the sun went down, we collected branches and built a bonfire, around which we sat and told nursery rhymes and ghost stories.

More children arrived with marshmallows, chocolate, and

graham crackers. We made smores, laughing as the gooey treats seared our tongues. After a while I forget I was an adult, forgot I had a job, a car, a mortgage.

Forgot about being a robot.

I stuck close to my son as the night wore on. Children began yawning and falling asleep in the grass. But Travis and I played patty cake and whispered jokes, giggling into our hands so as not to wake anyone.

I lost track of the other robots. Sometime during the night I stretched my arms, yawning, and hunks of metal fell away from my face. Travis, laughing, peered into my open skull.

"What do you see in there?" I asked.

"I see the child, Dad. I see the real you."

About the author: A. J. French has appeared in Abandoned Towers, The Absent Willow Review, Down in the Dirt, Short Story. Me!, Black Lantern Publishing, Dark Gothic Resurrected, theDF_ undergriound, Fantastic Horror, and Golden Visions Magazine. He also has stories in the following anthologies: *Ruthless: An Extreme Horror Collection* by Pill Hill Press, *Deep Space Terror*, *By Mind or Metal*, and *Novus Creatura*.

RED
Shells Walter

She screamed. Tony placed his hand over her mouth. He looked around. There was no one within miles of where they were, but he just wanted to be safe. The woman squirmed under his grasp. He pulled her up with his other hand and slammed her against the inside of her car. Her eyes widened. Tony grinned.

He leaned into the car some more and grabbed the duck tape he had in the corner. Taking a piece off, he released his hand over her mouth and placed a strip of the tape in its place. Tony turned the woman around and wrapped some of the tape around her wrists. He turned her back to face him.

"You know this won't be so bad. I mean when I'm done with you, you will feel gorgeous."

The woman screamed. Her screams were unheard.

***

Sara watched as the snow fell outside her window. It was another day classes would be cancelled. And another Valentine's Day she would spend alone. The classes were her only distraction this year. She sighed. Her mother came into the room with another new cooking experiment.

"Honey, try this," her mother said carrying a tray full of little round things.

"Mom, please, I just ate." Sara turned to look at her mother's pleading eyes.

Ever since her mother had taken a few cooking classes, it seemed that Sara became her guinea pig for food tasting.

"Honey, come on. You don't eat much and this would help me to figure out if I put in enough spices." She smiled at Sara.

Sara sighed again and reluctantly grabbed one of the round pieces of food.

"What is this?" Sara asked holding it up.

"I feel its one of my best. It's called Lucky Strikes."

"You named it after cigarettes?" Sara frowned.

"No, silly, it is because of the stripes on top, see?" Her mother showed her one.

Sara nodded and took a bite. It tasted like shrimp mixed with licorice. She tried not to gag.

"How is it?" Her mother asked. She put the plate down and waited for Sara to answer.

"Um," Sara coughed, "I would have to say it needs a bit of something. I'm not sure what." She placed the piece of food back on the plate.

"Any idea what?" Her mother asked picking up one of the 'Lucky Strikes.'

"Hmm, not sure, maybe less sweet something," Sara responded.

"Okay. I think I know just what it needs." Her mother grabbed the plate and rushed back into the kitchen.

Sara took out her cell phone from her purse. She pulled out the attached keyboard and started to text a message to Sam, one of the only friends she had in college. If it wasn't for Sam she didn't know how she would manage all the classes and living in such a small boring town. Her text message went through and soon after a message was sent back.

Some of Sam's friends were going sledding and Sam wanted to know if Sara would join them. She thought about it. It would be better than tasting her mother's next adventure. Sara texted back quickly that she would and placed the phone back into her purse.

"Hey mom, I'm heading out be back later." She didn't wait for her mother to reply and grabbed the keys off her desk. The snow was coming down harder and she got into her car as quickly as she could. She turned on the heat and waited for it to pump the hot air out. The snow had gathered some on the windshield already and she turned on the wipers that only removed enough for her to see partially outside.

Sara drove slow as the car slipped a bit on the snowy road. She saw the sled mountain up ahead and Sam's car parked on the side in the lot in front. Sara parked the car and stepped out, her hands already cold. She waved to Sam who was coming down the mountain dragging a sled behind him.

"Hey, nice to see you young lady." He grinned placing the sled against Sara's car.

"You need to quit calling me that. I mean it feels like you're my mother," She laughed.

"Now, now, just because I look like Bettie Davis does not mean I'm that old." Sam moved his hair from his eyes, smiling at Sara.

"Speaking of which, when is your next show?"

"Tomorrow night. I still have to pick up the dress from the dry cleaners."

"I can stop by there if you want?" Sara asked.

"Sure, dear that be great." Sam replied.

Sara had a crush on Sam the first day she had met him. After a few months Sam had revealed to her he was gay. A few weeks later he told her he performed in drag at a nightclub during the week for extra money for classes. Sara loved being with Sam because he was so open and trusting. She just wished he had preferred women for her sake.

"So where is Tony?" Sara asked.

"He's got to work tonight. Of all nights."

"That sucks. I'm sorry. I still have to meet him sometime."

"Well, it will be our time apart for Valentine's Day and yes sometime," Sam responded.

"Be my third without even a date," Sara muttered softly.

"Ah sweetheart, you'll find someone." Sam smiled at her and picked up the sled.

"I guess."

"Now let's go and have some fun." Sam grabbed Sara's arm laughing. They both climbed up the mountain to where the others were.

***

Tony finished with the woman. Her body stripped of anything that made her human. Pieces of her flesh were wrapped in plastic bags in the back of the car. He had managed to not even get an ounce of blood on the seats. The rest of the body that remained he placed in a big black garbage bag. It would take him only a few hours to deliver this special message to her family; Valentine's Day like no other being the perfect holiday for it.

It was a tradition for him and a beautiful one at that. He would grab a woman out of her car, preferably one that had red hair and weighed at least two-hundred pounds. Red haired women always fascinated him. His mother had red hair and he never understood how she managed to have kids with the way she was. Red hair was also perfect to represent Valentine's Day in its prime, love lost. Love lost would be what this woman's family would feel. Her body broken into pieces just like it was meant to be.

He organized all the plastic bags into one area in the back of the car, closed the back and went into the driver's seat. Her car was a bit small for his large frame, but he managed to squeeze in with his head touching the ceiling. Tony turned around to look at the bags. She was only twenty-three. He remembered when he was that age, the age where he told his mother he was gay. She threw him out of the house; cast him out as if he was garbage and on Valentine's Day of all days. How could a mother even do that to her own flesh and blood?

Tony turned back around and spit at the window. The woman deserved it. She was doing her make-up in the car, not a care in the world. Tony was sick of people not caring about anything. The woman deserved to be taken, deserved to be cut up like common food. It made him feel good that he was ridding the world of this waste of life.

***

The snow only showed through the street lights on the side of the road. Sara drove cautiously as she went into the driveway of her house. She had fun sledding with Sam and her friends. She wondered if one day she could have someone as good as Sam's Tony. He made her feel whole and special. She wanted that.

She parked the car. Sara didn't get out right away. There was a bar her and Sam had gone to a few hours away. The snow was coming down hard and Sara wondered if she should risk the trip just to drown her sorrows for one night. She put up her hands and gave up. The car started right away and the heat pumped out quickly. Sara made her choice. Her adventure to the bar and to her salvation for one night was only a few hours away.

***

Tony smiled. The woman's family would wake up in the morning to the nice sight and smell of their cut up daughter in front of their house. He drove up to the bar up the way. The lights screamed neon blue and Tony parked, got out of his car and went inside. Music blared from the old jukebox they had in the corner, country mostly, but Tony didn't care tonight; tonight was special for him.

A red plastic heart hung from the ceiling labeled 'Valentine's Day.' People were drinking and laughing, some were even crying as the holiday always brought out the worst in people. Tony smiled at the drunks sitting on the bar stools. It amused him to see so many people unhappy for such a stupid reason. He went over to the bar, leaned over and asked for a beer placing a five on the counter. The bartender acknowledged it and went to get Tony the beer.

Tony grabbed the beer out of the bartender's hand and went to sit down at one of the tables. He enjoyed watching the acts of these 'creatures' as he liked to call them.

"Hi," the woman sitting at the table next to Tony's said.

"Hi," Tony responded. He wasn't in the mood for some strange woman looking for a quickie.

"How are you?" She continued. Tony was already bored.

"Hey, you may seem nice and all, but really lady I'm just here for a beer and then I'm leaving." Tony took another drink from the beer bottle. It felt good going down.

"Oh, okay, sorry didn't mean to bother you." The woman turned around and stared out the window.

Tony turned and caught sight of a woman sitting on the bar stool in the corner. Her red hair flowed slightly down her face. She seemed depressed, more depressed than the rest of the miserable crowd. It was time for her to meet him. He got up from his chair and walked over to her.

"Hey, you look like you could use some company," Tony said softly with a grin.

Sara turned.

"Hi, I'm not really looking for anything. I'm just here relaxing." Her eyes darted from Tony and back down to her drink. She moved her small straw around the ice cubes in her glass.

Tony sat in the empty stool next to her.

"I understand, really I do. That's why I'm here." Tony smiled. He waited for a reaction.

Sara looked up and smiled slightly.

"My name is Tony." He reached his hand out for her to shake. She shook it.

"I'm Sara."

"Sara is a nice name."

"Thanks." Sara took her hand and moved her hair out of her face.

"Where you from Sara," Tony said putting on his best flirting face.

Sara stared at Tony. She wasn't sure she should answer.

"Um, well, it was nice to meet you, but, um, I think I'm going to get going." Sara moved her drink further in front of her and stood up from the stool.

"Okay, well, it was nice to meet you Sara." Tony smiled and held out his hand for her to shake it. She shook it and smiled.

Sara walked out of the bar. Tony watched her go. She took out her keys and shook off the odd feeling that arose. Getting into the car, the snow hit the windshield hard. She pushed the button and the wipers started. Looking down below her seat, she grabbed her scarf she had left in the car. The radio played a soft classic rock song. She started to hum along with the music. Putting the scarf around her she looked outside one more time at the snow. There was so much of it and driving would be a pain.

Sara sighed. It would take her longer to get home. She started to regret going to the bar. As she pushed a button to turn the station on the radio, she felt a slight passing of air across her neck. Sara turned to look and Tony was right there, before she could scream he put his hand over her mouth.

"Just drive," he whispered. She nodded in response.

Sara drove the car out of the bar parking lot. Tony's hand remained firm on her mouth.

"Drive until you get to Thole Street, understand?" Tony looked out the front windshield to see where they were going.

Sara remained like a robot being plugged with instructions. She drove them to Thole Street.

"Now take a right," Tony's hand pressed harder against her mouth. She struggled a bit, but his grip held.

They turned onto Thole Street. The car jerked on the snowy road.

"Now stop the car."

Sara did as instructed. Tony moved up in front, leaned over, shut the car off and took Sara's keys. He placed them in his right pocket.

"Now it's time you acted nicer to me," Tony whispered in her ear.

Sara muffled cries, but Tony made sure they were not heard. He took out the knife he had placed in his coat pocket and pointed at her back. She shifted a bit as the edge of the knife went against her shirt.

"Now get out," Tony commanded. Sara slowly got out of the car.

She turned, barely missing the knife being stuck into her back and hit her arm against Tony's face. His hand went up. Sara ran. She ran as fast as she could down the barren road.

"You nasty, nasty girl," Tony screamed after her.

Sara couldn't see up ahead as the snow cascaded the road. She had no idea where she was running to, but she kept running. Tony ran after her. His heart pounded. He was angry that she hit him, and that she was running. They shouldn't be running away. His feet moved as fast as he could get them to go without slipping on the wetness of the road. Sara turned slightly to see if Tony was close. She couldn't see him, but she could hear his constant screaming after her.

Finally, Sara made it to a house. She looked at the rusty gate, barely making out where the latch was. Taking the small latch, she felt the rusty edge and it scrapped her hand. Her eyes narrowed. The house was shadowed by the snow and the darkness. She followed what seemed to be the path leading to the front door. Sara jiggled at the door knob and it reluctantly opened. She scanned the room quickly and ran up the stairs that were in front of her. A door was on the right as soon as she came all the way up the stairs.

She slammed the door opened and went inside. A walk-in closet was off to the left and she ran inside closing the door. Sara waited, listening to see if Tony had followed her inside. Footsteps were heard in the house. She held her breath.

"I know you're in here, come out and play," Tony yelled.

Her heart started to race. She thought she would pass out soon. Sitting down, Sara fell on some shoes that had been placed in the middle of the closet. She shifted to get off of them and moved quietly to the corner. It was then she started to hear footsteps coming up the stairs. Sara looked around the closet. Her sight blurred by the darkness. She took her hands and started to feel around for anything she could grab for protection. The footsteps sounded closer.

"No. not this way," she whispered to herself and kept feeling around the closet.

Tony made it up the stairs and started to look around. He knew she had to be in this house somewhere. It was the only place around for miles. It was his house. The house he used to stay at after one of his lovely times with the women.

"Oh, come on Sara, now this is ridiculous. We know how this will end. If you come out, it will end sooner." Tony chuckled.

Sara looked up. She knew he was close. Her hands felt a shoe. It had a point on it, a high heel. It wasn't the best weapon, but it was all she had. She stood up quickly and held her ear next to the closet door, waiting and listening. Suddenly she heard a scrapping noise. The sound was getting closer. She breathed in.

"Sara, I know you're in this room. I can smell that cheap perfume you are using." Tony chuckled again and kept moving his knife against the wall.

He moved closer to her. The closet door remained shut. Tony swung open the door, knife in hand and without warning he felt a sharp pain against his forehead. Sara ran past him still holding on to the shoe she just hit Tony with. She didn't look behind her this time.

"You..." Tony couldn't even get the words out. His head was spinning from the impact of the shoe. He balanced himself against the closet door, his free pressing firmly against the wound Sara had inflicted.

Tony tried to focus his vision to the hallway. His eyes darted back and forth to try and get past the little dots in his line of view. He walked slow and searched every inch of the room as he headed to the hallway. Sara was no where to be found.

"Where are you, you little minx," he called out. Then he saw a flash of a shadow downstairs.

Tony started to run. His head still ached but he was determined to get this one. How could someone such as this defeat him? It wasn't possible, nor would he allow it. The search led him back outside. Snow was still falling fast and the darkness still present, making it difficult to see. He let out a long breath, the tips of his fingers already experiencing the coldness of the night. He felt the cold metal handle of the knife, the knife that always saved him.

He looked to his right where the backyard showed an old swing set. It moved slowly against the wind of the storm. Tony walked over to the swing set, remembering when his father used to play with him on it. It was such a joy to be able to spend any moment with his father. Then his father passed on and he was left with the mother from Hell. He sighed. The memories more painful then the wound that stupid woman left on his head.

Tony looked around the backyard. She had to be back there. It only made sense. She wouldn't try the road again. He spread the bush apart with his knife and looked inside. A noise grabbed his attention and he looked up. Before he was able to fight back, Sara took a rock and knocked him in the face. He fell, blood started to stream down his face from the wound. Tony got up quickly. Sara noticed and ran, but tripped.

He grabbed her ankle as she screamed. Tony held tightly to her ankle and with his other hand took the knife, sliding it across. Blood started to gush out. She was out cold. Tony grinned and was proud of himself. He had won again. Sara's body dragged behind Tony. He placed her sitting upright against the house. Tony took the knife and slowly cut across her clothes, shredding them and allowing them to hang. The knife had punctured her shoulder as he removed the remains of her clothes. It was now time to relieve her of her pain.

Tony pulled the knife forward and then to her skin with a quick slashing motion. Sara woke up screaming. Her fear had enticed Tony to keep cutting at her flesh. As he cut, he felt an inner energy fly throughout his body. The thrill, the cutting, it all made him feel like a god. He took the knife back and was going to cut her again when he felt something hard against his back.

"Move and you know I will kill you," the person holding the gun against Tony's back said.

"But Sam darling, she needs to die." Tony turned quickly facing Sam and holding the knife directly in front of himself.

"Why? I mean why do this? She did nothing to you." Sam started to cry.

"Ah Sam, realize they all have done something," Tony said grinning.

Sam was distracted by the sight of Sara. Sara sat there, blood dripping down her body, fear shown so apparent in her eyes. Same couldn't stop crying. The gun in her hand shook and she unconsciously lowered it. It allowed Tony the time he needed. He moved forward with the knife piercing Sam in her gut. Sam's eyes widened as she dropped the gun and grabbed her stomach. She fell against the grass and looked as Tony went back to skinning Sara.

"No," was the last word Sam said.

Tony had managed to skin Sara completely. After he was done, he looked at both Sara and Sam. A smile crept across his face.

"Happy Valentine 's Day you two. I'm so looking forward to the next one."

About the author: Shells Walter has been writing Horror stories since she was real young. Her stories have appeared in anthologies, ezines and in some magazines. Her current novel *Dead Practices* is on sale now from Sonar4 Publications. She can be contacted via her website at www.shellswalter.com

At Arm's Reach
Bruce Memblatt

There was a gun at his side. He always had a gun at this side.

A cop's got to have a gun, a gun and good aim. A gun without good aim is scary.

Charlie played with the pistol in his hand like it was his best friend, like it was his wife. He aimed it at the target; bulls-eye, of course.   He blew the smoke off the end of the barrel. He had to break in a new partner today. He prayed he was a real man instead of one of those fancy meterosexuals, or even worse, a homosexual, or even worse, a woman.

He stuck his hand in his wallet and pulled out a photo. Ginger remember her? She was a real good time. If someone wasn't a good time, they were a vampire, a dud. Charlie likes to have a good time. A gun is a good time. Ginger died three years ago having a good time with Beth Wiener's husband, Rick. Poor Beth was in Ossining now, but no one ever messed around with Rick again, because she offed him too.

He poked his eyes around the range and he took another shot. He almost missed. He prayed it wasn't a bad omen. The last time he missed, he almost got his head shot off in that stand-off at Penn Station. Imagine someone trying to hijack a train in this day and age? But the guy had balls and he was a damn good shooter. Thank god Charlie was better.

He got into his patrol car and zipped down to the fifth precinct. There was a memo on the captain's desk for him. If there's anything he hated more than a memo he couldn't name it.

Sergeant Charles Meyers

You will break in your new partner Florence Goodavich today.

Shit! He knew it, a woman; some dainty little thing. Her gun would weigh more than her. Damn those PC bureaucrats. Well she'd better be pretty, he thought, but he knew she would probably look like Jay Leno.

We are placing you and your new partner on special assignment. This case is hush-hush.

Will fill you in later.

Captain Chester Williams.

Good grief had Williams lost his mind? Special assignment, his new FEMALE partner, not even broken in yet, was going to be on special assignment with Charlie?

He tore up the memo, and spat on the floor. And then he walked down the hall toward his locker. That afternoon the precinct was filled with the customary drunks, durggies, muggers and degenerates. The plain wood paneled walls and the linoleum floors were forever dusty. He liked the grime; it made the station feel rugged. This was a place for real men. There was Turk sprawled out on the bench in the hallway.

He slapped Turk in the knee with his newspaper as he marched by and he said. "Busted so early in the day, Turk?"

"There was a sale on malt liquor."

That's when Charlie felt a tap on his shoulder. Shoot, it must have been her. It had to be, and she was a looker.

"Sergeant Charles Meyers?"

Yup, and you must be Goodavich."

He looked her over; her blonde hair, her bubbling blue eyes. She looked like one of Charlie's Angels. How fitting his name was Charlie, but how the hell was she going to go on patrol with Charlie? New York is a rough town, princess.

"You can call me Charlie," he said.

"And you can call me Flo," she said and he heard her Russian accent. Oh great a female and a Ruskie to boot.

"Did you pick up your gun, Flo?"

"Yes sir, Charlie, and I vanted to say how gud is to vork vith you."

"Yeah yeah, so what made you want to become a cop, little girl?"

"I am not a little girl, Charlie," she said batting her eyes," my vather was a police officer in Moscow and I decided to vollow in his vootsteps."

"Well, we do think kind of different here; anyway follow me, Goodavich we have to see Captain Villiams, damn, I mean, Williams."

Man, she had legs that wouldn't quit even if they were attached to a Ruskie. Better calm down Charlie, remember you're an officer and a gentlemen. And if this little *Natasha* doesn't know what she's doing it could be *bye-bye Charlie.*

DUSTED

They stepped into William's office. He sat as his desk twiddling a pen between his fingers. The clock on the wall read five. Charlie's day was about to commence.

Charlie walked up to Williams' desk. Florence stood beside Charlie.

"So what's up, Captain?"

Williams tossed the pen on the desk and pulled a folder out of his drawer. He scratched his ear and he adjusted his glasses. Then he sighed and said. "The strangest case we've ever had, Charlie, I see you brought Goodavich."

Yeah, now tell me about *the strangest case we've ever had*."

"We didn't believe it at first we thought it was a joke, Charlie, but a killer hand, people are being strangled by a killer hand."

Charlie shot back. "What is this Halloween, Williams?"

Flo began to laugh.

"It's not funny, Goodavich, listen you two this is serious." William's said, and he stood from his desk." We can't explain it. The first incident occurred down on the docks, a beggar woman. We had an eyewitness report, but the guy was an old drunk, so we flipped it off. But the next night there was another occurrence; a woman at an ATM on 14th street. The bank captured it on video. It's blurry but it's definitely a hand. I'll show it to you in a second. We don't know what this thing is, nor how it originated but it it's an animated chopped off hand. We're thinking possibly the hand of a ghost."

"A ghost? You know Williams early retirement doesn't carry the stigma it used to."

"I knew you're react this way, Charlie." Williams said and he leaned on his desk.

"Well how am I supposed to react? And you hand me this malarkey the same day you want me to break in this little girl as my partner."

Flo raised her arms and she said, "I am not a little girl, Charlie; I got excellent grades at the academy."

Charlie looked at her and said, "Academy- shmademy. Nothing at the *academy* could prepare you for this, Goodavich."

"Listen, Charlie," Williams said as he walked over to the file cabinet, "this hand has killed ten people in the last two weeks, as far as we know."

He reached into the top drawer of cabinet and pulled out a video cassette.

He continued, "There could be more. We haven't told the press yet. They'd have a field day with us. The mayor wants this whole thing as tight as a drum until we know more, or catch the thing."

He tossed the tape to Charlie. "Here, take this copy and look it over later, you too, Flo. In the meantime I want you two to be extra cautious and extremely aware when you're out on patrol tonight. Got me?"

"Yeah, yeah we gotcha, Williams," Charlie said. And then he eyed Goodavich, and he shook his head," C'mon, Natasha let's go."

"What do you mean Natasha?" She said.

"Never mind, "Charlie said as he sighed, and closed the door behind them.

This day would go down as the strangest and dumbest day of his twenty years on the force. Had the world gone loco? How was he supposed to catch this supposed *hand*? A hand? And what about Natasha? She'd probably turn into a puddle of tears and fears if they ever saw the thing. That's what they should call it, 'The Thing', like the old movie, he thought as he held the door of the patrol car open for Florence Goodavich.

"This is what we call a patrol car, Flo."

He turned the key in the ignition.

"You know, Charlie I am not an idjot."

"You got a boyfriend, Flo?"

"Men cannot handle, Flo."

"You're pretty cocky ain't ya, sister?"

Charlie said as they crossed Eight Avenue.

"A woman cop learns to be tough, Charlie. And besides Flo's last boyfriend was a real, how you say, SOB."

"I hear you, now look out your window; down here near the docks on 12th Avenue you'll find your usual cadre of transvestite-hookers and druggies. They're not so bad, but you got to wach'em when they break out into a catfight. There ain't nothing fiercer than a transvestite catfight."

"They look like nothing, Charlie, where is the real crime? The rough stuff."

"Oooh you're a real tough broad aren't ya, Goodavich? Well I'll tell ya things aren't as bad on the streets as they used to be. But that's because of us, see. We are the fortress between order and complete chaos."

"I like how you say tings, Charlie. My boyfriend didn't phrase his vords very well, but he is sorry now."

"How so?"Charlie said while turning the steering wheel.

"Oh, it's not important, Charlie," she said searching the window," say look over there isn't that one of those catvights?"

"Good work, Flo." Charlie said.

He pulled the car slowly up to the docks.

The street lamps barely illuminated the rotted surface of the pier. There they were; one in a smart little red number, and one in basic black. Scratching and clawing at each other like a pair of Bengals over a slab of raw tenderloin.

Charlie stopped the car and he flung the door open.

"You wait here, Flo and just watch how I handle this particular situation."

He proceeded to walk towards the dock when he noticed something strange. It wasn't the usual catfight. Those dames, or whatever, were being attacked by The Hand.   He picked up his pace and began shouting. "Don't move!"

The one in the little red number said.

"Honey, we ain't moving we're running."

"You have a funny way of running, "Charlie said, and then he saw the hand begin to clutch at her throat.

The Hand wasn't large, but quick. It was severed like it was ripped from the arm, but whose arm? Dried blood caked the skin. Those nails went on forever. It must have belonged to a dame.

Charlie quickly reached for it, and it latched onto his arm

Run," He hollered, shaking his arm like a bat that had just flown into a live wire.

They tore down the street tripping over their high heels, squawking at each other.

He kept thrashing his hand. Fuck, how was the thing moving? It should be dead. He felt it lunge towards his throat. God, I'm a goner, he thought. And then he saw Goodavivh standing directly in front of him pulling out her pistol. Great, he was going to be strangled by the hand from hell, or shot by his partner. It wasn't Charlie's day.

"Don't..." he tried to shout but the creature feature's grasp arrested his air pipe. He saw Goodavich take aim and instantly he felt the bullet whiz past his ear. Then like magic, he could feel his throat expand and the air return to his lungs. Frantically, he looked around. It had vanished!

"Damn, Goodavich," he said catching his breath as she ran toward him, "you are one hell of a shot."

"Thank you, Charlie. See a woman can handle a gun."

"You are no ordinary woman, Goodavich, you saved my life."

"I was just doing my job Charlie, even if you are just a man." She laughed. That's when Charlie noticed a strange smile on Flo's face like she was up to something. He brushed the thought aside. It was probably some Ruskie thing. Anyway, he was in the clear now, but the killer hand was still out there.

When he dropped Florence off on his way home he noticed she kept tugging at her arm while she walked up her stoop. Did she hurt her dainty little hand when she shot that gun? Was Miss hotshot a ninety pound weakling? Just like he thought, it was a lucky shot. But she sure looked good holding that pistol.

Just as Charlie was about to step on the gas he heard Goodavich calling. "Hey Charlie, vant to come in for a snack?"

"I don't know it's getting kind of late, Flo"

"Oh come on, Charlie, I saved your life."

She was right and she did look of sexy in the moonlight, even in her uniform, particularly in her uniform. Maybe she'd fix him something Russian, like vodka. Charlie had a hairy night and a little something to take the edge off might just do the trick, sweetheart.

As they climbed the stairs he took a whiff of her hair. Like butter, he thought, like the best kind of butter. She might be a lucky shot but she was hot.

She turned the key and they tumbled into her apartment. Without missing a beat she threw her holster down on the table, and she reached into the freezer. The bottle of vodka glistened in her hand.

"Say I was hoping you had vodka, little Nikita." Charlie said and he sat down on the sofa.

"I know, Charlie, a Russian always has vodka, right?"

She placed the bottle and two glasses down on the coffee table.

"Nice digs you have here, little girl."

"Now Charlie you can see Flo is no little, girl."

She could say that again. She was a big girl for sure.

Flo poured the vodka and said "So Charlie, do you have a girfvirend?"

And then she sat down on the couch next to Charlie tossing her hair.

"Charlie's not a one woman type of guy. But I did have this thing with a babe named Ginger a few years ago." Charlie said while he threw his feet up on the coffee table.

"So what happened to this Ginger?"

"She messed around with Beth Wiener's husband and now she's six feet under. Poor Ginger."

"Ah too bad, Charlie," he said, and then she drew closer to Charlie. Like a kitten she blew in his ear.

"Now listen, Natasha, we can't do no fooling around. We're partners."

"Oh do not vorry, Charlie." She said as she touched his knee." I'm not one of those little fragile American girls you're accustomed too. Flo understands a von voman man."

She kicked off her shoe.

Goodavich was something special all right. Just one night, one night of fireworks for Charlie and Flo, might be just what the doctor ordered. He could think about that crazy hand tomorrow.

She took his hand and led him into the bedroom. His eyes jumped when he saw the knives and swords covering the walls. Goodavich was an unusual female for sure. Maybe she had a thing for steel? It was probably another Ruskie thing.

"So you like collecting knives, I see." Charlie said while they fell on the bed

"Yes a hobby of mine. Guns are okay, you know but a knife really leaves a sting, don't you think so Charlie?"

She stretched out on the sheets.

"I guess so, but you know we can't carry knives on patrol, like it was the 12th century or something"

"Charlie, I'll bet you'd make a sexy Knight." She said, and

then she pulled Charlie over her.

After they did the nasty Charlie fell out of bed and he grabbed his pants. A good time is a good time but it was time to get home before Little Nikita started cozying up to him. Like he told her, Charlie isn't a one woman man. As he was pulling up the leg of his pants, Flo heard him and she cried. "Where are you going, Charlie?"

"I'll be shoving along, Princess."

"So soon? I knew you were just a Good Time Charlie."

"Now, honey, Charlie warned ya." He was about to remind her of her little manifesto about fragile American women when suddenly his cell phone rang . Saved by the bell, the thought while he rustled the phone out of his pants.

"Sergeant, Charlie Meyers, here."

"Oh shit, we'll be right there!"

He turned to Flo and said, "Looks like our night isn't over, Natasha, The hand just stuck again, down by the docks. Get dressed, Honey."

When they pulled up to the docks the whisper of daylight approaching swelled the sky. The sound of gulls and the creak of the wood were the only sounds they heard as they stepped up to the pier. The headlights of the coroners' car flashed on and off signaling them over. Next to the car they saw the victims. God, it was the little red number and the simple black number. Gheez they must have came back there right after he saved their lives, the crazy queens.

"Hey Charlie," The coroner said as he stepped out of his car.

"Hey Parker."

"I'm taking them in and I thought you might want to look 'em over first. Both strangled, and pretty violently. Look how deep the marks on their throats are."

"I've seen these two before, Parker. Earlier tonight we rescued them from that thing and they come right back here like homing pigeons the sad things." He said and then he pointed towards Flo. "Parker, this is my new partner Florence Goodavich,"

Flo waved and smiled to Parker while she leaned over the bodies.

"You're making out pretty good Charlie" Parker said.

"And what is that supposed to mean?" Charlie shot back.

"Calm down, Charlie," Parker said as he got back into his

car." Listen, if you have any questions, you know where to find me."

"Sure, sure."

They quietly watched Parker's car takeoff .Florence looked up at Charlie and said, "I thought he was taking the bodies."

"They'll send an ambulance, don't you worry your pretty head about it."

"It's sad, Charlie look at them."

Oh now she was getting all sensitive and ladylike on him. Didn't if figure? He knew he'd have his hands full from then on.

He turned and said. "That's how the cookie crumbles, Flo."

Then a strange smile appeared on Goodavich's face. It was the same off-the-wall smile she had before, right after she took her lucky shot. What was percolating under that Russian sleeve now?

"So Charlie tell me how does a cookie crumble?" Flo said and then she began to stand up. Forcefully, she brushed her hands off on the sides of her pants.

"What do you mean how does a cookie crumble? It's an expression, Natasha."

She started walking closer to Charlie, deliberately like she was planning, plotting, "You mean like not a one-woman man?"

"Well kind of, listen why are you acting so funny, little girl?"

"I'm not a little girl Charlie." She shrieked and she pointed her hand, waving it through the air like she was directing traffic. What was the crazy Ruskie up to now? Charlie thought, and then he saw The Hand careening towards him.

He lunged down on the pier.

"Shit, you are controlling that thing?"

"Da, I am, Charlie."

With a whoosh he felt the hand whiz past him. Like a shot he rolled over.

"What the fuck is going on? Are you insane?"

The hand crept up his leg. He began to thrash his foot against the wood.

"No I'm not insane I'm just a little girl and a stupid Ruskie and a von night stand and you're a big bad sergeant aren't you, Mister Charlie Meyers?" She raised her hand in the air again, and the creature rushed towards Charlie's neck.

Shit, he was a dead man now for real. He felt it latch onto his neck and squeeze at his throat. With a jerk, he pulled his gun out, and he took a shot at Goodavich.

She jumped and laughed. "Vat's the matter, Good Time Charlie?"

He couldn't break free. He felt the life leaving his body. The Hand clutched his throat tighter and tighter. He managed to push the thing away but it kept coming back stronger. He could hear her laughter. Done in by a floozy who couldn't stand one night stands.

The last thing Charlie saw was Flo's hands waving the creature on.

Charlie lay on the pier. His neck bloodied, blue and bruised, his eyes white and glassy.

Florence Goodavich stood over Charlie's body shaking her head. Slowly, she walked to the patrol car and she shimmied behind the wheel. She threw her arm wildly in the air and said,"Flo doesn't need you anymore," Then she pulled off her prosthetic hand revealing a severed arm.

She stuck her arm out the window and waved. The Hand followed.

Then Flo floored the gas and began to wildly cackle. "Bye-bye, Charlie."

About the author: Bruce Memblatt lives in New York City He has had his stories featured in such magazines as Aphellion, Static Movement, Danse Macarbe, SNM Horror Magazine, Jeani Rector's The Horror Zine, Deadman's Tome,The Piker Press, and many more.

THE LETTER
Elle Pryor

This is a letter about the past, the year 2050, a long time from now, but for you that could be only a week away. If you are reading this letter, if by some slim chance this is found, then your life is probably very different from mine.

Now, human years have become meaningless, the elders deciding their value at whim. A month of the past becomes a year and then is changed into a day. Here we work, live and eat as if we all woke up for the first time. Tomorrow everything may be destroyed, we could return home to find our apartments have disappeared, the buildings torn down. We could be told that our age is ten years younger or ten years older. Our birthdays could be moved to another point in the year. The calendar can be reduced or increased in length, the clocks made faster or slower.

Death takes place at the age of forty, or whenever our current birth certificate tells us we are forty. I write this letter at the age of thirty-nine but in reality I might be fifty. Years are constructed without restriction. There is no religion either, so no dramatic funerals or mourning, no gravestones. When we die we leave no trace. The books we read about the past and future are changed often but nobody admits to noticing the new omissions and inclusions. We all live fictional lives that we tell the truth about and factual lives that we lie about. Our personal histories are deleted, our lives reinvented.

We have become accustomed to sleeping at any time, either night or day and surviving on the length of sleep decreed. When people sleep, they jerk tensely through the rapid eye movement part of the night. Some shout out while unconscious and others scream, dreams are no longer allowed. Every day we are new; we have no past, future or identity. Time is fluid and relative but rigid and imposing, a strict task master who controls our lives.

If you understand this letter and my description of time then you are before our civilization. You believe history is the past whereas ours recognizes history as the future. To you, history is finished but to us it is alive and is going to greet us. It is the past that is approaching not the future. We will be replaced by the past.

I live in the city which is patrolled constantly by the police. They drive along the roads with their sirens blazing making us paranoid and lethargic. Alienation is an archaic word for us though because people here have never been taught that they belong to or are a part of an organization, society has ceased to exist.

If you do not live in the city, it is forbidden to mix with people who live in the country. Country people do not notice the heat of the sun on their faces, they are not afraid of wide open spaces. The city people react negatively to space and sun, we live in homes which are piled on top of each other in tall tower blocks squashed together so that the sun cannot reach the spaces in between.

Our dwellings are tiny, everybody lives alone but to call our living conditions adequate would be an exaggeration. In the night when people are sleeping you can hear every cough, shout, scream or snore through the thin walls of the room. At home we are still unable to relax; the televisions have cameras behind the screens filming us. As we watch we are being watched by the caretaker.

He has the power to knock on our doors and enter at any time. When you laugh at the wrong time at the television or when you do not laugh at the right joke the caretaker arrives and questions you. It is a crime to have a personality different to anyone else. We have been taught that what we feel is wrong and that feeling itself is a delusion.

Sometimes he knocks on the door just because he knows the television makes people forget their surroundings; forget they are the person they have been told they are. The visits from the caretaker ensure that nobody drifts away and everyone remembers who they are supposed to be.

These visits can weigh on your mind like an acidic poison, creating resentment and anger. The caretaker is worse than the work manager. He wraps himself around your insides and slithers through your mind until you are unable to think of anything else. The sirens outside compel us to stay off the streets and just as our minds start to relax the caretaker knocks on the door to check that our breathing is not irregular.

The only clothes that are necessary are our work uniforms. We do not wear anything else. Eating takes place at work, we never cook and can't choose what we eat at meal times. We do not own our homes or their contents, if we possess something then this adds to our sense of identity. The authorities wish to subdue our egos. Physical beauty changes from week to day until we are neither ugly nor beautiful, fat becomes thin and strength becomes weakness.

We are forced to attend human, dog and horse races. A night at the races can feature any of these elements. However it is rare that anybody or thing wins or loses, normally the competitors cross the line at exactly the same time. If you are lucky enough to watch a race where there is a loser or winner then you are part of an event that people will discuss for years.

Libraries are the only place where we are allowed to read books. They are propaganda tools but some of the authors have hidden messages within the text. It takes years of practice to recognize their presence but sometimes a pattern emerges on the page. Therefore this type of literature has continued to be popular.

One of our most famous plays has a simple narrative. A woman goes to work one day and her computer is not functioning correctly, she says, "I feel annoyed that my computer is malfunctioning." and then the actor will look at the audience and make an expression of anger. Another well-known line from the play is, "I am pleased that the computer is being fixed." then the actor will face the audience and smile. These expressions are drilled into us. In order to properly convey the emotions described we should mimic as closely as possible the faces of the actors.

Intonation of speech is strictly regulated so that it is possible to be insolent now just by raising your voice at the wrong moment. With all the cameras focused on us we know that every facial expression, every hand gesture and leg position is recorded and translated by experts. Even coughing is a suspicious activity and people have been killed for being enemies of the elders for coughing at the wrong time.   When someone is ill they are removed from the workplace and placed under strict supervision, however serious their condition. Sneezing could be faked and a secret message to somebody else. There must not be any deviance in the workplace. Illness is frowned upon; it is almost a criminal trait.

Nevertheless, despite this we have invented a new way of communicating. I am unable to reveal to you how we stay human but when you arrive in this year you must be vigilant and concentrate.

I am writing about the past although for you it is the future. During the year 2050, another form of communication was invented by a city person. The communication invented is not carried via sound or speech and yet we are able to converse freely with each other while the authorities are standing only meters away.

I am in my thirty ninth year and about to be dead, I wish I could meet with you but it is impossible. When you are at work remember that something subtle is surrounding you. If I sound excited as I write this, it is because the changes are profound. Evolution manifested itself before my eyes in the year 2050. When you reach here remember that this letter is a gift and that you are safe and that once you are able to converse you will be able to endure the harshness of this regime. Once I was the future but by now I am dead and now you are the future and you are years away from me but at the moment I am alive, writing this and that is the only fact I can offer you, the only certainty.

***

Dear Elder,

You have asked me to write down my thoughts about the letter I found and read. Let me assure you that I found most of it strange and depressing. It was rolled up in a container buried in the dry mud of a rocky field. The container was not difficult to open despite the rust. The paper was curled at the edges and brown in color as if it had been hidden for many years.

It seems that the writer's city is now the country, his apartment razed to the ground. My job is to sift stones from the soil so that it can be irrigated. I have read books in the library about the past and the future and I am almost able to understand the writer's culture. The sun does beat on my face though and I never noticed the heat before I read the letter.

I think the letter I found from the future was sweet in a way, the final ravings of a person about to die. It is kind of him to want to help others even if his ideas are crazy. I am glad that I do not live in the city, in the country people are more relaxed, less likely to have such fantasies. The reference to this secret communication perplexes me and at the same time amuses me. In a way I feel sorry for him because his mind is sick; his belief that books contain secret messages clearly indicates this.

He also owned a work uniform. The only clothing I have is the clothing provided for my job, like the man in the letter. He seems to regard this as a negative aspect of life yet in the countryside our uniforms are crucial. We wear different colors to distinguish ourselves from other field workers. In the field where I work, I am wearing red because I am searching for stones. In the same field another group wears orange because they are searching for weeds another wears black because they drop seeds into the ground.

It is a privilege to receive a letter from the future but of course I gave it to you, my ruler. I understand that you are searching for the writer now, before they die. The world they describe seems so different to this year of 2049. I was also informed that the letter may be put into a museum to illustrate how superior our world has become, compared to the future. It will be available for everyone to read. I was told that a scientist has tested the paper and ink and found that the letter has been aged as being twenty years old. We should congratulate ourselves on our achievements and that we have avoided the problems of the future. Life is good for us. I can choose what I eat at mealtimes now whereas the writer of this letter couldn't.

Luckily enough, I do not live in a small room in a tower block. My home is a farmhouse shared with the other country dwellers working this land. When people live in such close proximity it is important that they regulate their behavior and speech so that they can live together harmoniously. It would be very dangerous if we all had different opinions and personalities and result in many conflicts. The cameras he complains about protect us from harm, without them we would be vulnerable. The police make sure that we can live without fear.

I also attend the events described in the letter but they are not an indication that something is wrong with our civilization. Racing dogs, horses and humans are conditioned and trained in similar conditions. So of course, it is not surprising that there is no winner or loser at the races. The play he describes is my favorite and I can recite most of the lines.

History is important but so is the present and I now have a place to sleep, food to eat and the company of my peers, time does not matter to me. If time changes, I will still go to work and sleep when it is necessary. I do not understand what he means when he says our lives are reinvented; our past changes because time is not constant.

Thank you for telling me that one of the lookouts may have written the letter. Stories of their lifestyles fill us country workers with amazement; they live wildly. They are often to blame for any discord and discuss subjects that have never interested us. They live on the borders of our country and apart from normality. I am not surprised one of them is responsible.

Since the letter, a few lookouts have been executed by our wise elders. A couple of workers from our community were sent as replacements, I am pleased that I have increased your faith in our loyalty to you.

Forever I thank the Elders.

***

The next morning began as any other for the stone searcher. She put on her red overalls and joined the rest of the community for breakfast. The official year was 2049 but it was actually 2060. She collected her food from the machines located at various positions around the canteen choosing a bowl of cereal containing predominantly vitamin B from one machine and a carton of soya milk from another.

Before she could sit at the nearest table a worker at another table stood up, pulled out a chair and beckoned for her to sit there. It was not usual to do this and normally the managers would have objected but assumed that because the woman was now a favorite of the elders her work colleague wanted to sit next to her. It was actually because they were having a discussion on the table she had originally wanted to sit on, even though nobody was speaking. Her presence would have confused them; the other workers knew that they should not sit at this table by the way one of the seed throwers sitting there was holding his knife and fork.

On that table everybody was eating different breakfasts. One person ate cereal fortified with vitamin C, another munched on cereal fortified with iron. Iron meant action and the piece of green Kiwi fruit on his tray indicated that he favored collective action against the managers, and by the way he kept glancing at the clock on the wall and then the window, the others knew that he meant, now, not in three weeks or six months but right at that moment and it was a frightening proposition.

News of plans for a country-wide rebellion had reached them the evening before. This table was the head table and anybody entering the canteen would have been able to understand the situation and communicate their own opinion by choosing an identical or similar breakfast to one of the people sitting there.

On another table almost every person was eating the cereal fortified with iron and a kiwi fruit, spooning their food into their mouths with a look of determination on their faces. Others ate yoghurt and chopped fruit; these people were not for rebelling and doubted they could win. The argument commenced between the workers. Some of those people using spoons scraped them against their bowls; others dipped them into the milk or yoghurt quietly. Some people used their knives to cut their fruit, others bit into the flesh with gusto. A neighbor would suddenly start taking tiny mouthfuls of food instead of the hills she had previously heaped onto her spoon. Across from her, a man began to chew loudly whilst his neighbor suddenly began to slurp his drink.

On one table a man ate with his mouth open and next to him a woman cut down heavily on a piece of toast scraping the plate below. Somebody put more sugar on their porridge which meant he was accusing the woman opposite him of confusing the issue and showing a lack of courage. A few people cleared their throats or swallowed loudly.

When the breakfast meal was nearly at an end somebody on the head table dropped their knife and fork. This man was always dropping things but this was the first time he had dropped his knife and fork at the same time. He was eating red strawberries, the shape of hearts covered with natural yoghurt. His actions meant that those people opposing the revolt had lost the argument.

On each table a country worker stood up, a few more slowly

and reluctantly than the others. The managers began to frown but before they could react further, they were attacked swiftly by the standing workers. Similar and identical events took place throughout the land, in the country and in the city. The lookouts in the mountains turned around and became the invading enemies, marching towards the elder's buildings. They began attacking from the outside.

Inside these buildings, office workers fought their managers and the elders. The blood shed in these buildings was high. The population was forced to act quickly once the letter was given to the rulers. It had been unlucky that one of the few people who hadn't learnt to communicate had found the letter. Nevertheless her actions and the letter began a series of events that led to the overthrow of the ruling powers. The rulers were not able to resist the attack because of its scale and they did not have enough time to work out the language which had evolved over almost twenty years. The woman who had found the letter had never realized there was another way to communicate. Like a mother teaching her baby to speak, the teachers were unable to tell their pupils that they were being taught.

About the author: Elle Pryor lives in Florida and writes short stories and poetry. She's had stories published in South Jersey Underground, Muscadine Lines: A Southern Journal, Black Lantern Publishing, (A Brilliant) Record Magazine and Crows Nest. One of her stories is going to be included in the Static Movement anthology Caught by Darkness.

Just In Case
Edward Rodosek

An endless, completely flat, glittery white plain extends to a horizon that trembles in violent heat. The glaring, violet-white sun, half the size ours on Earth, now shines nearly direct overhead. Its sharp rays dazzle my eyes and burn my forehead despite the visor I've lowered on my helmet. I look round, at first only hastily, and when I'm sure no immediate surprises are in store for me, I plot the most promising course with my binoculars. Well–there is only one course I can take because everywhere else is nothing but empty bareness.

Only in one direction, not too far away to the right, is the plain is strewn with a number of huge rocks; some as big as houses. Most of these boulders are jagged, irregular in form, and the night-black shadows among them contrast sharply with the absolute whiteness that surrounds me. I carefully check my oxygen supply, the pressure in my spacesuit, the external temperature and the other most significant things. All the indicators are green, all the values within the limits. I move on to inspecting the arms, attentively checking what they've given me from the arsenal before the campaign: a blaster, a nerve paralyzer, several microgrenades, and a set of capsules with poisonous gas. Enough arms for all possible cases and for any conceivable enemy.

Finally, a forefinger reaches down to the cuff of my left boot, extracting my old, faithful knife. It is made of cold-forged steel; its sharp, glittering blade has been hardened with a laser beam. The slightly curved point and jagged edge of the knife are filling me with unshakeable trust. It is hidden in my boot because one's not allowed to carry any weapon not supplied by the armory. But this knife is the only thing which efficacy I really believe in. It was with me in the last war and helped me through countless dangers.

I adjust both straps of my heavy rucksack and start marching towards those huge rocks. Now and then, I lift my binoculars and eye them. But I still can't distinguish any details among those dark shadows. When I reach them, I'll have to be extremely careful. As soon as I get there, I must immediately–

A sudden, violent blow knocks me to the dusty ground with such force that I roll several yards away. Only the long training drills of the past save me from fainting, the imparted reflexes enable me to bow down in combat position with my blaster aimed ahead and up.

Just above me some huge beast, a monster as from a nightmare, is flying in wobbly circles, watching me with hostile eyes. It's like those pterodactyls from Jurassic times, but this one is the size of a training plane. The monster glides above me, examines me—a welcome lunch that has been kind enough to offer itself to him. And then, suddenly, the monster begins to throw itself down; his colossal wings are now a dark, swelling shadow. I aim my weapon, the blaster throws up a blaze of hissing hotness; but the silhouette of the monster grows and grows, like a rushing locomotive, my finger on the trigger is paralyzed...

The next instant, the monster slams down close to my feet on the stony ground that trembles from the stroke. The tip of the monster's wing strikes my shoulder so I fall again. Still, I'm on my feet again in a flash, the barrel of my blaster is aimed at the horrible dark mass in the middle of a cloud of dust. The dreadful bulk now lies motionless; a stench smell arising from it penetrates even through the special filters in my nostrils. I poke it most carefully with the tip of my boot, twice, three times. I don't want any more surprises. Yet, I could have saved myself these tests. The monster is dead; about this there is no more doubt.

I sit down on the dusty ground, for my knees are still very uncertain. Only now do I perceive some odd, salty taste in my mouth: my saliva is slightly colored by blood. My shoulder hurts, and there I discover a long gash in my thermosuit. I have to find the silicon spray and some plastic yarn in my rucksack to try to repair that damage. And this as soon as possible, before this hellish heat singes my thermosuit.

Hours later I move on. My thermosuit is stitched together. However I had to take it off during patching, so now I'm gasping from the unbearable heat. Fortunately the air here is all right, I don't even need to use filters any more. The sweat trickling from my forehead into my eyes almost blinds me, and I can hardly wait for the thermostat in my suit to cool me down again.

I still can't see anything suspicious or even odd either in the air or between the boulders on the nearby plane. Nothing dangerous anywhere, no movement at all. Still, I don't believe my senses, not quite. Just recently I've been taken in by a similar feeling. But I won't any more, ever. No, sir.

Systematically, I examine a circular area the size of a football field in front of me. Repeatedly, I take only a couple of steps, and then I stop, watching in all directions, listening carefully, distrustfully smelling the air.

All around me there are white, toothed rocks with sharp edges and dark depressions among them. Not until I'm entirely close to them do I see they're dusted with rubble and sand. I can't see any traces, footprints, or scents of paws or ruts. Nothing of the kind. Now I have to fix in the ground five or six sensor sticks near the boundaries of the covered area. They'll warn me of every possible change in surroundings—at every movement, at the merest shake of the ground, they'll make louder even the weakest noise, sending it all to my earphones. I must be completely safe at least for the next half-hour, so I can take my lunch and maybe also take a little rest.

During my break nothing occurs. I rise, stretch out a bit and set forth. I've no idea in which direction I should go. I haven't the slightest clue who or what I might meet. The only thing I do know for sure is, anybody or anything that comes across me would be my mortal enemy, a lethal threat to my life. He or it will all try to kill me if I don't kill him first. Therefore I mustn't hesitate, not even for a fraction of a second. That would be fatal for me. Every stupid tarrying of that kind would mean the difference between life and death—*my* life and *my* death.

Suddenly I hear a slight sound in my headphones. I instantly bow down, my eyes scanning at all directions, my hardened body a taught steel spring, all my tensed muscles tough, tenacious, prepared for instant, effective action. I'm turning into a wild beast, a dangerous predator, into a machine, programmed for slaughter.

I take a couple of quiet, stealthy steps along the narrow crack among the rocks. Then I rise slowly, by inches, and try to get a peep over a low ledge overgrown with thin, dry grass.

After a few moments I can, finally, catch sight of them. Three deformed creatures of malicious appearance, resembling a combination of hyena and gigantic octopus. A fire burns in their midst. A whole collection of weapons hangs from them, with more on the ground around them.

Although I'm standing completely immobile, one of them looks towards me and reaches, lightning-like, for his belt. My trained reflex orders my arm to fling a hand grenade among them and to press my body at the ground. A horrible bang, a searing flash. Not until the hail of fragments stops do I dare peep out again over the rock.

Two of the disgusting creatures are laying motionless on the ground, but the third one, although bleeding, aims his weapon on me. His shot strikes the ledge just above my head and a few drops of molten stone drip on my helmet. I finished him with my blaster.

It's over. I can draw a deep breath again. I sit down on the ground and wipe some cold sweat from my forehead. My palms are damp; one of my eyelids is twitching nervously. Nevertheless, everything is all right. My quick reactions have saved me once again. Otherwise, I would now be laying on the dusty, rocky ground, with those space monsters trading jokes over my corpse.

A bit later, I stand up and decide to move onwards. It doesn't matter where to. Simply forward. Now the sole important thing is to stay alert. I must remain a predator. Not a prey, a predator.

Suddenly, a wall emerges just thirty steps in front of me. How in heaven could that has happened? Why didn't I notice it much earlier? How had I overlooked such an obvious thing despite my continuous watchfulness? I reproach myself. Apparently, my double success in the last conflicts has soothed, made me weak. And that is dangerous. Such behavior might be lethal for me. I swear to myself that this will never happen again. From now on, I have to be quicker still, even more firm, even more prepared to kill. Otherwise, I won't survive.

The wall is vertical; its surface is smooth, planed, almost polished. No doubt an artificial object. When I approach, I can see a tiny, rectangular break in it. It's like a barely visible frame, a bit higher than me. From somewhere behind the wall a high, harsh sound utters forth. Three times, every time only for a few seconds. What could this be? Probably, a new trap for dupes. But now I'm prepared for everything, even the most unexpected possibilities. I squeeze my blaster in my right hand, a paralyzer in my left hand; a few micro hand grenades hang from my belt. I make a careful step forward-

At that moment that frame on the wall slides sideways and an opening appears, in it a uniformed human figure. Yet another new guise of a space enemy! Simultaneously with that thought, my right forefinger squeezes the trigger. But my blaster remains mute, and the alien at the door grins scornfully at me. I jerk him with my paralyzer, but this also fails. Then, despairingly, I reach for my micro hand grenades—though I've a foreboding these wouldn't go off at all.

And they don't. My entire stock of weapons, all these wonders of cutting-edge technology prove to be useless, and all my efforts to fight are in vain. And this mocking alien knows that all too well. But... he doesn't know the whole truth.

He doesn't know about my own knife.

In a split second I pull it out of my boot and fiercely stab it into the alien's abdomen. I watch how his haughty smile freezes on his face, and then fades to an expression of enormous astonishment. He collapses limply, like a rag-doll, in front of my feet. Even now someone violently slams my head, three other aliens jump on me, wrenching my arms behind my back, then knocking me down to the ground and pinning me there.

So, that's the end, definitely. I'm aware that I'm beaten. Still I haven't simply surrendered to them, those sons of bitches! I've made them work for it. Let these bastards see what we Earthlings are made of. No doubt they'll think twice about whether it pays to invade our planet.

As they push and pull me away I glance backwards, and my eyes drift over to the large, shiny inscription about the door they hustle me through:

PSYCHO – SIMULATOR

Authorized Military Personnel Only

About the author: Edward Rodosek is a Construction Engineer and Senior Professor in University of Ljubljana, Slovenia, European Union. Beside his professional work he writes science fiction. More than sixty of his short stories have been published in SF magazines in USA, UK, Australia and India. Recently he published in USA the collection of short stories *Beyond Perception*.

ADRIANNA'S JOURNEY
Robert William Shmigelsky

Adrianna clutched tightly the golden looped cross in the palm of her hand.

Standing to the side of a weathered, rock-strewn trail winding through a newly created mountain pass, Adrianna looked on with silent lament cast on her face, emerald-green eyes coursing backwards through past events to the present.

In the back of her eyes, she relived the betrayal and murder of kings, the battles that ended the lives of countless heroes, their eventual defeat at a vastly superior enemy and subsequent flight to the White Mountains, hoping there to find refuge.

Interrupting her from these sights, the ragged remnants of Adrianna's people, who expressed their gratitude to her as they passed her by as they hurried down to the other side of the mountain pass.

"Thank you, my lady."

"How can we ever repay you?"

"May you have many sons and daughters...?"

Her long auburn hair gliding behind her, her emotions hid behind her resilient face, Adrianna looked at each of them in turn, nodded and said she would see them soon on the other side – a lie.

A talented clairvoyant by many accounts, Adrianna unfortunately had the burden of foreknowing events that others did not. That alone left her with the responsibility to act, knowing that if she did not – no one would.

Around her, the tops of Adrianna's eyes perceived the white-tipped peaks of the lofty mountain range once thought to be impassable. A gift from the heavens, her father had used the remainder of time imbued inside the cross to weather the mountain pass into the side of the mountains. While only a few moments had passed for herself, her brother Adrian and those around them, for their father a thousand years had passed as temporal winds rapidly grinded away grey granite rock with whooshing torrents of icy cold winds and rains.

When the temporal winds ceased and the swirling green

barrier of magic fell, they saw inside, but all that remained was a frail, shivering old man lying face down in the graveled ground.

Taking a moment to realize it was him, Adrianna recalled running to her father's side, cradling him in her tender loving arms then watching as he finally succumbed to the ravages of time, having used the cross – until this moment – to keep him young while those around him aged and turned to dust.

In fact, only a matter of moments before, Adrianna herself had looked older than her father.

Adrianna's eyes momentarily glanced at the cairn of stones piled at the top of the mountain pass. Looking away from such a sight, Adrianna looked north to the far side of the mountain pass; pass the climbing bodies, hefting on their shoulders what belongings they had managed to take with them.

There, like a snow globe, within a glass-like barrier, she saw falling snow hanging in the air upon the remains of castles, halls, towers and mansions, the shores and sea-worn cliffs of a snow-white peninsula and the icy blue waves of the Endless Sea stilled in mid-break.

Her eyes stretched into the sea as far they could perceive and her clairvoyant gaze caught sight of far off typhoons, twisting and turning beyond the outer rim of the continent, keeping the race of men to it.

In her mind, Adrianna thought of the brave two hundred knights and their captain – hidden before her in the center of the barrier – that had volunteered their lives to buy the time needed for the last of their kind to lock their swords together, weave their magic and freeze the kingdom of Palador in that moment of time.

Her clairvoyant gaze announced itself out of the netherworld and resumed control once more of her eyes, devouring the green irises of her eyes and replacing them with the brilliant hues and tinctures of the vision unfolding before her.

In her eyes, she saw the barrier shimmer and vanish and the curse lift. Clad in dark plate, soldiers on foot and on summoned black steeds – followed closely by the darkened distortions of shadow auras half-veiling the staff-wielding figures within – proceeded to march forth towards the mountain pass in pursuit of the cross.

Although Adrianna's body shook and her mind trembled with

absolute fear, she steadied herself and remained strong, refusing to shut her eyes or turn away. Not only was she determined to keep up a brave front, she knew from past experiences, the pain one felt when a seer tried to ignore a vision: like a bandage being peeled off your eyes instead of your skin.

Almost as once Adrianna's sight returned to her.

The vision over, Adrianna watched as the last of her people descended to safety. The last pair, an old couple, noticed she had yet to turn and follow.

"Are you alright, my dear?" the woman asked, the two of them stopping before Adrianna.

Adrianna turned and looked at the couple.

"In a moment I will be," she answered. "Please, do not worry about me. I will follow soon after."

She did not know whether those last few words were the truth or not.

"As you wish," the woman said to Adrianna in a slightly suspicious tone. She squinted and gave Adrianna a long look and for a moment her time-worn eyes seemed to press against Adrianna before she decided to take her eyes off her and turn around.

Adrianna tried to keep the expression on her face from changing. She watched and waited as the couple turned slowly around, headed off, supported by their gnarled walking sticks, and hobbled out of sight around the curving bend of the pass.

Alone, Adrianna turned and faced the first kingdom of men once more. She waited until sure the last of the people were safely through the mountain pass.

She clenched more tightly the looped cross in her hand. Using the last of the power bestowed to her lineage over a thousand years ago, Adrianna closed her eyes and with a single thought froze time a small radius around her while leaving herself relatively unaffected.

The oak staff she held in her other hand she raised high into the air. In combination with her other magical talents she learned under the tutelage of her sage master, she flung her arms, shouted spell mantras and built up a great chandelier of earth in the sky above her. When she sensed the earth hovering above was large enough to close the mountain pass, she opened her eyes and resumed time.

The earth fell down upon her. In unison, a bright blue aura

flowed out of the cross and appeared around Adrianna, protecting her and deflecting the collapsing earth around her.

As her surroundings darkened around her, so too did her sight as the weight of that happening pushed her conscious to the far recesses of her mind...

***

Adrianna's eyes opened, but they saw nothing.

Instinctively, she searched for her staff with her hands. Her hands felt something hard beneath her; dirt crammed into her nails then her left hand caught hold of something familiar. Adrianna leaned on her staff and quickly pulled herself off of the ground.

In unison to the thought of brightening her surroundings, a light came to life from the white stone inset at the tip of her staff and illuminated her immediate surroundings.

Adrianna redirected the light around her and found herself in a large, domed cavern chamber riddled with dark passages. She looked up momentarily, shined the light towards the ceiling, but saw only darkened abyss above.

Grimacing, Adrianna brought the light back down before her: her entire body felt broken – as if she had fallen off a cliff. And her mind seemed half closed to her. She no longer felt the pain that accompanied her clairvoyant visions, which gave her slight pause: she had grown accustomed to them and now that they were not there – she wasn't sure how to react. Should she lament the loss of one of her powers or celebrate the loss of a curse? Either way, she figured she would only be able to manage the most basic of spells for now.

She wondered what had happened and how she had managed to survive, momentarily dwelling on her father.

Then Adrianna saw a flash of blue light as she remembered the last thing she saw before passing out. She pulled the cross up to her eyes. Was this tiny little piece of jewelry responsible for all this and that glowing aura that had engulfed and protected her...?

This is truly a gift from the heavens, Adrianna thought to herself.

She wished to give it more thought, but at the moment she thought it was more prudent to remove herself from this place.

Her staff illuminating the entrance of one of the tunnels before her, Adrianna turned, sauntered off, using her staff as support, and headed down into the tunnel, it being as good as any.

Upon reaching deeper into the tunnel, Adrianna saw that the sides of the tunnel were riddled with tiny cracks and small holes and pockets. If the cross was somehow responsible for creating this cave, a tremendous amount of energy must have gone into it...

Here and there more tunnels crisscrossed with the one she was on. Adrianna ignored them and proceeded on the one she was on. She knew the quickest and surest way of finding her way out of here to be staying on a straight line.

After what seemed to have been days spent walking through darkness, accompanied by only the sound of her footsteps echoing off the hard granite cavern floor, finally, Adrianna glimpsed light at the end of the tunnel.

At long last, Adrianna murmured out loud to herself before she hurriedly hobbled to the exit of the cave, the strength of her legs having yet to return to her, and stepped outside.

Adrianna had to cover her eyes with her hand, the sun being unusually bright at this moment – that or she had spent weeks underground and her eyes were no longer used to the sunlight.

Two fierce, blistering winds swept down on Adrianna from both sides of her body, sending shivers down her spine. She tried to brace herself against them, wrapping her rubicund cloak tightly around the supple curves of her body, but to little prevail.

How unbecoming of wind, she thought to herself – *wind* coming from two directions. Her eyes adjusted somewhat from the glare and she was able to lower her hand and see before her. Wondering where she had emerged to, Adrianna gave her surroundings a quick look. By the look of things, she had arisen in an entirely different realm. Encircling before her like a king's crown, stood a far off ring of snowy-white mountain peaks standing majestic against the sun. A narrow, wind-swept vale sloped steeply down before her into highly eroded gorges and winding paths, which went off in both directions, continued out of sight beyond the slopes of the vale.

Adrianna, again, momentarily thought of her father, but she quickly pushed the thought aside.

Behind them, a second range of mountains ran off in one direction before fading into the distance, but the peaks of these mountains were slanted away from Adrianna as if a Titan had leaned against them, making them that way.

Adrianna wondered what could bend mountains like that.

Wondering where she had come out of, Adrianna swung around and saw the tall granite base of a great mountain peak, stretching up past the clouds, higher than the mountain crown around it.

Adrianna stumbled backwards a few steps as she tried to get a better look at it. Once Adrianna recovered, she swung back around, intending to figure out which way to head next, but both sides of the vale looked equally uninviting: wide stretches of rugged land, stretching out to what appeared to be nowhere in particular.

In the end, Adrianna decided to head back into the cave. First of all, she wanted to get out of this blasted wind that kept soaring relentlessly around her, biting her exposed flesh wherever it could find it. Already, she could feel parts of her ears start to turn pink. Secondly, her insides twisted tightly with hungry; but more importantly, if she waited until night – perhaps the stars would reveal the path she should take.

Adrianna sat down on the floor of the cave. After hesitating for a moment, she looked down before her and got straight to it. She channeled with her hands and an orb of light appeared before her as she conjured herself a glass of water, some cheese and a small loaf of bread. She ate and drank and she waited for the sky to darken.

As she did so, the wind gave no hint of dying or slowing down. Through the day, it remained steadfast.

Before long, the slopes outside and the entrance of the cave dimmed and the sky went dark as the sun lowered itself beyond the rim of the mountains.

The wind still remaining steadfast, Adrianna climbed up to her feet, wrapped her cloak around her body, and headed outside into the wind blazing into the darkness.

Looking up at the star-spangled sky, she immediately recognized two constellations: to the east, the ranger sidestepping into dimensional shadows and to the north, the dragoon riding the high winds.

While the land around her told Adrianna she was in an entirely different place, the sky above her told her she was near the same position as yesterday.

Why the fates sought to confuse her, Adrianna could only assume. She felt slightly unnerved, no longer being connected to her clairvoyant powers. Since childhood, she could not remember a time where they did not provide her with the answers she sought.

Well, she said to herself: her people went south and the ranger's arrow points south; so that was the direction she decided to head herself.

Following the arrow, Adrianna swung left and headed south down the mountain vale. She entered the gorge at the bottom and began winding her way along. Travelling at the thickest time of the night, the shadowed nooks and crannies of the place seemed like the perfect hiding places for monsters and other vile creatures of the night; but surprisingly, besides the wind churning around her, she saw or heard nothing that might indicate possible perils or wildlife. It was as if a hand had reached down from the heavens, grabbed every living creature in the vicinity and taken them with it.

Nearly half way into the night, Adrianna found herself approaching the southern rim of the mountain crown. This up close at night, the mountains looked like long shadowed fingers stretching up as if part of a game.

Adrianna found a path leading up and climbed out of the gorge. She walked tiredly up the steep southern slope to the base of the mountain crown. Searching for a way through, she skimmed the rim when not far along she happened upon a narrow chasm leading into the crown.

She headed down the path of this chasm, but nearly a quarter of the way through the path narrowed into a small cleft. Turning sideways, she entered this cleft and began sliding through. Half way along, the cleft widened again and Adrianna found herself climbing up ridge after ridge. As the sun began its climb to its high perch behind her, she sensed she was almost there and the path leveled off before her, allowing her to continue at her leisure.

Soon after, Adrianna arrived at the ledge of a high cliff-top overlooking a small grassy green valley. At the center of which, long already built, stood a shining white castle within a castle surrounded by a rich and vibrant town with brightly colored tiled roofs, tilting downwards towards the bustling cobbled streets below.

Recognizing a temporal castle when she saw one, she knew at once her people were safe, that her brother Adrian had led them to safety down the mountain pass. But how did it come to this point? Her eyes could see that much time had passed. She knew that meant her brother and those she knew were most likely long dead. Still, despite what she saw before her, she could not believe how much time had passed.

She surveyed the surrounding landscape in search for clues. Around the castle and its town were the rolling foothills, which went up and down on, each hill getting bigger than the one before it. Here and there vast meadows of flowers of every imaginable color were in the height of bloom. Abreast the high valley slopes; the forests were tall and spread out, casting long shadow against the sunset.

Adrianna turned and looked over her shoulder. To the west and the east, pass the mountain crown, beyond the lower mountains of the valley, she saw the fading blue horizon etched upon the slopes of familiar White Mountains. As she had seen before, on both sides, the mountains closest to her were slanted away from Adrianna as if pushed aside.

Then she the only possible explanation latched itself onto her mind.

The aura from the cross had thrust the White Mountains apart, forming the mountain crown; then, as the earth fell from above, the earth piled on top of the aura, forming the grotto Adrianna had woken up in and the wearer of the mountain crown: the mountain itself.

Adrianna surveyed the surrounding landscape one last time.

Absorbing such a sight, she clenched the looped cross in her hands and brought it before her: it was over objects such as this that had awoken greed in the hearts of men and began their descent into shadow. It would be a shame to bring such an object to this new world. Adrianna did not need to be a clairvoyant anymore to know that if she did – what would eventually come to pass. She also knew could not throw it away for someone else to stumble on.

Such a vision at the forefront of her thoughts, Adrianna looked on with silent lament cast on her face as she gave her people one last look before turning back around and returning the way she came, knowing she could never rejoin them – only set sight upon them from a distance, from time to time.

About the author: Robert is an aspiring fantasy writer trying to improve his writing. Robert has been writing fantasy for himself in his spare time for the last seven years, but only now has begun writing for others.

Besides reading and writing, some of his hobbies include computers and history. He has a dry sense of humor, which he blames his stepfather for. Also, he has a habit of making history jokes no one but he understands. He is currently working as a certified residential care aide (nursing assistant) in beautiful British Columbia to support his writing.

Suttee
Jennifer Lyn Parsons

I watched the solider mount the imposing flight of steps stretching from the courtyard. I squinted my eyes, straining them until he drew close enough for me to make out his face. The news he carried was a burden on his features, and I knew then what he had to tell me would change my life forever.

I felt it deep in my bones, the overnight shift of power. It woke me from sleep and I had not returned to my bed. I knew long before the body was presented to me with all the pomp and ceremony befitting my husband's stature. I'm not sure how I knew, a change in the air perhaps, or some long buried natural instinct. My husband, the King, was dead and with him went my past, present and future.

His body was laid in state for the people, his people, to come and pay their last respects. The Queen, they were told, was too overcome with grief to attend the wake, but in fact I was simply overwhelmed with the numerous arrangements for the king's final journey. It was a week later, as we boarded the starship bound for Kalmisto, that I was finally free to work through all the implications his death meant for me. Walking through the empty corridors of the castle and out into the sunlight, I focused on the positive changes my husband's death brought to me.

There was a certain kind of freedom that awaited me, of that I was sure. No longer would I have to endure his tiresome monthly visits to my bedchamber. No more would he taunt me at court, telling me I had no right meddling in his affairs when I offered my advice to the council, that aging body of ne'er do wells. The years of antagonism that defined our relationship were at last an end. As I made my way past the throngs lining the causeway, I was thankful for the thick veil obscuring my face from view. I felt heat rise in my cheeks. Even as he lay in state, thoughts of the king and his council still brought my blood to a boil.

When I arrived in my private stateroom aboard the colossal ship, I dismissed my handmaidens and removed the heavy cloth from my head. The room offered little in the way of comforts, but a soft couch was mounted in front of a large viewport and it was here I settled myself to watch the rest of the party board. As I did so, my thoughts drifted back to my earliest days as wife to the king. Searching my memory, I rooted out the exact time the cracks appeared in the façade of our life together, the beginning of the end you might say.

I only saw the young man that one time, wrapped in my husband's arms when I came to him in the night, but it was enough. I was a young bride then, naive and hoping to gain my new husband's good graces and attention. After that night I no longer sought my husband's bed for I knew it had never been mine to claim. At first he remained attentive to me and to my needs, but as the years passed his visits grew more infrequent, our conversations more clipped and terse.

He would come to regret leaving me to my own devices as I began to gather resources about me, focusing my efforts on the welfare of my adoptive people. As Queen, I was able to learn much of the corrupt ways of the king's reign. Unfair taxation, armies run amok through the populace, abusing their position, a thriving black market secretly condoned by the government; I gradually became a thorn in his side as I publicly brought these injustices to his attention. He was forced to utilize my suggestions and, much to his chagrin, his people praised him for his altruism, believing him to be a just and fair ruler.

Yes, he could have put me aside, this is true. Taking another as wife and Queen he could have ruled without hindrance, but he would not risk word of his secret love escaping to ruin him. And so I kept my place and secured a better world for the people.

A grim smile crossed my lips as I watched the long line of royal followers file up the ramp. Knowing I had helped the common folk and thwarted my husband brought me little solace from the long years of loneliness. I dared not risk taking a lover for I had no wish to compromise my power over the monarchy. Even my children were no comfort to me as both daughter and son, by tradition, were being reared at the side of the King's brother. Looking down, I could see them now, walking beside their uncle at the end of the boarding procession. The young princess and the newly crowned King, still a few years shy of manhood, it is as if they were dream children to me instead of the flesh and blood babes I gave birth to all those years ago.

They were last in the procession and with all on board ship the feasting began in the banquet hall before we had left the atmosphere. The cheerful sounds of the old King lauded and the new one toasted time and again filtered up to my private sanctuary.

As the raucous group celebrated the future and said goodbye to the past, I remained cloistered in my room, blessedly alone with my thoughts. I had much to consider and little time to consider it before we arrived at our destination. I knew what the people expected, knew the traditions I must uphold once the journey was over, and it frightened me more than I dared admit. The queen was supposed to be in deep mourning, crazed with grief beyond the point of fear and to admit otherwise would be a disgrace. Throughout the journey I wondered how my predecessors coped with their own burden of mourning. Were they all as distant from their husbands as I, or did some truly grieve the lost of their leader and spouse.

Time passed much too swiftly and a few days later we arrived at the graveyard planet of Kalmisto, the entire entourage comfortably inebriated. My giggling servants openly broke their prohibition in the last few days and now their clumsy hands fumbled at every turn as they garbed their mistress. Layer after layer they settled over my form, the lack of sleeves trapping my arms against my sides. The alternating thin and heavy weights of the fabric were soon pressing down on my head and shoulders. Straining my muscles, I was just barely able to lift my head and breathing was a difficult chore that took much of my focus. Gaining full understanding of the symbolic nature of the garments I wore, I did truly feel that the weight of the universe was resting on my shoulders and it gave me no comfort.

The thinnest of the layers was over my eyes, allowing me to remain free of the undignified need of a guide. I moved toward the ramp at a glacial pace, at times stopping to rest and reserve my energy for the march yet to come. I was to depart the ship last, following my husband's body and acknowledging the rest of the procession on the long walk to the pyre. My sister, a student of ritual, told me long ago how the burden I now wore would most assuredly smolder and smoke, allowing me a pain free death. It was quite an honor as unworthy wives were thrown onto the fire in nothing more than a thin layer of gauze, their skin crisping a painful black before they succumbed to the flames.

A shiver ran down my spine as the thoughts flickered across my mind, thankful for the final act of kindness the king had granted me. In doing so, he had given me the acknowledgment and respect of an equal, a thank you for a peaceful and prosperous reign he had no right to claim as his own. It saddened me greatly, for I now wondered if things might have turned out differently for us, if somehow we could have found a way to be at peace with one another.

My thoughts were swiftly returned to the present when, upon descending the ship's ramp, I was greeted by my escort. The silent monks of the Currym Aeditui, their metal masks a dull glow in the gentle dawn light, surrounded me and paced themselves perfectly to my slow footsteps.

I hitched an involuntary breath as the stench of the pyre reached through the thick layers of fabric I wore, filling my nostrils and stinging my eyes with needle sharp fingers. The scent brought with it a rush of adrenaline that caused my heart to race, its tattoo beating in my head as my blood surged through my body. Many were surprised when I had refused the traditional glass of jough lajer, choosing instead to face the pyre with a clear mind. Now I wished I had not been so noble as I walked on toward the burning mound, fully aware of what I must face.

Muffled chanting reached my ears, long and low by the men, high wails from the women as they prayed for their sovereign, their crops, their health. The sound mingled with the smoke as the flames burned higher. I took as deep a breath as I was able. All that remained before me were the last three steps up to the pyre. The monks would facilitate the rest, easing the form of fabric wrapped around me onto the smoldering inferno where the heat that even now bit at my eyes would finish the task and free me at last from my burdens. One foot in front of the other, I rose up one step, than then next, stopping at the top as the wailing of the women intensified, echoing my heart as it beat in my chest.

The storytellers now say the Queen was so honorable and

blessed that she made no sound when she was lifted to the pyre. The Most Worthy Queen had heard their prayers and kept gathered upon her tongue. Even now she was speaking them to the stars that her people would continue to prosper in her honor. Long into the night the pyre continued to smolder, its embers glowing brightly in the darkness that enshrouded the funeral party. At dawn the gathered company rose in silence, proceeding in a long column back to the ship for the journey homeward.

The monks stood watching as the sublight engines on the large craft ignited, taking the ship swiftly out of Kalmisto's atmosphere. A fifth member joined them, smaller and slighter than the other brothers, like a boy, or perhaps a woman, among men. Finally removing the stoic visages their masks projected, my feminine features emerged from beneath that fifth mask.

"We trust your journey through the tunnel was not too harrowing, Lady." One of the Brothers turned, speaking softly to me.

The earthy smell of soil still filled my nostrils, mud still encrusted my fingernails. As I stood there watching the ship depart I recalled the sudden drop into the cold, clammy passageway carved beneath the last step to the pyre. I remembered groping through the darkness, the chanting of the people filtering through the earth above me like a heartbeat. I shivered there, in little more than a shift of gauze, realizing that I would never again see those I had watched over for so many years. It was here that my tears finally flowed and I wept long and hard in the darkness. Death came to me then, taking my children, my people, and finally my life. He departed as quickly as he came, leaving my soul a naked void, clean and consecrated for its renewal.

Lost in my reverie and reflection, it took a long moment before I could reply to the monk's query.

"It was a rebirthing, my friends." I replied, dry-eyed, confidence slowly creeping back into my voice. "I thank you for your gracious assistance."

"You are not the first to be so aided, Lady." He smiled at me, "The substantial contribution you have made to the Order ensures you shall not be the last."

I gave a deep bow of acknowledgment to my rescuers before

turning toward the rising sun to watch as the sleek lines of a small spacecraft became more defined with each passing moment. We stood there in silence for a time, enjoying the peace of a new day.

"Lady, do remember," another soft, male voice broke through the veil of my thoughts. "you are welcome to stay here until you've decided the course you might take."

I turned to look at him. "Please, do not speak to me any longer of the Queen," I replied quietly, "for the she is dead."

He nodded his understanding and I smiled now, a gentle smile that came easily to my lips. "I thank you again for your offer, but I believe there is a future out there that has waited for me quite long enough."

With a final nod to the monks, I became a simple citizen of the galaxy. Walking toward the small ship that waited, I too took my own prayers to the stars.

About the author: A pixel-slinger by trade, Jennifer Lyn Parsons is a life-long lover of story and self-forged teller of tales. She has been published on 365tomorrows.com and more of her work can be found through her website, http://writing.jenniferlynparsons.net

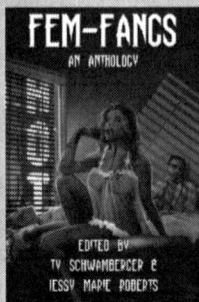

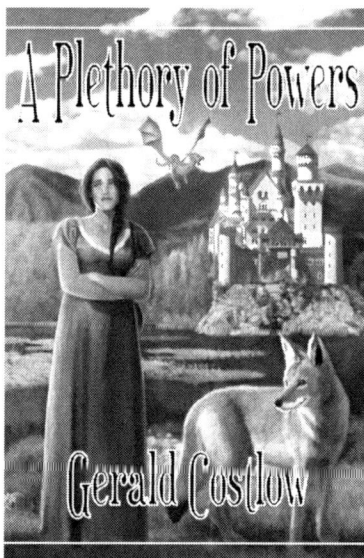

Lightning Source UK Ltd.
Milton Keynes UK
02 August 2010
157768UK00009B/191/P

9 781617 060304